A Life Stolen

Based on Historical Events

David Lee Corley

DEDICATION

Dedicated to all the men and women that fought and
sacrificed for their country.

Table of Contents

Quote

"All War is a symptom of man's failure as a thinking animal."

– John Steinbeck

Prologue

October 24, 1929 – Oslo, Norway

The bitter wind howled through the bustling Oslo harbor, carrying with it the mournful cries of seagulls as they circled overhead, their wings outstretched against the leaden sky. Dr. Sebastian Kristiansen stood upon the gleaming deck of the majestic ocean liner, Bergensfjord, his heart heavy with the weight of the decision that had brought him to this moment. In his hands, he clutched two battered leather suitcases, their worn surfaces confirmation of the years of tireless research and countless hours spent hunched over his desk, chasing the secrets of the universe.

Beside him, his wife Marthe stood, her delicate features etched with a mixture of excitement and trepidation, one hand resting gently on the slight swell of her belly, where their unborn child lay nestled. Their young son Erik clung to her hand, his wide blue eyes taking in the bustling activity of the docks with a child's innocent wonder. "Norway is beautiful, and we will miss it," Marthe said softly, her voice barely audible above the din of the harbor. "But I'm ready to start our new life in America, my love."

Sebastian drew her close, inhaling the familiar scent of her perfume, a delicate blend of lavender and vanilla that seemed to chase away the chill of the Norwegian autumn. "As am I, my dear," he murmured, his gaze drifting out over the cityscape of steep peaks and terracotta rooftops that had been his home for over three decades. "The future of physics lies across the sea, though I will miss these fjord-carved shores."

As they settled into their cramped cabin, Sebastian carefully arranged his precious cargo atop the floral bedspread, his fingers quivering as he unlatched the cases. Inside, a lifetime's worth of knowledge spilled out, journals, notebooks, and mathematical proofs that represented the culmination of his groundbreaking work in nuclear physics.

"Is it all there, Papa?" Erik asked, his small hands running over the weathered leather and yellowed paper with reverence.

Sebastian smiled, ruffling his son's strawberry blond hair with affection. "Nearly, my boy," he said, a sudden realization dawning upon him. "I'm afraid I've forgotten my personal notebook back in my campus office. All my latest designs reside within those pages. Not to worry though—we shan't set sail for another hour at least. I shall return swiftly."

Marthe's face clouded with worry, her delicate brows knitting together in concern. "Must you go alone?" she asked, her voice tinged with apprehension. "The docks seem so frantic this evening. Allow us to join you."

But Sebastian merely squeezed her hand, his rough

callouses a stark contrast to her smooth skin. "I won't be but a moment, my love," he assured her, his eyes alight with determination. "Watch over our boy while I'm gone."

As he stepped out onto the passageway, the cacophony of the docks faded away, replaced by the eerie silence of the university hallways. His footsteps echoed off the polished floors, the only sound in the deserted building. But as he approached his office, a sense of dread settled over him, a leaden weight upon his chest.

There, silhouetted against the weak light filtering through the window, stood Dr. Svein Knutsen, his junior colleague. In his hands, he held the very notebook Sebastian had come to retrieve, its pages open and exposed.

Svein Knutsen's emotions swirled within him as he watched his mentor, Dr. Sebastian Kristiansen, enter the room. Betrayal stung, a bitter poison that left his mouth dry and his hands trembling. How could the man he had devoted five years of his life to, the man who had promised him a bright future in the world of physics, abandon him so callously?

But beneath the anger and the hurt, there was a glimmer of something else, a sense of pity for the naive idealism that had led Sebastian astray. Knutsen had seen the way the world was changing, the rise of new powers and new ideologies that demanded loyalty and sacrifice. He knew that the future belonged to those who were willing to seize it, to mold it in their own image.

And yet, Sebastian remained blind to the truth, clinging to his outdated notions of scientific integrity and international cooperation. He believed that knowledge should be shared freely, that the pursuit of understanding transcended national borders and political allegiances. It was a beautiful dream, but one that had no place in the harsh reality of the modern world.

As he clutched Sebastian's notebook in his hands, the pages filled with groundbreaking theories and revolutionary designs, Knutsen felt a surge of determination. He would not let this knowledge slip away, would not allow it to be lost to the tides of history. He would take it for himself, use it to build a new future for Norway, one that would make his country a power to be reckoned with on the global stage.

And if that meant betraying the man who had once been his mentor, his friend? So be it. In the end, Knutsen knew that he was doing what was necessary, what was right. The world was changing, and he would change with it, no matter the cost.

Sebastian's face reddened in anger, his blood pounding in his ears. The sight of Knutsen with his notebook filled him with a deep sense of unease. In recent years, Norway had changed, and men like Knutsen had embraced the dangerous ideology of fascism. It was a philosophy that Sebastian could not abide, one that he feared would lead his beloved country down a dark and treacherous path. The thought of his groundbreaking research falling into the hands of those who would use it for their own nefarious purposes was a nightmare he could not bear to contemplate. "You were leaving without saying goodbye?" Knutsen said, his voice dripping with disdain. "Five years I worked for you, and this is the thanks I get? You and your family slinking off without notification?"

"That research is not meant for your eyes, Knutsen!" Sebastian shouted, his voice raw with emotion. "Return it at once!"

But Knutsen merely smiled, a cold, cruel twist of his lips. "You may run away to America, Dr. Kristiansen, but your research belongs here in Norway, to benefit our homeland," he replied, his tone as icy as the fjords that carved the coastline. "I cannot allow such knowledge to leave these shores."

In a desperate, futile attempt, Sebastian charged forward, his hands grasping for the notebook. But Knutsen was younger, stronger, and he easily deflected the attack, slamming Sebastian backwards against the corner of a wooden support column with a sickening crunch. As he slumped to the cold tiles, blood pooling beneath his matted hair, the last thing Sebastian heard was the distant sound of the ship's steam horn, bellowing its farewell to the land of gods and giants.

As the Bergensfjord steamed towards the open sea, carrying with it the hopes and dreams of a family seeking a new life, the fate of Dr. Sebastian Kristiansen's groundbreaking research fell into the hands of a man whose ambition knew no bounds, a man who would stop at nothing to claim the power of the atom for himself.

A Lifetime of Secrets

Chicago Suburbs - December 7, 2009

In a quiet suburb on the outskirts of Chicago, nestled among snow-covered lawns and freshly shoved sidewalks, sat a modest, two-story house. Its creamy white exterior was adorned with dark green shutters and a red brick chimney. A paved walkway, lined with empty flower beds, lead to the front porch, where a weathered rocking chair swayed gently in the breeze. Americana.

Inside, the hardwood floors creaked softly beneath the weight of years. Bathed in soft, natural light filtering through the windows, photographs of grandchildren and family each telling a story of its own. The tranquility was broken by cabinet doors opening and closing mixed with the shuffling spice bottles and cookie sheets.

In the cozy confines of her kitchen, eighty-year-old Elsa gathered the ingredients for her favorite Norwegian pastry, skillingsboller. With a nostalgic smile, she recalled the countless times she watched her mother make the delicate cinnamon buns, the scent of cardamom and butter filling the air. Her hands covered in flour, Elsa mixed the dough, kneading it gently, and prepared the fragrant filling. She rolled out the dough, spread the filling evenly, and carefully cut the log into perfect spirals. As the skillingsboller baked, the aroma of cinnamon and cardamom wafted through the house, evoking memories of home and family. When the timer chimed, Elsa removed the golden-brown pastries, their surfaces glistening with a sugary glaze. Taking a bite of a warm skillingsboller, the flavors of her heritage danced on her tongue, a comforting reminder of the love and tradition baked into every bite.

She carefully placed two layers of rolls in a Tupperware container and sealed the lid. Skillingsbollers in hand, she walked to her next-door neighbor's house and knocked. No answer. The family that lived there was always busy with soccer practice and piano recitals. She set the Tupperware on the welcome mat, considered for a moment, then moved it to the side so anybody coming out of the house wouldn't trip over it. No note. It wasn't necessary. Everyone loved Skillingsbollers in the winter. Back to her house. They would return the container when they were done which would probably be thirty minutes after they opened it.

Back inside her house, she poured herself a cup of coffee and settled at the kitchen table, the newspaper spread out before her. The headlines spoke of the U.S.

governments war on Wikileaks and the arrest of Julian Assange in London. War on Wikileaks? Clearly the editor did not understand the meaning of actual war. She did. She had lived through several. A war was hard to forget. A waste of life and precious resources. A shame on humanity. "If it bleeds, it leads" as the saying goes. She didn't like reading the news anymore. She folded the paper, moved into the family room, and tossed it next to the fireplace as a starter. It now had a new purpose and that suited her. She pointed a threatening finger at the television and said, "Watch out or you're next."

With a sigh, Elsa turned her attention to the photographs scattered across the living room coffee table, images of her children and grandchildren, their smiling faces a reminder of all that was good in the world. She picked up a particularly cherished photo of her newest grandchild, a tiny bundle of joy with bright eyes and a gummy smile. Carefully, she placed the photo in a silver frame to be set on the fireplace mantel, a position of prominence. She glanced at the clock on the wall. It was time. She rose and walked upstairs.

In her bedroom she finished packing a well-worn suitcase on her bed. The last article of clothing was recently purchased formal dress. She studied it for a moment and shook her head. What a waste of money that she could use to pay for grandchildren's braces or a new set of tires. She neatly folded the dress inside the suitcase and closed it snapping the locks shut. She left the suitcase on the bed and went downstairs. She wondered if she should make herself a baloney sandwich. The doorbell rang. Too late. The baloney would need to keep until her return.

Before she could reach the front door, it opened

and a woman's voice said, "Mom?" It was her daughter and son-in-law. Seeing Elsa approaching, her son-in-law said, "Where's your suitcase?"

"On my bed," said Elsa kissing her daughter on the cheek.

Pushing past his wife to enter the house, her son-in-law sniffed the air, "Someone's been baking."

"Skillingsbollers. I left one for you on the kitchen counter."

The son-in-law shifted direction and headed for the kitchen. Everyone loved Skillingsbollers.

"How are you feeling?" said her daughter with concern.

"I'm fine."

"No more dizzy spells?"

"None that I care to mention."

"You know, you don't have to go."

"I already accepted. It would be rude to be a no-show. They might keep the check."

"They wouldn't keep the check. I'm sure they would understand."

"I already bought a dress."

"I know, I was with you. It's beautiful but we could return it."

"I hate returning things. It seems so indecisive."

Her son-in-law rounded the corner licking his fingers covered with sugar glaze and headed upstairs to fetch her suitcase.

"Make sure you wash your hands. I hate a sticky handle."

"Right-o," he said stomping up the stairs.

"I don't know that this is such a good idea," said her daughter.

"It'll be fine," said Elsa, then called into the living

room. "Bill, you ready to go?"

Elsa's daughter looked alarmed and said, "Mom, dad's not here anymore."

"I know. I'm just messing with you."

December 10, 2010 – Stockholm, Sweden

The Stockholm Concert Hall, an architectural gem in the center of Sweden's capital, was resplendent on that crisp December evening, its grand facade illuminated by the soft glow of streetlights. Inside, the Main Hall was a breathtaking sight, its soaring ceilings adorned with intricate frescoes and glittering chandeliers. The stage, flanked by towering columns and draped in rich blue velvet, was set with a simple lectern bearing the iconic Nobel medallion.

As Elsa took her seat among the distinguished guests, dressed in their finest attire, she could feel the palpable sense of anticipation that filled the air. Beside her, her daughter Ingrid sat, eyes wide with wonder as she took in the grandeur of the surroundings. The rows of plush, blue velvet chairs were occupied by some of the world's most brilliant minds - scientists, writers, and luminaries from every corner of the globe. The gentle murmur of conversation ebbed and flowed around them, punctuated by the occasional burst of laughter or the clink of champagne glasses.

Elsa leaned over to Ingrid, whispering, "Can you believe we're here, surrounded by all these incredible people?" Ingrid smiled, squeezing her mother's hand in response, and said, "And you're one of them."
Elsa smiled at the thought, then said, "I suppose you're right. I am one of them. Bout time someone realized that."

At the front of the hall, Elsa noticed the royal box, glorious in gold and azure, where the Swedish royal family sat in regal splendor. Their presence lent an air of timeless elegance to the proceedings, a reminder of the rich history and tradition that underpinned the prestigious event.

As the hour approached, a hush fell over the audience, the silence broken only by the soft rustling of program pages and the occasional discreet cough. Elsa's gaze was drawn to the stage, bathed in a warm golden light, which seemed to shimmer with an almost otherworldly glow, a fitting backdrop for the momentous occasion that was about to unfold. With Ingrid by her side, she knew that this night would be etched in the annals of history, proof of the enduring power of knowledge, creativity, and the indomitable spirit of human endeavor, a legacy she had worked so hard to build and one that she hoped would inspire generations to come.

As the ceremony began, the hall fell silent, all eyes fixed on the stage. The King of Sweden, resplendent in his formal attire, took his place at the lectern, his presence commanding the attention of all in attendance. With a warm smile, he began his speech, his words echoing through the grand hall, paying tribute to the extraordinary achievements of the Nobel laureates.

Elsa listened intently, her heart swelling with pride as the King spoke of the groundbreaking discoveries and contributions that had earned her this prestigious honor. Beside her, Ingrid's eyes glistened with tears of joy, her hand never leaving her mother's.

As the King concluded his speech, he invited Elsa

to the stage to receive her Nobel Prize in Physics. With a deep breath, Elsa rose from her seat, her steps measured and confident as she made her way to the stage. The audience erupted in applause, a thunderous ovation that filled the hall, confirmation of the respect and admiration they held for her.

Elsa stood before the King, her head bowed as he placed the Nobel medal around her neck and handed her the diploma. The weight of the medal was a tangible reminder of the decades of hard work, dedication, and sacrifice that had brought her to this moment.

As she turned to face the audience, Elsa's eyes found Ingrid's, a silent exchange of love and gratitude passing between them. With a trembling voice, Elsa began her acceptance speech, her words filled with humility and grace as she first thanked the king, then her colleagues, her family, and all those who had supported her throughout her journey.

"Science has the power to unite nations, to bridge divides, and to illuminate the darkest corners of the universe," Elsa said, her voice clear and strong. "But with this power comes great responsibility, the duty to use it wisely and for the betterment of all humanity."

As she spoke, a sudden memory flashed through her mind – a memory of a mysterious man from her past, a man who had been her partner and confidant during a tumultuous time in her life. The secret mission they had undertaken together, the risks they had faced, and the sacrifices they had made in the name of a greater good.

Elsa faltered, her words trailing off as the weight of the memory threatened to overwhelm her. She gripped the podium, her knuckles turning white as she fought to maintain her composure. But it was too late.

Without warning, Elsa's eyes rolled back in her head, and she collapsed, her body crumpling to the stage floor. The audience gasped, a collective cry of shock and horror filling the hall.

Ingrid, seated in the front row, leapt to her feet, her heart pounding as she raced towards her mother. "Mother!" she cried, dropping to her knees beside Elsa's still form.

Paramedics rushed onto the stage, their movements swift and precise as they assessed Elsa's condition. The audience watched in stunned silence as they worked, their faces etched with concern and fear.

As the paramedics loaded Elsa onto a stretcher, Ingrid followed close behind, her hand never leaving her mother's. Tears streamed down her face as she watched them wheel Elsa out of the hall, the flashing lights of the ambulance illuminating the night sky.

In the hospital, Elsa lay motionless, her life hanging in the balance. Ingrid sat by her bedside, holding her hand and whispering words of love and encouragement. The doctors worked tirelessly, their faces grim as they fought to save the life of the woman who had achieved so much, who had touched so many lives.

As the hours passed, Ingrid's mind filled with questions, with fears, and with a growing sense of desperation. She couldn't lose her mother, not now, not after everything they had been through together.

And so, she prayed, her whispered pleas filling the sterile hospital room, a desperate plea for a miracle, for a second chance, for the opportunity to unravel the mysteries of her mother's past and the secrets she had carried with her for so long.

In that moment, as Elsa hovered on the brink of death, the memories of the mysterious man and the mission that had defined her life, a legacy that would forever be remembered, even if the full truth had yet to be revealed. Half in a dream and half conscious, Elsa remembered…

Breakthrough

1942 – University of Chicago

Dr. Elsa Kristiansen hurried across the University of Chicago's Gothic-styled campus, her mind a whirlwind of equations and possibilities. The crisp autumn air filled her lungs as she wove between the ivy-covered stone buildings, the bustling metropolis of the South Side a distant backdrop to her singular focus. The weight of her research pressed down upon her, a constant companion that both exhilarated and terrified her.

As she veered from the central courtyard, Elsa's footsteps echoed through the looming Gothic arch of Foster Hall, home to the physics department. She kept her gaze downcast, avoiding the curious glances of her fellow students, their youthful exuberance a stark contrast to the heaviness that settled in her chest. The burden of her work, the endless hours spent hunched over chalkboards and journals, had left her feeling isolated, disconnected from the world around her.

With a sigh of relief, Elsa slipped into the sanctuary of her small office, the familiar scent of chalk dust and musty books enveloping her like a comforting embrace. The room was a testimonial of her brilliant, restless mind, every wall crammed floor to ceiling with chalkboards on wheels, a hodgepodge of old, new, and slightly broken. The slate surfaces were filled with endless lines of calculus and nuclear physics notations, a dizzying array of symbols and equations that held the key to unlocking the secrets of the universe.

Late fall sun filtered through the room's single, mullioned window, casting a warm glow across the worn leather stool where Elsa perched, her mind already churning with possibilities. She loved this space, this tiny corner of the world where she could lose herself in the intricacies of her work, free from the expectations and judgments of the outside world.

But despite the promise of a new day, Elsa found herself slumping in defeat, staring hopelessly at the incomprehensible equations scrawled across her army of blackboards. Weeks of tireless efforts had yielded nothing but frustration, a mounting sense of failure that gnawed at her insides. She could feel the weight of her own expectations bearing down upon her, the fear that she would never be able to live up to the legacy of her brilliant father.

With a shove, Elsa pushed back from her desk, her body protesting the sudden movement after hours of stillness. She began to pace, her mind churning through possibilities even as her weary limbs begged for respite. The equations danced before her eyes, taunting her with their complexity, their refusal to yield to her probing intellect.

And then, as she passed the central blackboard, something clicked. A subtle interrelation that had eluded her before, a glimmer of understanding that set her mind whirling. Elsa snatched up a nub of chalk and a well-used eraser, the familiar weight of the tools a comfort as she began to erase a segment of calculations, her mind whirring with newfound clarity.

The equations flowed from her fingertips, a stream of refined expressions that took shape before her eyes. Elsa worked feverishly, her breath coming in short gasps as the sequence unfolded, a beautiful, elegant solution to the problem that had plagued her for so long. She rechecked her work again and again, hardly daring to believe that she had finally cracked the code.

With a clatter, the chalk fell from her fingers, forgotten as Elsa bolted for the door. She raced through the hallways, dodging startled colleagues and students alike, her mind still churning with the implications of her discovery. The cool autumn air stung her cheeks as she pelted across the leaf-strewn campus, her destination clear in her mind.

She burst into the auditorium, her heart hammering in her chest as every head turned to stare at her. Dr. Sanders, his bushy eyebrows raised in surprise, paused mid-lecture, the smoke from his cigarette curling lazily towards the ceiling. Elsa froze, suddenly aware of the unwanted attention, the weight of her discovery pressing down upon her like a physical force.

"Elsa? What's going on?" Dr. Sanders asked, his voice tinged with concern.

Elsa swallowed hard, her throat suddenly dry. She could feel the eyes of the students boring into her, their curious glances making her skin crawl. "I... I think I've got it, Dr. Sanders," she managed, her voice barely above a whisper. "The equations, the neutron flows... I think I've figured it out."

Dr. Sanders's eyes widened, his lecture forgotten as he stepped towards her. "Are you sure, Elsa?"

Elsa nodded, her confidence wavering under the weight of his gaze. "I'm sure. I've checked and double-checked. It all fits."

Dr. Sanders turned to his class, his voice apologetic. "I'm sorry, everyone, but I'm afraid we'll have to cut today's lecture short."

As the students filed out of the auditorium, their curious glances lingering on Elsa, she could feel her cheeks burning with embarrassment. She hated being the center of attention, hated the way their eyes seemed to see right through her, exposing all her flaws and insecurities.

Dr. Sanders turned to her, his expression serious. "Show me what you've got, Elsa."

With a deep breath, Elsa stepped up to the blackboard, the chalk clutched tightly in her hand. She began to write, the equations flowing from her fingertips in a stream of elegant, refined expressions. Dr. Sanders watched, his eyes widening with each passing moment, his mind struggling to keep up with the brilliance unfolding before him.

As Elsa finished, she turned to him, her heart in her throat. "Well? What do you think?"

Dr. Sanders was silent for a long moment, his gaze fixed on the blackboard. Then, slowly, he began to nod, a smile spreading across his face. "I think you've done it, Elsa. I think you've really done it."

Elsa felt a rush of pure, unadulterated joy, the weight of her discovery lifting from her shoulders. She had done it, had achieved the impossible, and nothing would ever be the same again. And as Dr. Sanders clapped her on the shoulder, his voice filled with pride and admiration, Elsa knew that this was only the beginning, the first step on a journey that would change the world forever.

But even as she basked in the glow of her achievement, Elsa couldn't shake the feeling of isolation that clung to her like a second skin. She had always been an outsider, a misfit in a world that didn't quite understand her. And as she left the auditorium, her mind already racing with the implications of her discovery, she couldn't help but wonder if she would ever truly belong, if she would ever find a place where she could be herself, without fear of judgment or rejection.

Elsa walked across the University of Chicago campus, her mind lost in a maze of equations and theories. The crisp autumn air swirled around her, carrying the scent of fallen leaves and the distant echoes of laughter from the quad. She pulled her coat tighter around her slender frame, a futile attempt to ward off the chill that seemed to emanate from her very core.

As she rounded the corner of the physics building, a cacophony of noise and activity jolted her from her thoughts. A large crowd of students had gathered in the plaza, their faces alight with excitement and purpose. Elsa slowed her pace, curiosity drawing her closer to the commotion.

A charismatic man in a crisp military uniform stood atop a makeshift stage, his voice booming through the crowd. "Remember Pearl Harbor! Join the fight, defend your country, and protect the freedoms we hold dear!" He gestured to a line of eager young men and women, their eyes shining with determination as they signed enlistment forms.

Elsa felt a knot form in the pit of her stomach, a palpable reminder of her pacifist beliefs. The attack on Pearl Harbor had shaken the nation to its core, but even in the face of such a devastating blow, she could not bring herself to embrace the call to arms. Her father, a brilliant physicist, had instilled in her a deep reverence for the power of diplomacy and understanding, a belief that had been reinforced by her Norwegian heritage, a nation known for its neutrality.

As she tried to slip away unnoticed, a recruiter approached her, his smile warm and inviting. "Hello there! Have you considered joining the war effort? We need bright young minds like yours to help us defeat Hitler and his Axis allies."

Elsa's throat tightened, her words caught in a web of conflicting emotions. "I... I'm sorry, but I don't believe in fighting. War is not the answer."

The recruiter's face darkened, his smile faltering. "But surely you understand the threat we face? The attack on Pearl Harbor proves that the Axis powers will stop at nothing to destroy us. We need everyone to do their part."

Elsa shook her head, her voice growing stronger as she found the courage to speak her truth. "Violence only breeds more violence. My father always believed that there must be another way, a path to peace that doesn't involve bloodshed."

The recruiter's eyes narrowed, his voice taking on an edge of frustration. "Peace? There can be no peace until we've avenged the lives lost at Pearl Harbor. If you're not willing to fight for your country, then what kind of American are you?"

Elsa felt the weight of his words, the accusation of disloyalty hanging heavy in the air. She glanced around at the other students moving closer to listen to the conversation, their faces now etched with suspicion and disapproval. In that moment, she realized just how isolated her beliefs had made her, how far removed she was from the patriotic fervor that gripped the nation.

Elsa turned and pushed her way through the crowd, their murmurs of discontent echoing in her ears. She walked until she found a quiet spot beneath an old oak tree, its branches bare and skeletal against the gray sky.

Tears stung her eyes as she replayed the confrontation in her mind, the recruiter's words a painful reminder of the chasm that existed between her and her fellow Americans. She had always known that her pacifist views set her apart, but never before had she felt so utterly alone, so disconnected from the world around her.

And yet, even in the face of such hostility, Elsa knew that she could not abandon her principles. Her belief in the power of peace, instilled by her father through his writing and reinforced by her Norwegian heritage, was a part of who she was, woven into the very fabric of her being. She would not compromise her values, no matter the cost.

With a deep breath, Elsa squared her shoulders and wiped away her tears. She would continue to stand for what she believed in, to be a voice for peace in a world consumed by war. And though the path ahead would be difficult, she knew that she could not waver, could not lose sight of the hope that burned within her, the hope for a better tomorrow, a tomorrow her father and mother had always believed in.

December 2, 1942

The secluded halls of the University of Chicago bustled with activity, even as the semester drew to a close. Within the imposing gothic facades, physicists like Elsa migrated between nondescript laboratories, their work too vital to the war effort to halt for holiday respite. Armed guards stood frozen at every entrance, their stern faces a stark reminder of the secrecy that shrouded the groundbreaking discoveries being made daily in the basement labs.

Elsa emerged from the windowless subterranean chambers, her eyes squinting as they adjusted to the weak winter sunlight that filtered through the clouds. She had lost track of time, her mind consumed by the equations and theories that danced across the chalkboards, the numbers and symbols etched into her brain like a permanent tattoo. As she trudged through the snowy quads in her tweed skirt and overcoat, the wind whipping at her face, the Harper Memorial Library clock tower chimed the late hour, its bells echoing across the ivy-draped buildings like a haunting melody.

Within the cramped basement laboratory hidden beneath the abandoned football stands of Stagg Field, Elsa and her fellow scientists prepared for the momentous experiment – the first sustained nuclear reaction in world history. The drab green walls and concrete floors of the lab felt more like a bunker than hallowed halls of academia, the air thick with the scent of coffee and stale cigarettes. Dozens of the nation's most brilliant minds clattered about, their neckties and sweater vests belying the gravity of their work, the intensity of their focus palpable in the cramped space.

At the center of it all stood the reactor nicknamed "Chicago Pile-1," a twenty-foot-tall stack of graphite blocks peppered with hundreds of smaller blocks of uranium, its presence both awe-inspiring and terrifying. Elsa double-checked her calculations, ensuring that every detail was perfect. She knew that the success of this experiment could change the course of history, and she was determined to make her father proud.

As the technicians finished assembling the palisades of brick around the reactor core, Enrico Fermi, the head of the Theoretical Physics Division at the Metallurgical Laboratory, made his final inspection, his forehead creased in concentration. Fermi was a man of contrasts, his brilliance and intensity tempered by a quiet, unassuming demeanor. He stood at the heart of the Manhattan Project, a towering figure in the world of physics, yet his modest appearance belied the sharpness of his mind and the depth of his knowledge. With his thinning hair and wire-rimmed glasses, he looked more like a kindly professor than a man who held the fate of the world in his hands. But beneath that gentle exterior lay a fierce determination, a relentless drive to push the boundaries of science and unlock the secrets of the universe. His eyes, dark and piercing, seemed to see beyond the present moment, to the limitless possibilities that lay ahead. And when he spoke, his voice was soft but commanding, a barely restrained energy thrumming beneath each carefully chosen word. To those who worked alongside him, Enrico Fermi was a force of nature, a man who could inspire both awe and terror in equal measure. But to Elsa, he was a mentor, a guide, and a constant reminder of the incredible power and responsibility that came with their work on the Manhattan Project.

The air was thick with anticipation as the team prepared to initiate the chain reaction. Suddenly, an alarm sounded, and the room fell silent. One of the control rods had jammed, threatening to derail the entire experiment. Panic filled the room as the scientists scrambled to find a solution, but time was running out.

Elsa stepped forward as she examined the problem. She had spent countless hours studying the reactor's design and had a deep understanding of its intricacies. With a calm and steady hand, she reached for the control rod, but Fermi grabbed her wrist.

"Elsa, no! The radiation levels are too high. It's too dangerous," he warned, his eyes filled with concern.

Elsa met his gaze, her determination unwavering. "I know the risks, Dr. Fermi. But if we don't fix this now, the entire experiment could fail. We've come too far to let that happen."

Fermi hesitated for a moment, then nodded, realizing that Elsa was right. He handed her a pair of thick, lead-lined gloves and a protective apron. "Be careful, Elsa. We can't afford to lose you."

Elsa smiled reassuringly, then donned the protective gear. She took a deep breath and carefully reached into the reactor core, her anxiety heightened as she maneuvered the control rod back into place. The seconds felt like hours as she worked, the heat of the reactor palpable even through the thick gloves.

Finally, the control rod slid into position, and the alarm fell silent. Elsa withdrew her hands, her body trembling with a mixture of relief and adrenaline. She knew that she had potentially exposed herself to dangerous levels of radiation, but it was a risk she was willing to take for the sake of the experiment.

Fermi clapped her on the back, his eyes shining with admiration. "Well done, Elsa. You may have just saved the entire project."

Elsa smiled weakly, suddenly feeling the weight of her actions. She knew that the long-term effects of radiation exposure were still largely unknown, and she couldn't help but wonder what price she might pay for her bravery.

As the team resumed the experiment, Elsa monitored the radiation levels, her hands shaking slightly as she adjusted the dials. She tried to push the thought of her own safety to the back of her mind, focusing instead on the historic moment unfolding before her.

Suddenly, the clicking device leapt upwards as atomic fission spontaneously initiated. Elsa gasped, glancing to Fermi. His stern lips turned upwards into a proud smile as years of secretive efforts now came to life, the needle steadily climbing. It was historic.

After only twenty-eight minutes, they had done it — the world's first self-sustaining nuclear chain reaction. The team exchanged relieved laughter and handshakes after hours of nail-biting tension, although Elsa held back shyly from the rowdy celebration. This breakthrough stretched far beyond science and security concerns, she believed — it could remake civilization.

Elsa felt a rush of pride and accomplishment wash over her, but it was tinged with a sense of unease. She knew that her actions had helped make this moment possible, but at what cost?

In celebration, the team drank Chianti from paper cups and signed the straw wrapping around the bottle to prove that they were indeed there on the day the power of the sun was harnessed. Forty-nine signatures

- the first to welcome the age of the atom.

After securing the precious reactor safely, the scientists emerged from the basement, hunger and relief dulling the chill night air. Their strides stretched longer past the guards down oak-lined campus halls out to the bustling city street where Fermi led them to Durley's Pub.

Inside, the smells of spilled beer and tobacco entwined with animated student chatter. Fermi waved over the bartender who began lining up pints as the lab coats crowded around a corner table, laughing with an uncharacteristic giddiness.

"To the future!" boasted the normally stern Fermi, hoisting his foaming glass.

"Hear hear!" came the echoes down their frothy line.

Bottoms up and slam, slam, slam rang the emptied mugs against worn oak. Elsa ran her tongue over the faint sweet malt traces, unaccustomed to anything stronger than tea, feeling limbs loosen and normally self-conscious thoughts now glowing.

Another chorus rose around Elsa as her inner wallflower faded under camaraderie and hops. Tomorrow the sober gravity would return. But tonight, success and possibility thrummed electric under Chicago's yellow streetlights. They had taken God's building blocks in hand. What might humanity build next?

Elsa watched her male colleagues noisily reenacting the day's breakthrough reactor experiment across the bar. Though she had devised the crucial stabilization calculations herself, fame skipped the mousy pens behind such advances. It seemed whomever boasted the loudest gained the honor.

Sipping courage from her second pint of beer, Elsa spied engineer Arlo McMahon weaving towards her holding several fresh pints. The prodigal engineer whose sharp insights had stimulated her own theories for months surely grasped her full talents?

As he drew closer, she interjected tipsily - "Arlo! I was hoping we could discuss palladium filter geometry? I've scribbled plans for novel packing you might find intriguing."

McMahon blinked politely down at the usually timid physicist emboldened by spirits. "Appreciate the offer Elsa, but I'm just grabbing drinks for colleagues. Maybe later this month when we both have a moment."

Her eager smile fractured as he moved past her. The awful truth sunk in watching his ready laughter round the bar - she would remain resigned as a sexless research asset. Though ideas within shown promise, no admiring gaze yet turned her way in this academic world.

Finishing her second pint, Elsa made her way to the restroom, looked in the mirror at her drunk face, then vomited in the sink. Twice.

After cleaning herself, she exited the restroom to find a tall man standing at the entrance. "If you are waiting for someone, there's nobody in there," she said pointing to the women's door.

"Actually, I was waiting for you," said the man.

"Me? Why?"

"My name is Culper."

"Culper? Is that a first name or a last name?"

"Both."

"That's a bit strange."

"I get that a lot."

"I suppose a person has the right to call themselves whatever they want."

"That's my feeling on the matter."

"Okay. So, you found me. What can I do for you?"

"I was hoping to take you to coffee tomorrow."

"Coffee? Why?"

"To talk."

"If you're the press you want Dr. Fermi, not me."

"I'm not the press. Just the opposite, in fact."

"What's that mean?"

"Come to have coffee with me tomorrow and you'll find out."

"Mysterious."

"Yep."

"All right. Where?"

"Do you know Promontory Point?"

"Doesn't everyone? It's where couples go to make out."

"Not during the day."

"Oh, right."

"I'll bring the coffee… and maybe some bagels. Something tells me your stomach is going to be a little queasy."

"I wouldn't know. I've never drunk before."

"Well, I have, and bagels are a good idea. Trust me. 10 AM okay?"

"Sure."

"I'll see you then."

"Do I need to bring anything?"

"Nope. Just you."

"Okay, Culper. You got it."

With a nod, Culper moved past her and exited through the back door. Elsa stood for a moment wondering. He wasn't asking her out on a date that was for sure. Selling encyclopedias? Obviously, she didn't have any money. Murderer? Maybe, but he didn't look the type. There was only one way to find out.

As she made her way back toward the bar, Elsa couldn't shake the feeling that this man was about to change her life in ways she could never have imagined.

The Offer

Elsa woke with a groan, her head pounding in rhythm with the dull ache behind her eyes. The celebratory drinks from the night before had seemed like a good idea at the time, a way to forget the weight of responsibility that came with their groundbreaking achievement. But now, as she struggled to sit up, the room spinning around her, she couldn't help but wonder if it had been worth it.

She stumbled out of bed, her stomach churning as she made her way to the window. The weak winter sunlight filtering through the pane did little to ease her discomfort, and she pressed her forehead against the cool glass, willing the nausea to subside.

It was only then that she remembered her meeting with Culper, the mysterious man who had approached her at the bar the night before. A glance at the clock confirmed her fears - she was already running late.

With a muttered curse, Elsa hurried to dress, her fingers fumbling with the buttons of her blouse. She splashed cold water on her face, hoping to clear the fog from her mind, but the pounding in her head only intensified. She wished she had declined his invitation to meet. It was risky meeting a stranger in a secluded place like Promontory Point. But she had agreed and was not one to give her word lightly, and besides, she was curious about what he wanted to discuss.

As she pedaled her bicycle along the winding lakefront trail, the towering spires of campus fading behind bare-branched trees, Elsa couldn't shake the sense of unease that settled over her like a shroud. The frosty sunlight glittered across the churning steel-gray waves as she neared Promontory Point, but the beauty of the winter day was lost on her. Her mind thrashed with questions about Culper's intentions, her hangover only amplifying the uncertainty that gnawed at her.

She spotted him sitting alone on a stone bench overlooking the azure ice shelf rimming the lakeshore, holding two steaming cups and a paper bag. As she pulled up beside him, her toes numb inside sodden leather Oxfords from the slushy trail, she couldn't help but feel a sense of trepidation.

"You made it. I was beginning to wonder," Culper grinned, his breath forming frosty plumes in the sea-tinged air.

"I'm sorry I'm late," said Elsa sitting on the opposite side of the bench but still within his easy reach.

"Understandable," he said handing her a cup, then offered a bagel from the bag. "A bagel should help with your nausea."

"How do you know I'm nauseous?"

"Like I said, I've tied one on before. Nausea goes with drinking too much."

"I differ to your experience."

Fishing a bagel out of the bag, she took a big bite

and immediately thought of retching.

"Might want to slow down a bit. Smaller bites and don't forget to chew."

"Right… chew."

She gazed out at the granite boulders bracing against the roiling lake beyond, hoping the dark roast warmth seeping through her mittens would help clear the cobwebs from her mind. "Thank you," she murmured, taking a tentative sip. "I have to admit, I'm a bit curious about why you wanted to meet."

Culper chuckled, reaching into the paper bag and pulling out a bagel. "Straight to the point. I like that." He took a bite, chewing thoughtfully for a moment before continuing. "I've been following your work, Elsa. Your contributions to the Manhattan Project are nothing short of remarkable."

Elsa felt a flush of pride, but it was quickly tempered by suspicion. "How do you know about that?" she asked, her voice tight. "That information is classified."

"I have my sources. But that's not what I wanted to talk to you about." He leaned forward, his eyes intense. "I heard you turned down an offer to join Oppenheimer's team. Why?"

Elsa bristled at the question, her hangover forgotten in the face of her rising anger. "That's none of your business," she snapped. "My reasons are my own."

Culper held up his hands in a placating gesture. "I'm not trying to pry, Elsa. I'm just trying to understand. A brilliant mind like yours, turning down the chance to work on the most important scientific project of our time? It seems...strange."

Elsa sighed, rubbing her temples in a futile attempt to ease the throbbing in her head. "I have my principles. I won't be a part of something that could lead to the destruction of innocent lives."

Culper nodded, his expression thoughtful. "I can respect that. But what if I told you that there was a way to use your skills for good? To help prevent the Nazis from developing their own atomic weapon?"

Elsa's eyes widened, her heart skipping a beat. "What are you talking about?"

Culper leaned back, his gaze drifting out over the churning waves. "The Nazis have their own atomic program, Elsa. They call it Uranverein, the Uranium Club. And they're close, dangerously close, to developing a bomb of their own."

Elsa felt a chill run down her spine, a sense of dread settling in the pit of her stomach. "How do you know this?"

Culper turned to face her, his expression grave. "Because I'm with the OSS, Elsa. And we need your help."

Elsa's mind reeled, the revelation hitting her like a physical blow. She had suspected that Culper was more than he seemed, but this? This was beyond anything she could have imagined. "You're OSS?"

"Yes."

Elsa rose and moved toward her bicycle.

"Wait. Just hear me out."

Elsa stopped, considered for a moment, then sat back down. "You've got one minute."

"We need someone with a strong knowledge of nuclear physics."

"You've got Oppenheimer."

"Yeah, well… he's a bit busy. Plus, he's not right for this mission.

"Mission?"

"Yes. And we need a woman about your age."

"For what?"

"To stop the Nazis from achieving their goal."

"I don't understand."

"Not yet, but you will… if you accept."

"You want me to accept without knowing what you want me to do?"

"Yes."

"I'll pass."

"Elsa, if Hitler develops an atomic bomb before the Allies, the fate of the free world will hang in the balance."

"It's that "before the Allies" that bothers me, Culper. You and the war department are no different from the Germans. You both want to create a weapon that can kill tens of thousands in a blink of the eye."

"You're right. We do. But that is not what I am asking you to do."

"What do you mean?"

Culper considered his argument before uttering his next words, "If you could stop either side from developing an atomic bomb, wouldn't you do it?"

"Yes, of course."

"That's what I am asking you do to… stop the Germans from developing their bomb."

"And what about the Americans?"

"You remain neutral concerning the Americans. You don't help and you don't hurt our efforts. Elsa, you could be the key to ending the war, to saving countless lives."

Elsa took a moment to think. The concept was complex and absorbing.

"If you were standing next to a man about to throw a grenade into a city bus full of passengers, would you stop him?"

"Of course I would. I'd talk him out of it."

"And what if he didn't listen and pulled the pin. Then what would you do? How far would you go to save those passengers?"

"You want me to kill?"

"No. I want you to stop our enemies from killing innocent civilians."

"Culper, we're not talking about a bus load of passengers. We're talking about a weapon with the potential for unbelievable destruction."

"All the more reason to stop Hitler from developing it. He will use it, Elsa."

"And Roosevelt won't?"

"I would trust our president far more than Hitler when it comes to the use of atomic weapons."

"And I fail to see the difference. Whoever detonates an atomic bomb will kill multitudes. Intentions won't matter."

"Elsa, you're being naïve if you don't see the difference."

"It's my prerogative, Culper. Your minute is up."

Elsa climbed on her bike and rode down the hill.

"The world needs you, Elsa," he called out as she pedaled away, but she couldn't bring herself to reply. The tears flowed freely now, freezing against her cheeks as she rode back to campus, her head a battleground of conflicting emotions.

Elsa's anger burned bright, a fire stoked by the arrogance of this OSS officer who thought he could sway her with appeals to patriotism and fear.

And yet, beneath the rage, a small voice whispered in the back of her mind. What if he was right? What if her pacifism, her unwavering commitment to non-violence, was nothing more than naivete in the face of a world consumed by war and brutality?

Elsa shook her head, trying to banish the traitorous thoughts. She had made her choice, and she would stand by it. Her work, her brilliance, would be a beacon of hope in a world gone mad, a tribute to the power of science to uplift and enlighten, not destroy.

But as she neared the weathered spires of Foster Hall, the doubts continued to gnaw at her. The path ahead was uncertain, fraught with moral dilemmas and impossible choices. And though she clung to her convictions like a lifeline, Elsa couldn't shake the feeling that her world, and her place in it, were about to change forever.

Inside her cramped office, she slumped at her desk where equations still covered the blackboards in expectation. She knew she must push aside messy emotions to reclaim logic's anchor. There lay certainty and purpose. In time, her fiery confrontation with Culper would fade before relentless curiosity.

It was late. Elsa rubbed at the crick in her neck as she gathered notebooks together, finally forced by exhaustion to leave the haven of diagrams and formulas on her chalkboards. Stepping into the midnight quiet of the corridor, she secured her office door, shuffling papers into her worn leather satchel.

Elsa started at an unexpected looming silhouette engulfing the hallway's dim corner - Culper stood leaning against the bricks, arms casually crossed as if standing silent vigil for hours. What in heaven was he still doing here?

Their eyes caught and held for a tense moment and Elsa swore she glimpsed his flinty glare soften briefly. But she knew better than to endure another round of righteous posturing tonight. Squaring her tired shoulders, Elsa glared straight ahead into the gloom as she strode briskly past the imposing agent. Culper's steely gaze and unwavering determination were forged in the fires of the Great Depression, where he lost his family and learned to rely on his own wits and tenacity to survive, qualities that now made him an invaluable asset to the OSS.

Maintaining a rapid clip toward her dormitory, she refused to acknowledge the heaviness of Culper's expectant stare still boring into her retreating back. Didn't he have more willing recruits to intimidate?

A bone-deep chill hugged the shadowy grounds as newly fallen snowflakes swirled around her legs in tiny whirlwinds. The dark Gothic halls of the university stood as dim bastions now, scattered lamps in high windows warding off full surrender to the icy night. Only the crunch of her shoes cracking ice on the cobblestones broke the palpable silence.

Passing the twin stone lions guarding the philosophy building, Elsa tugged her coat tighter against the frigid air, yearning for the refuge of her tiny dormitory room and narrow bed ahead. At this late hour, the dark halls would be deserted except for a few oddball physics wonks still arguing quantum theory over tepid coffee and a wheezing radiator.

Tucked under her threadbare wool blanket, Elsa lied awake staring at the ceiling of her bedroom. The complex equations that she used to tire her mind like counting sheep no longer manifested themselves. Instead, she was left with the conversation she had with Culper earlier that day. Her head throbbed. He was a barbarian and a warmonger for sure, but he wasn't wrong and that was what bothered her most. And there were other things…

Elsa had heard the rumors of relocation camps outside the cities where the Nazis herded dissidents and undesirables in the countries they had captured. A barbaric practice.

At first, Elsa imagined the reports were exaggerations borne of wartime fears, doubtless some measure of temporary detainment awaited dissenters in any embattled nation. But whispered conversations with European colleagues hinted a bleaker reality — entire districts gutted overnight without explanation, terrified refugee accounts of specialized settlements hemmed in by concrete and barbed wire.

As Elsa wrestled to reconcile the accounts, she clung to the lifeline of clear evidence and reason against rumors and ambiguity. There must be some misunderstanding. No civilized people could tolerate such violations against humanity for long without outcry.

But with each new report, her skepticism eroded. She knew she would have to choose between naive denial and facing harsh truth if her ideals hoped to withstand the coming darkness.

Elsa questioned if her own pacifistic outlook had contributed to the Nazis' denials. By refusing to accuse the Reich had she allowed it to continue its covert activities? And what else had Hitler done that she hadn't heard about?

Elsa turned to her side, pulling her covers tight against the draft creeping through the warped window frame. She watched the faint pulse of the streetlights beyond the deserted snow-lined road.

She had read every paper her father had ever written

as if somehow those words would connect her with him. She squeezed her eyes shut trying to summon his gentle wisdom that had soothed her restless mind in the past. But instead of comforting familiar physics equations, Culper's icy images of corpses burned from radiation simmered behind her eyelids.

Elsa shuddered. In the name of science, she had advanced the destructive weaponry destined to threaten mankind. If the world ended, was she partly to blame?

She rose hastily to click on her desk lamp, seeking light to banish the visions but also clarity from the jumbled books and papers around her. Titles on ethics, quantum mechanics, and Tolstoy scattered over a newspaper with headlines about fresh Nazi atrocities in the East. The clock's hands cruelly reminded her that no respite would come before the dawn.

She sank back into her chair gazing outward through the frost-lined window. The stars of Orion shone brightly between scuttling clouds over the silent campus. What answers lay beyond this tiny world of Chicago streets and dorm rooms she had accepted as the entirety of existence just twenty-four hours before? For she could no longer pretend neutrality nor inaction was still a choice.

A storm passed over Chicago's skyscrapers. The university woke as it always did for early morning classes. Dark rings under her eyes, Elsa hurried through the swirling snow towards campus, fatigue weighing down each step after the long restless night. She spotted Culper's unmistakable form on the Physics building's cement bench as she drew closer, two steaming paper cups and a bag beside him.

Bristling internally, Elsa kept her eyes fixed ahead as she navigated the slippery path right past him. Several paces beyond, Elsa hesitated despite her ire, curiosity slowly turning her chin to glance back. Culper watched her with that intense hawk gaze, breath fogging the frigid air, silently waiting to see if she would break first.

Damn the man. He clearly intended setting up camp indefinitely. Elsa stalked back to stand imperiously over his bench. "For argument's sake, what exactly would you want me to do?" said Elsa.

"So, you accept?" said Culper.

"No. But I sure as hell am not going to commit to anything without knowing what I am getting myself into first."

"That's fair. But for that, we're gonna need a bit more privacy," said Culper.

"Okay. Five minutes of my time so you'll leave me in peace."

"Let's make it fifteen minutes. You may have questions."

"Fine," said Elsa picking up one of the cups and fishing a bagel from the bag. Culper rose and followed Elsa.

Inside her office, Elsa dusted off an extra chair covered in eraser dust. Culper sat, sipped his coffee, and said, "Have you thought about what we discussed?"

"I've thought of nothing else. You're a real bastard, you know that?" said Elsa. "But there is some logic to your arguments. You are right about Hitler if he gets the bomb first, he'll use it and millions may die."

"Good. We have a basis for discussion."

"What discussion? Just tell me what you want me to

do."

"Alright. I want you to help me sabotage the Norsk heavy water research facility at Telemark, Norway."

"What?!"

"I didn't stutter."

"Me? You want me to help you sabotage a research facility?"

"Yes."

"That's ridiculous. I've never fired a gun or blown anything up in my life."

"And yet, you designed a nuclear reactor that could be the basis for an atomic bomb."

"Two different things – technology development and sabotage."

"Not that different."

"Now, who's being naïve?"

"To sabotage a research facility you need to know what to destroy, right?"

"I suppose."

"You know what's important, or at least you will once you see it."

"What? Are you going to show me photographs or something?"

"No. You'll need to go there… to Telemark."

"To Norway?"

"You speak the language. Quite fluently I'm told. And your heritage is Norwegian."

"Norway is under German occupation, you know?"

"I am aware of that fact."

"I would be going behind enemy lines."

"Yes. It's not as big of a deal as you think. I've done it many times. As long as your paperwork is in order, and it will be, you shouldn't have a problem."

"Jesus, you want me to be a spy?"

"Yes. You're highly intelligent, Elsa. You can do this."

Elsa sipped the coffee slowly, letting the warmth infuse her chilled bones as she contemplated Culper's outrageous request. "Your confidence in my aptitude is flattering, but I'm no covert operative. You must have professionals trained for these types of missions?"

Culper leaned forward, "We do - brave souls. But none possess your rare genius for particle physics. We've intercepted intelligence about a new heavy water extraction design far more productive than current technology and Germany's brightest minds are building it under a mountain at Telemark. I need someone who not only speaks Norwegian, but speaks the language of atoms and quarks to decipher their advancements."

He withdrew a technical diagram scrawled with cryptic notations and German words circling a cylindrical vessel. Elsa's scientific curiosity couldn't help but be piqued, even as her conscience recoiled instinctively.

Culper continued his appeal. "With your insights into exactly which processes and equipment to sabotage, we could potentially save millions of lives by hindering the Nazis' nuclear program for months or even years."

Elsa traced the reactor's cooling pipes and ion chambers, personal dreams of future clean energy admiring Germany's engineering prowess before revulsion rose anew. These same brilliant constructs destined to drive Fascism's horrific vision across the world. "So, how would it work... me helping you?"

"Have you ever heard of Dr. Paula Aadland?"

"The physicist?"

"Yes."

"I think I read one of her papers on advanced heavy water extraction techniques, but I don't know much about her."

"She's a Norwegian Fascist that's been working in Finland heading up their nuclear research program. Since Germany's invasion of Russia, Finland has become a German ally. Aadland has been chosen for a key research position at the Norsk Research Facility. She will be heading to Norway shortly by train through Sweden."

"What does that have to do with me?"

"We want you to impersonate Dr. Aadland and occupy her position at Norsk. The switch will take place aboard the train to Norway," said Culper handing Elsa a photo of Dr. Aadland – a striking woman with sharp cheekbones and a cascade of golden curls gazed back confidently. The photo could have been a glamorous magazine cover if not for the utilitarian lab coat. Aadland looked born for the spotlight.

Elsa laughed, "You gotta be kidding? I look nothing like this woman. She's more than beautiful. She's stunning," Elsa managed, shifting self-consciously. All gangly limbs and muted academic attire, she felt instantly dwarfed by this Amazonian goddess's aura even just through paper and ink.

"I admit. It's gonna be a challenge, but you underestimate yourself."

Elsa laughed, "And you're in dreamland."

"My people assure me your face's bone structure and slender figure are close to hers and they can make your appearance close enough to Aadland's that it will work."

She traced a trembling finger over the photo woman's elegant velvet dress under lab coat, then glanced down at her own rumpled wool sweater and trousers.

"Do they have magic wands? Cuz they're gonna need them."

"Let us worry about the physical stuff. The hard part will be learning Aadland's unique persona and mannerisms in the limited amount of time available."

"How long do I have?"

"Eighteen days."

"Is that even possible?"

"I believe it is."

"And if I am found out?"

"They won't find out. I'll make sure of it."

"But if they do?"

"You'll probably be tortured and shot."

Elsa was in shock. "I'm a physicist, not a spy."

"You can learn. I'll teach you everything you need to know."

Culper could see that Elsa was overwhelmed and sought to calm her, "I'll be near you the during the entire mission."

"You'll be going with me?"

"Mostly, yes. I can't actually get into Norsk. You'll need to do that part on your own, but I'll be in the town of Telemark if you need my help."

He could see she was on the cusp of rejecting the mission.

"I need to think about this," said Elsa her eyes darting around, unsure.

"There isn't much time," said Culper.

"You just informed me that I could be tortured and shot. I'm gonna need to process that before I can make a decision."

"I understand, but I hope you realize what is at stake."

"Yeah, my life."

"…and the lives of millions if we fail."

"You really don't let up, do you?"

"No. It's not in my nature."

"Yeah, I got that. How long can I have?"

"The day."

"And if I say no?"

"You are the only one that can do this, Elsa. Believe me, we looked. There is no plan B."

"The day then."

"I'll see you at 5:00."

Culper left.

Sunlight filtered through high clerestory windows as Elsa stood peering down from the university pool's overlook at the several lanes of swimmers splitting the turquoise waters below. She inhaled the soothing scent of chlorine before descending to take her usual lane for laps.

The familiar routine of stretching on deck then fastening her trusty faded silver swim cap into place grounded Elsa as her thoughts continued wrestling over Culper's audacious mission proposal. Slice through the water, turn, kick - could she truly brave enemy terrain wearing another woman's identity to enable a targeted attack? Even in service of the greater good, she would be abandoning her pacifist principles. There would be no denying it - she would be taking sides in a war. Even if successful, she wondered who she would be when it was done.

Focusing on controlling the splash her fingertips

made cutting into the pool at each stroke, Elsa tried weighing the millions of lives she could help save against the brutish idea that her single life held prohibitive worth. And what about the Germans that might die during the sabotage or if the Americans achieved the atomic bomb first because of her efforts. Every soul carried the luminous spark. Who was she to measure one flame over another? Even those in Fascist uniforms.

Approaching the wall in a frenzied sprint at set's end, Elsa clung there as if the mission's risks and moral quandaries might drown her if she could not anchor to some less turbulent philosophic harbor in her mind. How could she possibly decide in the hours that were left when so much was at stake?

She caressed the fading tiles, the comfort so palpable of this campus sanctuary. With all her heart, she wanted to return to the comfort of her blackboards. But she knew, nothing would be the same, not even her blackboards, if she turned down the sacrifice demanded of her.

As the university's clock struck five, Elsa walked toward Culper sitting on the bench in front of the physics building. As much as she enjoyed seeing the brash soldier suffer, she got right to the point ending his turmoil. "If I do this, I want to make two things clear – First, I won't kill anyone or blow anything up. That's your job."

"Agreed," said Culper.

"Second, I will be helping you prevent Hitler from developing an atomic bomb. I will not be helping America develop an atomic bomb."

"Agreed."

"Then, I'm in."

Culper offered a slight smile. He had done the impossible.

Transformation

OSS Training Facilities – USA

Elsa stared at the pistol Culper was attempting to hand her, feeling her chest tighten like a caged bird desperate for freedom. The metal gleamed in the cold light, a stark reminder of the violence that seemed to permeate every aspect of this war. "No," she said, her voice barely above a whisper. "You said I didn't have to shoot anyone or blow up anything. You were going to handle that stuff."

Culper's eyes narrowed, a flicker of annoyance passing over his chiseled features. "And I will, but I can't plan for every eventuality. You should be prepared in an emergency."

Elsa felt a surge of frustration, her hands clenching at her sides. "What kind of emergency?"

"Elsa, we don't have time for this. Just take the pistol and let me teach you how to fire it." Culper's voice was tight, his patience wearing thin.

But Elsa couldn't let it go, couldn't ignore the sickening twist in her gut at the thought of taking a life. "What kind of emergency?" she repeated, her tone insistent.

Culper sighed, running a hand through his hair. "Fine. What if I get shot during the mission?"

Elsa's eyes widened, her breath catching in her throat. "You expect me to defend you?"

"It would be nice."

She shook her head, a bitter laugh escaping her lips. "I'm not going to kill for you, Culper."

"Okay... just wing 'em. Now, pick up the damned gun and shoot the target."

Elsa's hands shook as she lifted the stubby pistol, the checkered handle cold and unyielding against her skin. She squinted through the tiny iron sights, her breath forming clouds in the frigid air as she aimed at the makeshift paper target dangling from a tree in the snowy woods. The scent of pine and gunpowder filled her nostrils, a jarring contrast to the sterile labs and musty books that had been her world for so long.

"Both eyes open," Culper instructed, his breath hot against her neck. "And use the front sight as your point of focus, not the target itself. You'll shoot better instinctively that way."

Elsa inhaled deeply, the cold air burning her lungs as she let out half her breath, just as Culper had taught her. Her finger tightened on the trigger, the metal biting into her skin as she fought to keep her aim steady. The loud crack of the gunshot sent a flock of crows flapping from the bare branches overhead, their harsh cries echoing through the stillness of the forest.

She peeked anxiously at the target, her heart jumping as she saw the smoking hole through the periphery. A part of her knew she should be appalled at the idea of firing a weapon, at the thought of causing harm to another living being. But another part of her, a part she hadn't even known existed until now, felt a thrill of exhilaration at the power that coursed through her veins.

Elsa fired again and again, the recoil of the pistol sending shockwaves up her arms as she emptied the gun. The acrid scent of gunpowder filled her nostrils, the taste of metal lingering on her tongue as she lowered the weapon, her chest heaving with the effort.

Culper nodded, a glimmer of approval in his eyes as he surveyed her first cluster. "Remember, shooting accurately matters far less than learning to draw, aim, and fire without hesitation when lives depend upon swift action. Shall we run the drill again?"

Elsa reset her stance, her feet planted firmly in the snow as she tried to ignore the guilt that gnawed at her insides. She had always believed in the power of the mind, in the ability of science and reason to solve even the most complex problems. But here, in the heart of the forest, with the weight of the pistol in her hand and the echo of gunshots ringing in her ears, she couldn't help but wonder if violence was the only language that mattered in this war.

As the training continued, Elsa felt herself slipping further and further from the person she had once been. The timid scholar, the pacifist who had raged against the brutality of the world, seemed like a distant memory now. In her place stood a new Elsa, a woman who could field strip a pistol in under twenty seconds, who could navigate treacherous terrain in the dead of night, who could blend into any crowd and disappear without a trace.

But even as her skills grew, even as Culper's approval became a source of pride and satisfaction, Elsa couldn't shake the sense of unease that settled in the pit of her stomach. She had always believed that science should be used for the betterment of humanity, that knowledge was a gift to be shared and celebrated. But now, as she prepared to infiltrate the most secure fortifications of the Reich, to unearth the secrets that could shift the tide of the war, she couldn't help but wonder if she was betraying everything she had ever stood for.

The relentless sun reflected off the snowpack as it beat down upon the vast expanse of the OSS training compound, its scorching rays painting the barbed wire fences and the glistening faces of the recruits in a shimmering haze. Elsa collapsed onto a weathered wooden bench, her lungs burning and her muscles screaming from the brutal morning's hand-to-hand combat drills. Every fiber of her being ached, a physical manifestation of the mental and emotional toll this training had taken on her.

Culper sat beside her, the wax paper of his sandwich crinkling as he unwrapped it, the sound a jarring contrast to the heavy stillness of the afternoon. He took a contemplative bite, his gaze distant as it swept over the snow-covered training grounds, a man lost in his own thoughts.

"I know it's a lot to take in, but you're making progress," he said at last.

Elsa felt a heavy sigh escape her lips, her hand instinctively running through her sweat-soaked hair, a futile attempt to tame the wild strands. "I don't know, Culper. There's just so much to remember, so many skills to master. I feel like I'm barely keeping my head above water."

Culper turned to face her, his eyes locking onto hers with an intensity that stole her breath. "I won't lie to you, Elsa. This training is tough, tougher than anything you've ever done before. But I've seen the determination in your eyes, the strength in your spirit. You have what it takes to succeed."

A flicker of warmth ignited within Elsa's chest at his words, a spark of pride that burned through the exhaustion and the doubt, illuminating the darkest corners of her soul. Culper's praise was not given lightly, and she knew that he meant every word.

"But what if I'm not ready?" The question fell from her lips in a breathless whisper, her deepest fears laid bare. "What if I make a mistake, and people get hurt because of me?"

"You'll be ready, Elsa. I'll make sure of it. You have a gift, a brilliance that the world needs now more than ever. I'm just here to help you unleash it."

He stood, brushing the crumbs from his lap and extending a hand to her, an invitation and a challenge all in one. "Come on, let's get back to it. We've got a lot of work to do."

Elsa grasped his hand, allowing him to pull her to her feet. As they strode back out onto the training grounds, she felt a sense of destiny, of purpose, that she had never before experienced.

An ice cliff rose before them, a towering behemoth. Its surface shimmered in the wan light, a tapestry of glacial blues and crystalline whites, each jagged contour a specimen of the relentless forces that had carved it over countless winters. At its base, a chaotic jumble of shattered ice and compacted snow whispered of the perils that lay in wait for those foolhardy enough to test their mettle against the mountain's might. The air surrounding the frozen monolith hung heavy with an eerie stillness, broken only by the occasional gust of wind that sent a flurry of snowflakes swirling across the cliff's face.

"Today, we climb," Culper said, his breath misting in the cold air as they stood at the base of the towering cliff.

Elsa stared up at the frozen wall, her head already starting to spin. "Climb? Up there?"

Culper nodded, handing her a pair of ice axes, their metal gleaming in the pale light. "First, you need to understand the ice. It's not just a barrier. It's your path, and you have to trust it."

Elsa gripped the axes, the cold of the handles seeping through her gloves. She nodded, a silent acknowledgment of the respect she must pay to conquer the cliff.

"Position your feet right," Culper instructed, demonstrating a stance that balanced agility with strength. "Kick in with your toes. Make every move deliberate. One careful step at a time."

Elsa followed, the spikes of her crampons biting into the ice, the crunch of compacted snow underfoot. She swung an axe, its point sinking into the cliff face. Then another. Step by step, she ascended, her breaths coming in short gasps, mingling with the snowflakes that danced around her.

At the top, Culper waited, a solitary figure against the gray sky. He didn't help as she summited the cliff pulling herself up and over the edge. It was her honor and he wouldn't take it away from her, not one bit. He let her catch her breath and bask in her achievement, then said, "Now, for the descent. Rappelling is about trust. Trust in your equipment, trust in your training, and above all, trust in yourself."

He showed her how to set the ropes, how to harness herself in, and how to lean back into the void, letting the rope and gravity guide her descent. "The key," he explained, "is to let go, but with control. It's a balance of forces – tension on the rope and gravity."

Elsa leaned back, her body suspended, her fate in the hands of the physics she knew so well, yet had never applied in such a raw, primal form. She descended, the rope running through her gloves, her boots bouncing off the icy face of the cliff. Her feet touched down, a reunion with solid ground.

Culper offered a slight nod, an unspoken acknowledgment of her accomplishment. Elsa, with a smile that fought through the cold, realized that the ice had taught her more than just how to climb. It had shown her a new way to understand her world, not through equations and theories, but through the raw, unyielding laws of nature itself.

As they made their way back to base, the sun dipping below the horizon and casting long shadows across the snow, Elsa couldn't help but marvel at the strange twists of fate that had brought her to this moment. Just days ago, she had been a pacifist, a woman who believed that violence was never the answer. But now, as she prepared to embark on a mission that could change the course of history, she knew that sometimes, the only way to fight darkness was with darkness of your own.

"Just keep putting one foot in front of the other, and you'll get through it," said Culper.

"I don't know if I'm cut out for this, Culper. I'm exhausted all the time. I can't even think."

"That's just your body conserving energy. It'll get better in a couple of days as your muscles rebuild and become more efficient."

"God, I hope so."

"You're exactly what we need, Elsa. Your mind, your skills, your courage – they're all going to be crucial to the success of this mission."

Elsa sighed, her breath misting in the cold air. "Nice pep talk. I just hope I don't let you down."

Culper squeezed her shoulder, his eyes intense. "You won't. I believe in you, Elsa. And more importantly, you need to believe in yourself."

As they reached the base, the lights of the compound glowing in the distance, Elsa knew that Culper was right. She had to believe in herself, had to trust in the strength and resilience that had brought her this far.

As she lay in her bunk that night, the sounds of the base fading into the distance, Elsa closed her eyes and let the memories wash over her. The crack of gunshots, the bite of the icy wind, the weight of the pistol in her hand. They were all a part of her now, woven into the fabric of her being. She wasn't sure she wanted them but they were there none the less and she couldn't deny them.

As another day of training drew to a close, Elsa found herself utterly exhausted, her mind reeling from the sheer volume of information she had been forced to absorb. It was like cramming for a final exam, every detail vital, every fact a potential lifeline in the perilous mission that lay ahead.

She stumbled into her room at the safehouse, kicking off her shoes and collapsing onto the bed, her body aching for the familiarity of her cozy dormitory. A knock at the door shattered her momentary reprieve, and she dragged herself to her feet.

Culper stood in the hallway, his face a mask of urgency. "I know you're tired," he said, his voice low and insistent, "but I need to review Aadland's research papers."

Elsa sighed, the prospect of venturing out into the cold night almost too much to bear. "They're in my office on campus. I can get them for you in the morning."

But Culper was unyielding. "It can't wait. I can give you a ride."

With a reluctant sigh, Elsa slipped on her shoes, grabbed her coat, and followed Culper out into the frigid darkness.

The campus was a ghost town, the buildings looming like silent sentinels in the night. Elsa made her way to the physics building, her footsteps echoing in the empty corridors. A sliver of light spilled from a partially open door, the sound of whispers drifting from within.

Elsa's senses were heightened by the training that had consumed her every waking moment. She pushed the door open, her body tensed for danger, only to be met with a chorus of "Surprise!" Balloons bobbed against the ceiling, and a cake proclaimed "Congrats, Double Doc!" in cheerful letters.

Tears sprang to Elsa's eyes as she took in the smiling

faces of her colleagues, their pride and admiration washing over her like a warm embrace. Dr. Fermi wrapped an arm around her shoulders, his voice filled with warmth and affection. "Just received word that the review board officially approved your second dissertation. You've done it - two doctorates by twenty-three! That's got to be some kind of record."

As the others crowded around, offering hugs and handshakes, Elsa caught a glimpse of Culper watching from the hallway, his usually stern features softened by a hint of pride. In that moment, she understood with startling clarity why she had to risk everything for his cause - he was one of the good guys, fighting for a world where moments like this could still exist.

With a deep breath, Elsa turned back to her colleagues, determined to savor this last moment of normalcy before her fateful leap into the unknown.

When she woke early the next morning, Elsa stumbled into the kitchen in hopes of coffee. The safehouse walls, covered in maps and grainy photos, had become a second home, a constant reminder of the weight of her mission. Culper sat beneath the flickering light, his eyes clouded with concern.

"What's happened?" Elsa asked, her voice trembling with trepidation.

Culper gestured for her to sit, his sigh heavy with the burden of command. "The mission timeline has been moved up. Aadland leaves for Norway within the week. We're out of time."

Panic gripped Elsa, the enormity of the task threatening to overwhelm her. "But... I'm not ready."

"We don't have a choice," Culper said, his voice firm but not unkind. "Once she enters Norsk, there won't be another opportunity to replace her."

Elsa's thoughts twisted and turned, searching for a way out, a glimmer of hope in the darkness. "This was impossible from the start. What makes you think I can fool anyone into believing that I am this woman?"

Culper leaned forward, his gaze intense. "Because you need to, Elsa. She's the key to getting into Norsk and stopping the Nazis from finishing their bomb. You are the only one that can pull off the physics convincingly."

Elsa felt the weight of his words settle on her shoulders, a mantle of responsibility that she had never asked for but could not refuse. "The physics I can handle," she said, her voice barely above a whisper, "but there's a lot more than physics needed to pass me off as Dr. Paula Aadland."

"How do you know what's required?" Culper asked. "Have you ever done it before?"

"Well... no," Elsa admitted, her cheeks flushing with embarrassment. "But come on... look at her."

Culper shook his head, his eyes never leaving hers. "I don't need to look at her. I see you. And I know deep down that you can pull this off. You just need to have faith in yourself."

Elsa fell silent, her mind a whirlwind of doubt and determination. There was no turning back now, no escape from the path that fate had laid before her. "Alright," she said at last, her voice barely a whisper. "I'll do my best."

Culper nodded, his expression a mix of pride and apprehension as he unrolled the map that would guide them towards Telemark and the destiny that awaited them both.

Elsa sat nervously in the hotel suite's embroidered bar stool. Claire, the OSS master stylist scrutinized her mousy strands against Dr. Aadland's photo. Culper observed from the suite door and said, "Well?"

"I agree with you. It's all there. It's just hidden," said Claire keeping her focus on Elsa.

"Alright. Uncover it."

"These things take time."

"That's not something we have a lot of."

"Okay. We best get started then."

Elsa tensed as Claire slid her scissors around one of her chestnut locks. Snip. It fell in Elsa's lap. She could hardly breath as she looked down at it.

"Relax. It's just hair. It will grow back if that is what you choose," said Claire.

"It'll take years," said Elsa tears welling up in her eyes.

"We must all sacrifice. You can buy a wig if it means that much to you. But I don't think that will be necessary."

"What do you mean?"

"You'll see." Claire continued to cut, trim, and angle with the scissors. A master of style.

Flinching with each new strand falling to the tile floor, Elsa slowly relaxed as a new image emerged in the mirror. Someone she had never seen before. A stranger. A beautiful stranger.

Elsa was mesmerized. Claire worked swiftly, brow knit with artistic concentration, angling and shearing further up Elsa's scalp. The snips of hair became smaller and smaller as she honed her design, glancing at the photo of Aadland, then snipping a bit more. Finally, she was done. "What do you think?" said Claire.

"It doesn't look like me," said Elsa staring in the mirror.

"Is that such a bad thing?"

"No. I suppose not."

"If you ladies are done critiquing, I'd like to get on with this. We have a schedule to keep," said Culper tapping his watch.

Elsa glared at him in the mirror. Not even the slightest compliment. Unfeeling man beast.

Claire escorted Elsa to the bathroom and closed the door to prevent Culper from upsetting her patient. She washed and dried Elsa's hair, then wheeled over a tray table arrayed with foils, bleaches and dyes. "Just a bit more work." She said as she whipped a stained cape around Elsa's neck briskly.

Over the next hour, Elsa choked back reflexive gags against the noxious ammonia fumes invading her nostrils as Claire massaged chemicals across her tingling scalp. "I need to dye your eyebrows and pubic hair," said Claire.

"My pubic hair? Why?" said Elsa.

"Because details matter. They can keep you alive when you least expect it."

"But nobody is going to see down there."

"If there is one thing I have learned in all the years of doing this, it's that you can't predict what is going to happen during a mission."

"You mean I might have to seduce someone for information?"

"I don't know. That's the point. It's like being a Boy Scout… always be prepared."

Elsa considers for a moment, then opened her towel… "Alright. Do whatever you need to do."

"You have a nice figure. That should work well for

you."

"You mean in the spy game?"

"That… and life. The war won't last forever."

"I hope not. I'd hate to think I need to bleach my nether regions for the rest of my life."

Claire laughs as she goes to work on Elsa's nether region.

The last swirling rivulet of dye disappeared down the sink. Claire toweled the result dry gently, easing Elsa back to face the final result. "It seems darker than I imagined," she said afraid to touch her hair.

"It will lighten over the next few days," said Claire. "Trust me. It will match Aadland's hair color."

"I do… trust you. It's amazing."

Claire gave a slight bow in appreciation. "We won't curl it until you are ready to leave. The color needs time to set in before we apply heat."

"Okay."

"Shall we let Culper have a peek?"

"Do we have to?"

"Be brave."

Elsa and Claire left the bathroom. Busy reading a report, Culper looked up at Elsa. He did everything he could to hide his astonishment, but Elsa could see it in his eyes… desire.

"Well?" said Claire.

"She looks… good," said Culper.

"Good?"

"Okay, better than good. We need to keep on schedule."

"You and your damned schedule."

"It's how I get things done."

"Fine."

Claire sat Elsa back down and wheeled over a cart filled with makeup and pieces of disguises. "Are you going to give me a new nose?" said Elsa.

"Your nose is fine, as is everything else. We just need to add a bit of definition here and there. You need to watch how I apply your makeup, especially the scar. You will be doing this on your own once you get to Norway."

"Scar?"

"Aadland has a small half-moon shaped scar on her left cheek that she hides with her hair and makeup. She got it when she was a teenager climbing a fence to pet a horse. She slipped and her face hit the top of the fence post. It must have been very traumatic for her. We'll start with the scar, then cover it up with makeup as Aadland would do."

"Okay."

Claire started with a dab of wood glue on the end of a small, pointed brush. She drew a small crescent-mooned shape on Elsa's left cheek and gently pinched it together to form the scar as the glue dried. "We don't know the actual size or location of the scar beyond her left cheek. She is very self-conscious about the scar and has never let anyone see it let alone photograph it."

"So, how do you know this is correct?"

"I don't. But neither does anyone else. At times, a best guess is all we have."

With the glue dry, Claire examined her work and was satisfied. Next, she dabbed another small, pointed brush across red lipstick covering the tiny bristles. She made a single stroke in the center of the scar turning it pink, then dabbed a cotton ball to soak up any excess liquid and give the scar a slight rough look. She leaned back and studied her work. It was convincing.

"Done."

Elsa moved up to the mirror and studied the scar. "It looks real. It's kind of sad. She has such a beautiful face."

"She's a fascist helping the Nazis. Don't forget that," said Culper, not looking up from his reports.

"She's still human," said Elsa defiantly.

"I'm not sure about that. Wait until you meet her."

"Wait… You've met her before?"

"Yeah. Once. We keep track of people like her."

"Scientists?"

"Collaborators."

Claire's skilled hands moved with a meticulous precision as she applied the foundation to Elsa's face, her touch as light as a whisper across her skin. With a careful hand, she crafted the illusion of a scar being covered up, a subtle blemish that would serve as evidence of the identity Elsa was to assume. The faux imperfection, a masterful blend of artistry and deception, sat upon Elsa's face like a secret waiting to be unveiled, a silent nod to the woman whose life she was about to step into.

Powder settled like a gossamer veil, softening the contours of her face. Bronzer accentuated Elsa's cheekbones, narrowing her nose, sculpting her features into Aadland's likeness. But it was the eyes that truly captivated, the makeup creating a gaze that held the mysteries of another life.

Claire stepped back, examining her work with a critical eye. Elsa's anticipation built, nerves and excitement dancing beneath her skin. When Claire handed her the mirror, Elsa's breath caught in her throat.

The face staring back was a stunning amalgamation

of herself and Aadland. Elsa's gaze darted between the photograph and her reflection, a giggle of disbelief escaping her lips. "I don't believe it," she breathed. "It's her."

Claire smiled, pride glimmering in her eyes. "Like I said, it was all there. It just needed to be uncovered."

Culper approached, his presence an annoying anchor. As he stood behind Elsa, his eyes met hers in the mirror. "Amazing," he whispered, reverence in his voice.

Elsa and Claire exchanged a glance, a silent communication passing between them. In unison, their voices rang out, a chorus of triumph and relief. "Finally."

Elsa fought the urge to flinch as Claire leaned in close, a contact lens poised on the tip of her finger. The sterile solution glistened in the harsh light, a promise and a threat.

"Just look straight ahead," Claire instructed, her voice a soothing balm. "Try not to blink."

Elsa gripped the chair, her knuckles white, as the lens drew closer. Its cold kiss sent a shiver down her spine, panic rising in her chest. She bit her tongue, tasting copper, as Claire maneuvered the lens into place.

Her vision swam, the world a blur of colors and shapes. Elsa reminded herself to breathe, to trust in the process. Claire's deft hands worked quickly, preparing the second lens.

"One down, one to go," Claire said, a smile in her voice. "You're doing great."

As Claire leaned in with the second lens, Elsa focused on her breathing, on the steady rise and fall of her chest. Each inhale brought her closer to her new reality, each exhale a letting go of the past. The second lens settled into place, a perfect match for the first.

"There," Claire said, stepping back to admire her work. "That wasn't so bad, was it? You have lovely eyes, but green will suit you better."

Elsa forced a smile, her stomach churning. She knew that vanity and stagecraft often required sacrifice, but the lenses felt like a betrayal, a stripping away of her identity.

"Done!" Claire proclaimed, swiveling Elsa's chair to face the mirror. "Have a look!"

Elsa hesitated, fear and anticipation warring within her. When she finally met her own gaze, she gasped. Paula Aadland stared back at her, a stranger wearing her face.

With trembling fingers, Elsa touched her cheek, marveling at the transformation. She was no longer the timid physicist, but a woman of power and purpose. "Hello, doctor," she whispered. "Shall we change the world?"

The lifts in her shoes added inches to her height, a physical manifestation of the change within. As Elsa slipped on the lingerie, she felt a blush creep up her neck. The silk and lace clung to her curves, a second skin that both empowered and unnerved her.

She stood before the mirror, a stranger and yet more herself than ever before. The chromatic barriers of her past had fallen away, revealing a woman ready to embrace the uncharted possibilities of her future.

Elsa stood before a sea of dresses, each one more luxurious than the last. The OSS seamstress flitted around her, placing pins with practiced precision, marking where the fabric needed to be taken in or let out.

Bracelets, necklaces, and purses followed, their opulence foreign to Elsa's modest sensibilities. She felt like a child playing dress-up, her mother's clothes engulfing her in a world of grown-up glamour. The seamstress watched, a knowing smile on her lips. "Remember," she said, her voice a gentle reminder. "Less is more."

With the transformation complete, Elsa turned to face the floor mirror, her breath catching in her throat. The woman who stared back at her was a stranger, beautiful and sexy, a femme fatale in the making. A flicker of confidence ignited within her, a spark of hope that maybe, just maybe, she could pull this off.

The door opened, and Culper stepped inside, his eyes widening as he took in the shimmering replica of their target. "You look just like her," he breathed, his voice a mixture of awe and disbelief.

Elsa paused, her fingers poised to reapply the ruby lip stain. "I think that's stretching it a bit," she said, doubt creeping into her tone. "But I have to admit, I'm in the ballpark. What if I meet someone who knew Aadland before she went to Finland?"

Culper shook his head, his expression reassuring. "It shouldn't be an issue. Aadland left for Finland before Hitler invaded Poland. Memories fade with time." He stepped closer, his gaze intense. "As long as you have Aadland's core persona and mannerisms down, you'll pass their scrutiny."

Elsa nodded, a sense of determination settling over her. She had come too far to let doubt creep in now. With a final glance in the mirror, she squared her shoulders, ready to embrace the role that fate had thrust upon her.

The seamstress watched, a knowing glint in her eye. She had seen transformations like this before, had witnessed the birth of legends in the making. And as Elsa stepped out of the room, her head held high and her stride confident, the seamstress knew that she was witnessing the beginning of something extraordinary.

In the final days before her departure, Elsa found herself hunched over a flickering screen in the safehouse backroom, her eyes fixed on the grainy films of Aadland's public appearances. She watched, transfixed, as the glamorous scientist wove a spell over her audiences, her charm and eloquence a weapon as potent as any bomb.

Aadland's voice, whether in English or Norwegian, held a rapid-fire confidence that left listeners enraptured, her accent shifting like a chameleon to suit her needs. One moment, she was the poised authority, unraveling the secrets of quarks with a deft hand and a textbook diagram. The next, she was a sultry temptress, her whispered words and coy glances leaving men starry-eyed and eager to pledge their funding to her cause.

Elsa saw through the façade, her keen eyes discerning the cool manipulator that lurked beneath Aadland's beguiling surface. To her, men were nothing more than steppingstones, their weaknesses and desires a means to an end. With each lingering handshake and manufactured laugh, Aadland ticked off a mental checklist, her piercing emerald eyes always searching for the next advantage, the next admirer to be collected and discarded.

A twinge of envy, unexpected and unwelcome, stirred in Elsa's heart. She had always shied away from such games, her polite withdrawal a shield against the attention she so desperately craved. But as she watched Aadland work her magic, Elsa couldn't help but wonder what doors might have opened had she cultivated such irresistible charm herself.

And yet, beneath the refined allure, Elsa sensed something ferocious, a hunger that made her recoil. If she were to inhabit this rapacious splendor, even temporarily, would the remnants of it cling to her psyche long after she had shed the false skin?

The sound of footsteps drew her from her reverie, and Elsa turned to see Culper standing in the doorway, his face frozen in surprise as a throaty feminine laugh echoed from the screen.

"Enjoying the films, I see," he said, his voice cutting through the darkness.

Elsa rose from the couch, her movements unconsciously mimicking Aadland's feline grace. She crossed the room, her emerald eyes glinting with a predatory light that made Culper's grin falter.

He tensed as she drew closer, her unfamiliar persona piercing his stoic armor. "I should let you rest," he managed, gently extricating himself from her grasp.

"If that's all you want?" Elsa sighed, her finger trailing down his chest before she released him, her touch leaving a trail of fire in its wake.

She reclined on the cushions, her smile a faint curve of invitation. "Should you need anything else, my door will be open... all night."

Culper cleared his throat, his fingers fumbling with his rumpled collar. "Get some sleep, Doctor," he said, his voice gruff as he retreated from the room, unaccustomed to the challenge of a subordinate's feminine wiles.

Elsa smiled to herself, a thrill of triumph coursing through her veins. The new identity was already working its magic, its power intriguing and intoxicating in equal measure.

That night, as she lay in her bed, Elsa half-expected a knock at the door, an acceptance of the invitation she had so boldly extended. But the knock never came, and as she drifted off to sleep, she couldn't help but wonder if Culper's restless dreams were haunted by the same visions of emerald eyes and feline grace that danced behind her own eyelids.

University of Chicago

Elsa cinched her thrift-store peacoat tighter against the knifing wind as she crossed the snow-lined campus quad. Frosty breath plumes trailing students rushed past her, flushed cheeks bent over armloads of literature or mathematics texts. She allowed herself a faint nostalgic smile at their carefree exuberance that she had inhabited only weeks prior.

But now each laugh and shouted greeting to friends across the yard only accentuated how irrevocably distanced Elsa felt from their familiar undergraduate escapades. Days that once revolved around problem sets, scholarly debates over coffee, and the occasional attempt at romance.

Her world was equations and ethics no longer, but crackling pistols in a frozen forest and a tormentor named Culper.

She paused outside the windows of the crowded

dining hall, observing an impromptu indoor snowball fight break out amidst yelps and smiles. Beanie-clad scholars pelted friends courageous or foolish enough to try crossing the food line under fire. Just youth unwinding before crackling fireplaces awaited in dormitory common rooms along with hours of studying late into the night.

She felt different like she comprehended something that the others could not. Pride swelled within her, a fierce and unshakable sense of accomplishment that burned bright against the backdrop of her trepidation. She had pushed herself to the very limits of her endurance, and in doing so, had discovered a well of strength she had never known existed. But even as she reveled in this newfound resilience, a profound sadness settled over her, a bittersweet realization that the carefree days of her youth had been forever lost to the inexorable march of time. The innocence that had once defined her, the unbridled passion for knowledge and discovery, had been tempered by the weight of the mission that now consumed her every thought. The world seemed different now, its once-familiar contours sharpened by the knowledge of the dangers that lurked beyond the confines of her beloved campus.

Elsa tightened her scarf, her exhaled breath vanishing swiftly. She turned resolutely towards the shadowed Physics tower looming over stately ivy-clad edifices nearby. Within those unassuming weathered halls, new complex formulas now commanded focus.

Soon she would become an infiltrator behind enemy lines. But tonight, the flakes fell silently as she wandered once familiar campus walkways, a stranger already irrevocably changed within.

Elsa stepped into her once-cherished sanctuary, her

gaze sweeping across the army of blackboards adorned with intricate equations, their chalky scent lingering in the air like a fading memory. The symbols and numbers that had once held such promise, such allure, now seemed diminished, their magic tarnished by the weight of the impending mission. A part of her, the scholar, the scientist, yearned to immerse herself once more in the comforting embrace of her work, to lose herself in the intricacies of the universe's secrets. But her heart, heavy with the burden of what lay ahead, could not summon the passion, the drive that had once consumed her every waking moment.

Exhaustion seeped into her bones, her muscles aching with a weariness that went beyond the physical, proof of the relentless training and the emotional toll of her newfound path. The mission, once a distant abstraction, now loomed before her, a monolithic presence that demanded her every thought, her every breath. Culper's warnings echoed in her mind, a grim reminder of the dangers that awaited her, the sacrifices she might be called upon to make. The specter of her own mortality hung heavy in the air, a constant companion that whispered of the fragility of life, the fleeting nature of existence.

With a heavy sigh, Elsa reached for the light switch, her fingers trembling as she plunged the room into darkness. She stepped back, her hand lingering on the doorknob, a final, fleeting connection to the world she had once called her own. As the door clicked shut behind her, a sense of finality settled over her, a bittersweet acknowledgment of the path she had chosen. The future stretched out before her, a vast and uncertain landscape, and Elsa couldn't help but wonder if she would ever find her way back to this moment, to the comfort and solace of her beloved office. But even as the doubts and fears swirled within her, she knew that there was no turning back, no retreat from the destiny that called to her with an inexorable pull. For better or worse, she had set her feet upon this path, and she would see it through to the end, no matter the cost.

The Switch

Midway International Airport – Chicago, Illinois

Elsa stood before the mirror in the airport restroom, her eyes filled with exhaustion and her mind heavy with doubt. Gone was the confident, alluring woman she had become in recent days, the one who had so easily slipped into the skin of Dr. Paula Aadland. In her place stood a shadow of her former self, clad in the familiar comfort of her faded university cardigan and horn-rimmed glasses.

She had thought that shedding her disguise would bring relief, a chance to breathe and be herself again, if only for a moment. But as she stared at her reflection, Elsa realized that she no longer knew who that self was. The lines between Elsa Kristiansen and Paula Aadland had blurred, leaving her adrift in a sea of uncertainty.

With a sigh, Elsa gathered her belongings and made her way to the boarding gate. Each step felt like a monumental effort, her body weighed down by the sleepless nights and the constant pressure of the mission ahead. She climbed the stairs to the airliner, her mind a haze of exhaustion and self-doubt.

The plane was nearly empty thanks to Culper's influence, and Elsa made her way down the aisle looking for her assigned seat on the ticket. Culper was already seated, his eyes fixed on a map spread across his lap. Elsa paused as she noticed the empty seat beside him. Why wasn't he sitting next to her?

"You're not wearing your contacts," Culper said, his voice cutting through her thoughts.

Elsa sighed, her shoulders sagging. "No. I thought I'd give my eyes a rest. They hurt when they're in too long."

Culper studied her, his gaze searching. "Everything okay?"

"Sure, everything is fine," Elsa replied, her voice flat and devoid of its usual energy. It was as if the fire that had burned so brightly within her had been extinguished, leaving only the shell of the woman she had once been. "I just didn't get much sleep last night."

"Yeah, me neither." Culper hesitated, his fingers tapping nervously against the armrest. "About the other night..."

Elsa held up a hand, her eyes pleading. "You don't need to say anything. In fact, I wish you wouldn't."

"You just threw me a curveball, Elsa. I wasn't ready for it."

"Right... a curveball." Elsa turned away, her voice barely above a whisper. "I am going to try and get some sleep, if it's okay with you?"

"Of course," Culper said, his voice softening. "It's a good idea. It's a long flight."

Elsa curled up in her seat, her overcoat pulled tight around her shoulders as she turned her back to Culper.

She closed her eyes, willing sleep to come, but her mind continued to juggle thoughts of the mission ahead and the man seated just a few feet away.

Culper watched her, concern etched into the lines of his face. He needed Elsa at her best, confident and razor-sharp, but the woman who sat before him now seemed a mere shadow of the brilliant scientist he had come to know. The change in her appearance, the return to her old, comfortable clothing, was a red flag he couldn't ignore.

He wondered if the pressure of the mission, the constant need to be someone else, had finally taken its toll on Elsa. Or perhaps it was something else, something more personal, that had drained the life from her eyes and the energy from her step.

As the plane lifted off, the city falling away beneath them, Culper knew that he would have to find a way to bring Elsa back to herself, to reignite the spark that had made her so special in the first place. The mission depended on it, and so did she.

Finland

The airliner droned on, a monotonous hum that filled the cabin as it soared over Finland's snow-dusted forests. Elsa sat huddled in her seat, her faded cardigan wrapped tightly around her as she stared out the window, lost in thought.

Culper's voice, low and discreet, broke through her trance. "Meet Mr. and Mrs. Nilsen," he said, producing two Norwegian passports from his briefcase. "On honeymoon from Trondheim, visiting her family in Oslo."

Elsa took the passport, her fingers shaky as they

brushed against the unfamiliar name on the identity page. She studied the forged documents and stamps, each one a reminder of the new identity she would soon have to embrace.

"Before you enter Norway," Culper continued, his voice barely above a whisper, "you will become Dr. Aadland. You'll use her passport and travel documents."

Elsa nodded, her eyes still fixed on the passport in her hands. She could feel the weight of her impending transformation pressing down on her, a suffocating force that threatened to overwhelm her.

"And you're certain I can successfully impersonate her mannerisms and speech freely enough not to be exposed by those who know her?" she asked, her voice small and uncertain.

Culper leaned closer, his eyes searching her face. "Dr. Aadland hasn't been in Norway for quite some time. The few that knew her as a younger woman are unlikely to remember all her details."

"And what about memories shared? What if they ask me about them?"

"Fake it," Culper said, his tone firm but not unkind. "But be smart about it. The fewer details you give them, the less there is to be uncovered."

Elsa swallowed hard, her nerves fraying at the edges. She knew that Culper was right, that she had to maintain her cover until the moment came to switch identities with Dr. Aadland. But the thought of shedding her own skin, of becoming someone else entirely, filled her with a sense of dread that she couldn't quite shake.

Culper seemed to sense her unease, his hand coming to rest on her arm in a gesture of reassurance.

"You were made for this, Elsa," he said, his voice soft but insistent. "Once we pass the first checkpoints, any lingering risks depend more upon steady nerves than further theatrics."

Elsa managed a weak smile, her shoulders sagging beneath the weight of her fears. "Okay. I'll be alright. It's the waiting that unnerves me."

"It won't be long now," Culper said, his eyes holding hers for a long moment before he turned back to his own documents.

As the plane flew on, carrying them ever closer to their destination, Elsa tried to focus on the task at hand. She knew that she had to maintain her frumpy, unassuming persona, had to blend in and avoid drawing any unwanted attention.

But even as she sat there, her hands clasped tightly in her lap, Elsa could feel the first stirrings of something new and unfamiliar deep within her. It was a sense of purpose, a feeling that she was exactly where she was meant to be, doing exactly what she was meant to do. For beneath the faded cardigan and the horn-rimmed glasses, there beat the heart of a warrior.

Helsinki Central Station - Helsinki, Finland

The bustling platform hummed with activity as Culper and Elsa stood sipping their coffee, the steam from their cups mingling with the crisp Finnish air. Elsa, still disguised in her old clothes and without makeup, her blond hair tucked under a woven hat, felt a flicker of nervousness in her chest as she scanned the crowd.

"There she is," said Culper, his voice low and steady.

Elsa's gaze drifted across the platform, her heart

skipping a beat as she caught sight of Dr. Paula Aadland. The woman was a vision of elegance, her movements fluid and graceful as she eyed the steward loading her bags onto the train. Elsa tried not to stare too long, looking away whenever Aadland's eyes shifted her way, but she couldn't help but be transfixed by the aura of confidence that seemed to radiate from Aadland's every pore.

"She's different in real life," Elsa murmured, her voice barely audible above the din of the station.

And then, as if by some unspoken cue, Aadland saw a passing acquaintance and smiled. It was brilliant. All consuming. Perfect white teeth gleaming in the weak sunlight. Elsa felt a pang of envy, a longing to possess even a fraction of that self-assurance.

"Jesus, how do I imitate that?" said Elsa, her eyes still fixed on Aadland's radiant smile.

"You'll do just fine," said Culper, his tone reassuring. "We should get onboard."

Elsa nodded, tearing her gaze away from Aadland and tossing her empty coffee cup into a nearby trashcan. As they climbed aboard the train, one coach ahead of Aadland's, Elsa couldn't resist one last glance at the woman she was meant to become. She watched as Aadland tipped the steward without acknowledging him, her smile vanishing as quickly as it had appeared. It was a glimpse of the real Aadland, the one beneath the façade of white teeth and a pearl necklace. Elsa swore not to forget that moment as she disappeared into the train, the weight of her mission settling heavily on her shoulders.

As the train pulled out of the station, the Finnish countryside blurring past the windows, Elsa turned to Culper. "I need to listen to Aadland's real voice in different situations," she said, her tone urgent. "It means getting close to her, and that's risky."

To her surprise, Culper agreed readily. "The more you know about Aadland, the better chance you have of pulling off an impersonation," he said, his eyes meeting hers with a steady gaze. "Try the dining car. Wait until she sits, then come up with some excuse for sitting nearby."

Elsa nodded, grabbing a book from her suitcase and heading out of their compartment with a mixture of nerves and anticipation. She positioned herself near the restroom, pretending to read while she waited for Aadland to arrive. When the elegant woman finally swept into the dining car an hour later, Elsa seized her chance.

She approached the steward, asking to be seated facing the same direction as the train, citing motion sickness. As she slid into the booth across the aisle from Aadland, Elsa buried her nose in her book, straining to catch every inflection and nuance of Aadland's speech as she ordered her lunch. The woman's tone was imperious when addressing the stewards, a clear indication of the disdain she felt for those she believed beneath her social status.

Elsa risked occasional glances at Aadland, studying her expressions and hand gestures, noting how they varied with the tone of her voice and the person she was addressing. When a male friend joined Aadland, Elsa listened intently to the shift in her demeanor, the way her voice became warmer, more inviting. It seemed Aadland had a different persona for every situation, a chameleon-like ability to adapt and charm that left Elsa in awe.

But when Aadland's friend departed, leaving her

alone once more, Elsa caught a glimpse of vulnerability beneath the polished veneer. She watched as Aadland nursed glass after glass of Bordeaux, her displeasure evident in the set of her shoulders and the tightness around her mouth. It was a chink in the armor, a reminder that even the most vivacious of butterflies could be brought low by solitude.

As dinner service approached and Aadland prepared to leave, Elsa made her move. She stumbled into the aisleway, colliding with Aadland in a carefully choreographed dance of clumsiness and apology.

"Pardon me, miss!" Elsa stammered, catching herself on Aadland's mink clad arm. "I fear I misstepped upon our curve there."

Aadland's reaction was swift and cutting. "Quite inappropriate!" she snapped, flinching in disdain at Elsa's frumpy attire and hand upon fine cloth. "Do compose yourself before attempting dining cars if routine motion unsettles you so..."

The words stung, but Elsa realized she had learned precisely what she needed. Any perceived social inferior made a convenient public whipping post for Aadland's insecurities and vanities.

"Yes, madame, I apologize again," Elsa muttered, retrieving her book from amongst upset silverware. As she watched Aadland march away without a backward glance, spine straight like a sergeant, Elsa understood. The true template to channel authority over Nazis and misogynists alike was one of unwavering confidence, only dropping the façade out of sight from fellows and lessers.

For the moment, Elsa sank back into her faithful mouse disguise, the psychological keys she had gleaned from her sleuthing tucked away for when the time came to topple kingdoms. Little did she know that Culper had been watching from the shadows, his keen eyes alert for any sign of danger.

When a large man rose from a nearby booth, seemingly following Elsa as she left the dining car, Culper sprang into action. He waited until the man had passed, catching a glimpse of the German Luger concealed beneath his coat. It was all the evidence Culper needed.

He fell into step behind the man, waiting for the right moment to strike. As they moved between cars, Culper called out in German, "Did you lose this?"

The man turned, reaching for the proffered billfold, but Culper was faster. He grabbed the man's wrist, twisting it hard, his grip unbreakable despite the man's size and strength. With a swift, decisive motion, Culper pushed the man backward, sending him tumbling down the steps and onto the snow-covered gravel embankment below.

Culper watched as the man's body disappeared into the frosted bushes, the train speeding onward without pause. He had no idea if the man had been following Elsa with ill intent, but he wasn't taking any chances. As he made his way back to their compartment, Culper resolved to keep the incident from Elsa. She had enough to worry about, and so did he.

The mission ahead would require all of their focus and determination, a dance of deception and danger with the highest of stakes. But for now, as the Finnish countryside rolled past the windows and the secrets of Dr. Paula Aadland unfolded before them, Culper and Elsa could only prepare themselves for the challenges to come, their partnership a fragile thread of trust.

As the train hurtled through the night, the rhythmic clacking of the wheels a soothing lullaby, Elsa settled into her plush sleeper compartment, a cocoon of warmth and comfort amidst the chaos of the world outside. She read the detailed file that the OSS wonks had prepared on Aadland's family and history. As a brilliant scientist, Aadland was frustrated by the lack of opportunities and recognition for women in her field in Norway. When the Nazis rose to power, they promised her a chance to lead groundbreaking research if she worked for them. Aadland, who had grown disillusioned with the chaos and destruction of the war, came to believe that the Nazis were the only force capable of bringing order and stability to Europe. Seduced by the promise of unlimited resources and the chance to make a real impact on the world stage, she threw herself into her work for the Nazi cause, convinced that she was helping to build a better future for all.

With careful reverence, she spread the classified research files Culper had compiled across the quilt, the papers rustling softly beneath her fingertips. Dr. Paula Aadland's name seemed to leap from the title pages, the bold strokes of fountain ink evidence of the woman's indelible presence in the scientific world.

Elsa's lips moved silently as she mouthed the exotic vowel combinations, each syllable a step closer to embodying the scientific aptitude and European sophistication that were the hallmarks of her cover identity. She could feel the weight of Aadland's brilliance settling upon her shoulders, a mantle of responsibility and expectation that both thrilled and terrified her.

As she delved deeper into the documents, the

emerging nuclear applications spanning from reactor shielding alloys to particle acceleration techniques, Elsa's eyebrows rose in surprise. The security clearance levels stamped on even this censored selection spoke volumes about the true cutting-edge work of Nazi wonder weapon programs, the secrets that lay just beyond her reach, waiting for Paula Aadland's intuitive leaps to unlock their devastating potential.

But as the Alpine vistas rolled past the cabin porthole, the velvet midnight sky a backdrop to the grandeur of the mountains, Elsa found herself lost in the beauty of the equations and molecular diagrams that danced before her eyes. The opulent surroundings faded away, the plush fabric of the quilt beneath her fingertips no longer registering as she surrendered herself to the allure of pure scientific discovery.

Hours passed in a blur of photographic focus, Elsa's mind working to unravel the brilliant hidden machinations that lay at the heart of Aadland's work. Like a master jeweler working with the finest of gems, she sought to strip away the layers of dangerous ideas, revealing the elemental beauty that lay beneath. It was a delicate dance, a tango of the mind that required the utmost precision and care, but Elsa reveled in the challenge, consumed with the joy of discovery.

As the first blush of dawn began to paint the sky outside her window, Elsa came to a realization that sent a shiver down her spine. She knew that she must carry Paula's prodigious intellect onwards once the transfer was complete, but steering those mighty forces towards humanity's enlightenment would require a new kind of subversive creativity on her part. The ideas that bubbled up from the depths of her mind were perhaps too progressive for either warring side, too focused on achieving victory at any cost to see the potential for something greater.

Elsa carefully replaced the documents, her fingers lingering on the pages as if to absorb their secrets through osmosis. Somewhere on this train, her scientific doppelgänger lay unaware of the destiny that awaited her, the fate that would intertwine their lives in ways neither could have ever imagined.

As the Stockholm spires materialized on the horizon, their gilded tips catching the first rays of the morning sun, Elsa felt a sense of purpose settle over her, a clarity of vision that cut through the fog of uncertainty that had plagued her for so long. She knew that the road ahead would be fraught with danger, that the consequences of failure would be deadly for all involved. But in that moment, as the train hurtled towards its inevitable destination, Elsa felt a flicker of hope, a glimmer of possibility that she could be the one to change the course of history, to steer the world towards a brighter future, one equation at a time.

Once the train left Stockholm station, Elsa once again retreated to her private cabin, a sanctuary of solitude amidst the chaos of her mission. With trembling hands, she began the transformation, each step a ritual of becoming. She took her time curling her short locks to match Aadland's hairstyle, the golden strands slipping through her fingers like threads of fate. The makeup came next, a mask of confidence and allure, the crescent-moon scar a hidden reflection of the scars she carried within.

As she slipped into the lingerie, the silk and lace a whisper against her skin, Elsa felt a flicker of doubt, a momentary hesitation at the threshold of her new identity. But as she attached the stockings to the garter belt, each clasp a tiny act of defiance against the world that sought to define her, she felt a sense of power, a surge of determination that burned away the last vestiges of her former self.

The dress slid over her slender body like a second skin, the fabric a caress against her curves. Pearls, the accessory of choice, adorned her neck, a simple elegance that spoke volumes. Elsa stood before the mirror, her reflection a stranger and yet somehow more familiar than ever before. She was ready, a chameleon poised to blend into a world of danger and deceit.

A knock at the door shattered the stillness, and Elsa opened it to find Culper, his presence a reminder of the weight of her mission.

"Are you ready?" he asked, his eyes searching her face for any sign of hesitation.

"As ready as I can get," she replied, her voice steady despite the butterflies in her stomach.

"We've been over everything," Culper reminded her, his tone a mix of reassurance and urgency.

"A thousand times," Elsa said, a wry smile tugging at the corners of her mouth.

"Go to her cabin and distract her. I'll go the rest."

"Alright. You still haven't told me how you plan to get her off the train before we cross the border."

"That's because you don't need to know. Just do your job and I'll do mine."

"Okay. I trust you."

Culper leaned over and kissed her on the forehead, a gesture of affection and support. "Good luck," he whispered, his breath warm against her skin.

Elsa nodded, then checked the mirror to make sure Culper hadn't messed up her makeup. They slipped out of her cabin, closing the door behind them, and walked down the aisle, passing several passengers with polite nods. Nothing amiss. Nothing to see. They moved to the next carriage where Aadland's cabin was located, each step a crescendo of anticipation and dread.

As they approached the cabin, the door opened, and Aadland stepped out with her back to them. She closed the door and walked toward the dining car, her movements fluid and graceful. When she disappeared through the between car doorway, Culper turned to Elsa, his eyes intense.

"Probably just coffee. Do you have your lock pick kit?"

Elsa nodded.

"Good. You get into her cabin while I keep an eye on her."

Elsa nodded again, her palms slick with sweat. Culper followed Aadland, his footsteps a murmur on the carpeted floor. Elsa glanced down the swaying train corridors. Deserted. She slid the lock picking set Culper had provided from her coat pocket and knelt before Aadland's door as she selected two slender instruments.

With one tension wrench anchored, Elsa guided the half-diamond pick steadily into the keyhole, the clackety-clack of rail joins counting down urgent seconds. She focused on regulating her breathing against the adrenaline surge while feeling for familiar pins, each one a delicate ballet of pressure and release. It was taking too long. The lock was old, a stubborn guardian of the secrets that lay beyond.

Elsa worked the lockpicks in Aadland's door when echoes of jovial Finnish drifted down the passageway. She redoubled her efforts as an elderly couple emerged from their compartment ahead, their presence a threat to her mission. She swung around, keeping her body angled to conceal the tools as she manipulated the door's lock.

"Are you okay?" said the man in Finnish, his voice laced with concern.

Elsa didn't respond, her focus unwavering as she kept working on the lock.

"You seem in distress there, dear?" the woman ventured again in accented English, her tone gentle and probing.

Elsa strove to appear casually irritated. "Oh I'll sort this stubborn lock presently," she replied with an airy laugh, the sound foreign to her own ears. "Old mechanisms can prove so temperamental."

The husband gestured kindly as he drew nearer, his eyes filled with genuine concern. "I could fetch the conductor to assist if you wish?"

Just then, the pins aligned with a breathy click, a sigh of relief escaping Elsa's lips. "At last!" she proclaimed brightly, swinging the door open wide to preempt his intervention. "You are both so very kind, but I persevered! Just an aged mechanism as I suspected."

She waved appreciatively and slipped inside, pulling the door swiftly but casually closed behind her. That was far too close for comfort. Elsa leaned against the lacquered wood, straining to discern suspicious murmurs. But the couple's steps soon resumed down the groaning passageway, their well-meaning intervention averted.

Elsa studied the room, Dr. Aadland's domain in elegant repose - cashmere blankets askew over silk pajamas, bespoke luggage bearing gilt monograms stacked neatly awaiting the next global destination. She drank in every detail rapidly, committing the lifestyle intricacies to memory. She would stretch herself to blend here soon enough. Her lockpick tools vanished into wool coat lining swiftly. Unsure what to do, she sat on the bed and waited for Culper's return.

After twenty minutes that felt like an eternity, a key slipped into the lock from the outside. Elsa's blood ran cold. Culper didn't have a key. He would use their secret knock. That meant it wasn't Culper...

Elsa froze as the door swung open and Dr. Aadland entered, the scientist's sharp eyes widening with recognition. "You! The little mouse scurrying about my dining car?" Aadland exclaimed, her voice a razor's edge. "Explain this intrusion before I summon the authorities!"

Elsa stammered hopeless excuses – she wanted to talk with the famous Dr. Aadland and get her views on new physics' theories. But the words fell flat, a flimsy shield against the fury in Aadland's eyes.

"You're a liar. You were looking for something to steal. Jewelry I think. It doesn't matter. You're trespassing. The conductor will place you under arrest until the next station where he will turn you over to the authorities."

Elsa could tell that Aadland was enjoying seeing her twist in the wind, a true sadist reveling in her discomfort. But before she could respond, a garrote whip lashed round the blond beauty's porcelain neck, a deadly embrace that stole the breath from her lungs.

Culper had moved up behind her, the handles of the garrote gripped tightly in his gloved hands. The wire bit as it tightened, cutting into Aadland's skin, a ruby ribbon of blood against her alabaster flesh. Her strand of pearls snapped, the precious beads cascading to the floor like drops of spilled milk, bouncing and rolling in a macabre dance.

Aadland gagged brutally against the thin wire drawn ruthlessly tight by Culper's gloved hands. He held fast, sinews bulging against her frantic thrashing, her nails clawing at his face in a desperate bid for survival.

"What are you doing?" shrieked Elsa, her eyes wide with horror and disbelief.

"Shut up and stay back," Culper growled, kicking the door closed behind him.

Aadland's eyes bulged, but she wasn't through fighting. In a last, desperate act of defiance, she reached down and pulled a push dagger from a leather sheath attached to her garter belt. She swung wildly at Culper, the blade slicing his outer thigh, a bloom of crimson against the dark fabric of his trousers.

Elsa snapped out of her shock and moved toward Aadland's hand as it readied for another swipe at Culper. She slipped on several pearls and tumbled to the floor, her elbows and knees meeting more of the scattered beads in a jarring impact. Aadland swung the blade again and again, Culper pitching and gyrating to keep away as he refused to let go of the garrote.

Elsa lunged at Aadland, grabbing her wrist in a desperate attempt to stop the deadly thrusts. The dagger waved wildly in front of Elsa's face, just an inch from her nose, a glint of steel that promised pain and death.

Starved of oxygen, Aadland continued to struggle, her movements growing weaker with each passing second. Slowly, the thrashing stopped, her body going limp in Culper's unyielding grip. Culper held the garrote tight for another twenty seconds, a lifetime of agony, before releasing the wire, unwrapping it from her neck.

Aadland fell to the floor, her eyes wide open, staring at Elsa in a silent accusation.

"You killed her," said Elsa, her voice a whisper of disbelief.

"Don't forget who she was and what she was going to do, Elsa," Culper replied, his tone hard and unyielding.

"You lied."

"No."

"You said you were going to abduct her."

"No. I didn't. You said that. I just didn't correct you."

"So, deceit is better?"

"In this case… yes. You weren't ready for the truth."

"You keep saying that. When do I get to decide what I am ready for?"

"Soon."

"So, that's the truth in what we do? We're assassins?"

"At times, yes. We do what is necessary to carry out the mission."

"No. I can't accept that. I can't accept this. This is not who I am."

"Are you sure about that?"

"What the hell is that supposed to mean?"

"We don't know what we are capable of doing under the right circumstances."

"Excuse me, but I don't think I am ready for a lecture on morals with a dead body lying in front of me."

"Then blame me if you must. I did it, not you. Grab the silk sheets. We need to wrap her body in something."

Elsa didn't move, her mind reeling from the horror of what she had just witnessed.

"What is done, is done. Are you going to help or sulk?" said Culper, his voice a lash of impatience.

Incensed, Elsa grabbed the silk sheets from the bed, her movements sharp and angry. Culper stripped the jewelry from Aadland's corpse and handed it to Elsa to wear, a final indignity for the fallen scientist.

"I want her dagger and the sheath," said Elsa, her voice steel.

Culper was surprised by the request, a flicker of admiration in his eyes.

"You seem surprised. It was part of who she was. I want them."

"I'm just glad it wasn't a derringer."

Culper lifted Aadland's dress to reveal the sheath and her undergarments, a violation that made Elsa's stomach turn.

"Let me," she said, her voice barely above a whisper. "The woman still deserves some decency."

"She deserves nothing. She was betraying her country and our's," said Culper, removing the sheath and handing it to Elsa.

He rolled Aadland's corpse over, found the push dagger on the floor, and handed it to Elsa. A knock on the door shattered the moment, freezing them both in place. Culper snapped out of it first, removing a .22 Cal pistol and silencer from his coat pocket. He screwed the silencer into end of the pistol's barrel and chambered a round, the sound a death knell in the stillness of the cabin.

Elsa knew that Culper was going to kill whoever was on the other side of that door, another life snuffed out in the name of the mission. A second knock and a voice said, "Conductor."

Elsa moved toward the door, turned to Culper and said quietly, "Let me try."

Culper nodded, a silent acknowledgment of her bravery. One body to dispose of was bad enough.

Elsa pulled her dress off, revealing her lingerie, a display of vulnerability that belied the steel in her spine. She opened the door a crack and looked out at the conductor. "Can I help you?"

"I am sorry to disturb you, ma'am. There have been noise complaints."

"Yes, that would be me. I misplaced my lipstick and had a bit of tantrum. I apologize if I disturbed anyone."

"I see. Well, these things happen. Please be more mindful next time."

"I hope there isn't a next time."

"Of course," said the conductor, tipping his hat as she closed the door, a gesture of respect that felt like a mockery in the face of what had just transpired.

Culper waited until he heard the conductor's footsteps recede down the corridor and said, "That was impressive. You saved that man's life."

"I know."

Culper wrapped Aadland's body in the silk sheets, a final shroud for the fallen scientist. He used his garrote to tie one end of the cocoon, a mockery of a bow. He opened the closet door and removed a belt hanging on the rod, using it to tie the opposite end. Blood dripped onto the white silk sheets, a crimson stain that would never wash away.

"You're bleeding," said Elsa, her voice laced with concern.

"It's nothing," said Culper, his tone dismissive.

"Why do men always say it's nothing when they know it's something?"

"No idea."

Elsa began looking through the drawers until she found a sewing kit and said, "Pull your pants off."

"What?"

"Your pants... off."

"We don't have time for this."

"So, you're just going to bleed to death?"

"It's not that bad. I've had worse."

"Pull your damned pants off and let me have a look. I'm in no mood for your stubbornness, Culper."

Culper knew she wasn't going to let it go. He unbuttoned his trousers and let them drop to the floor, a display of vulnerability that felt out of place in the midst of such violence.

"Happy?"

"Ecstatic. Let me see the wound."

Culper turned, revealing a three-inch gash that ran down his leg, blood flowing freely from the wound. Elsa threaded a needle, her hands steady despite the adrenaline coursing through her veins.

"This is gonna hurt."

"I'm a big boy. I can take... Jesus!" said Culper as Elsa squeezed the cut together and pierced his skin with the needle, a flare of pain that made him grit his teeth.

"Is that thing sterile?"

"Not that I know of. You're gonna need to put some iodine on the wound as soon as you can."

"Right."

Culper yipped and ouched his way through the surgery, twenty-two stitches that felt like a lifetime. Elsa ripped and wrapped a pillowcase around the wound and tied it off, a makeshift bandage that would have to do.

"That'll do for now. You can put your pants back on."

Culper obeyed, a flicker of gratitude in his eyes.

"What are you going to do with her?" said Elsa, staring at the white coffin that held Aadland's body.

"Open the window."

"You can't be serious."

"Would you rather carry her corpse down the corridor?"

"No."

"Then open the window."

Elsa complied, the cold wind rushing in, a blast of reality that made her shiver.

"Shouldn't we say something?"

"No. But listen up. I'm going with the body. I need to dispose of it so the authorities don't find it. I'll catch up with you in Telemark. Until then, you're on your own."

"Wait... what?"

"You wanted to make your own decisions, well here it is."

"But... I don't know what to do?"

"You'll figure it out. That's why I chose you."

Culper picked up the silk shroud holding Aadland's corpse and unceremoniously shoved it out the window. It tumbled along the snow-covered embankment and well into the undergrowth paralleling the tracks. He followed, climbing out the window. At the last moment, he turned and said, "Good luck, Dr. Aadland."

Elsa nodded and watched as Culper disappeared into the night, his silhouette swallowed by the darkness beyond the train window. She stood there for a moment, a mix of fear and exhilaration coursing through her veins. She was alone now, truly alone, with nothing but her wits and her courage to guide her.

She turned back to the cabin, her eyes scanning the room for any signs of the violence that had just transpired. The pearls still lay scattered on the floor, a reminder of the life that had been snuffed out, the destiny that had been altered in the blink of an eye. Elsa bent down and began to gather them, one by one, a silent ritual of mourning for the woman she had never known.

As she slipped the pearls into her pocket, Elsa caught a glimpse of herself in the mirror, a stranger staring back at her with emerald eyes and golden curls. She was Dr. Paula Aadland now, a woman with a past she hadn't lived and a future she couldn't predict. The weight of her new identity settled on her shoulders like a mantle, a burden she would have to bear alone.

Elsa took a deep breath, steadying herself against the rocking of the train. She knew she had to act quickly, to erase any evidence of what had happened in this cabin. She began to move through the space, her movements efficient and precise mixed with deception that felt all too familiar.

She stripped the bed of its bloodstained sheets, bundling them up in a giant knot, then shoving them out the window like discarded trash, hoping the next snowfall would cover them up. She wiped down every surface, every doorknob and window latch, her fingers shuddering with the knowledge of what she was doing. She was erasing a life, a history, a legacy that had been cut short by Culper's cruel hands.

When she was finished, Elsa stood in the center of

the room, her chest heaving with the effort of her labors. The cabin looked pristine, untouched, as if nothing had ever happened here. But Elsa knew the truth, knew the secrets that lay hidden beneath the surface, the ghosts that would haunt her dreams for years to come.

She glanced at the clock on the wall, a reminder of the time that was slipping away. She had to move, to blend in with the other passengers, to become the woman she was meant to be. Elsa smoothed her dress, checked her hair in the mirror, and took one last look around the room.

Then, with a deep breath and a silent prayer, she stepped out into the corridor, her heels clicking on the polished wood. She walked with purpose, her head held high, a mask of confidence firmly in place. She nodded to the other passengers as she passed, a smile playing at the corners of her mouth, a charm that felt as natural as breathing.

But beneath the surface, Elsa's mind was racing, her thoughts a jumble of fear and doubt. She had no idea what lay ahead, no clue how she would navigate the treacherous waters of her new identity. She was a physicist, a scientist, not a spy or an assassin. How could she possibly hope to succeed in a world so far beyond her experience? And yet, she had no choice. She would have to find a way to make it all work.

As she made her way to the dining car, Elsa's hand slipped into her pocket, her fingers brushing against the cool metal of the push dagger. It was a reminder of the violence that had brought her to this moment, the blood that had been spilled in the name of a greater cause. But it was also a reminder of her own strength, her own resilience in the face of unimaginable odds.

Elsa took her seat at a table, her eyes scanning the room for any signs of trouble. There were none. She ordered a coffee, her voice steady and sure, a mask of normalcy that belied the chaos swirling within. And as she sipped the hot liquid, letting it warm her from the inside out, Elsa knew that she had no choice but to embrace the destiny that had been thrust upon her.

She was Dr. Paula Aadland now, a woman with a mission and a purpose. And no matter what challenges lay ahead, no matter what sacrifices she would be called upon to make, Elsa knew that she would face them head-on, armed with nothing but her intelligence, her courage, and the unshakable belief that she was exactly where she was meant to be.

The train raced on through the night, carrying Elsa towards a future she couldn't begin to imagine. But even as the darkness pressed in around her, even as the weight of her new identity threatened to crush her, Elsa held fast to the flicker of hope that burned within her.

She was a survivor, a fighter, a woman who would stop at nothing to see her mission through. And with that knowledge as her guide, Elsa knew that she could face whatever lay ahead, no matter how daunting the road might be.

So, she sat back in her seat, her eyes fixed on the horizon, her mind juggling possibilities and plans. And as the train hurtled onwards, Elsa felt a sense of purpose settle over her, a calm certainty that she was exactly where she needed to be, doing exactly what she was meant to do. Elsa knew that she would face whatever lay ahead with the same unwavering determination that had brought her this far, a force of nature that could not be stopped, a woman on a mission to change the world, one secret at a time.

Telemark

Norwegian Border

The train lurched to a stop, jolting Elsa from her thoughts as she gazed out at the snow-covered landscape. A sense of unease settling in the pit of her stomach as she realized they had reached the Norwegian border. This was it, the moment of truth, the first real test of her carefully crafted disguise.

Elsa took a deep breath, trying to steel herself for what was to come. She closed her eyes, reaching deep within herself to find the essence of Dr. Paula Aadland, the woman whose identity she had to embrace. But instead of confidence and cool assurance, she felt a chilling presence, a ghostly echo of the woman whose life she had helped to end.

The memory of Aadland's final moments flooded Elsa's mind, the struggle in the train compartment, the sickening sound of the garrote, the broken pearls falling to the floor, the lifeless eyes staring up at her in silent accusation. Elsa shuddered, a wave of guilt and fear washing over her. She was a scientist, not prone to superstition, but she couldn't shake the feeling that Aadland's spirit was there with her, a vengeful presence that could betray her at any moment. It wasn't logical or even possible, but it was a very real feeling.

As the sound of heavy boots echoed through the train car, Elsa tried to push aside her doubts, to summon the cool, confident persona of Dr. Aadland. But it was like trying to grasp smoke, the essence of the woman slipping through her fingers like water.

The compartment door slid open, revealing a pair of SS officers, their faces stern and unsmiling.

"Papers, please," the taller of the two barked, his voice cold and authoritative.

Elsa's palms were slick with sweat as she reached for her papers. Her hand trembled as she handed over her documents, the crisp pages feeling like a lead weight in her grip. She tried to meet the officer's gaze, to summon Aadland's haughty defiance, but she could feel the mask slipping, her own fear and uncertainty bleeding through.

The officer eyes shifted back and forth as he compared the passport's photo to Elsa. Moving on, he studied the papers, his eyes narrowing as he scanned the details. Elsa held her breath, every second feeling like an eternity as she waited for his verdict. Would he see through her deception? Would Aadland's spirit whisper the truth in his ear, exposing her as an impostor?

"Your purpose in Norway, Fraulein Doktor?" the officer asked, his tone sharp and probing.

Elsa opened her mouth to speak, but the words stuck in her throat, Aadland's voice a distant echo in her mind. She could feel the officer's gaze boring into her, his suspicion growing with every passing moment.

"I... I am here on official business," she managed at last, her voice trembling despite her best efforts. "I am to oversee a research project at the Norsk Hydro plant in Telemark."

The officer's eyebrows raised, a flicker of surprise crossing his features. "Telemark? That is a highly secure facility. What kind of research are you conducting there?"

"I'm afraid that information is classified, Officer," she said, her tone weak and unconvincing even to her own ears.

As the SS officer's questions grew more insistent, his suspicion palpable in the cramped confines of the train compartment, Elsa felt a rising panic threatening to overwhelm her. But then, in a sudden moment of clarity, she realized that her only hope lay in surrendering herself completely to Aadland's persona, in trusting the instincts and mannerisms of the woman she had so reluctantly come to embody.

With a deep breath, Elsa let go of her own fears and doubts, allowing Aadland's cool confidence to wash over her like a protective shield. She felt the shift in her posture, the subtle change in her expression, as Aadland's essence flowed through her veins, a potent elixir of charm and authority.

"Officer, I understand your need for caution, but I assure you that my papers are in order and my work at Telemark is of the utmost importance to the Reich," Elsa said, her voice firm and assured.

The officer's gaze remained skeptical, his eyes narrowing as he studied Elsa's face for any sign of deception. "Fraulein Doktor, your credentials may be impressive, but that does not exempt you from the necessary scrutiny. These are dangerous times, and we must be vigilant against all threats to the Reich."

Elsa met his stare unflinchingly, her chin lifted in a

show of quiet defiance. "I am no threat, Officer. I am a loyal servant of the Reich, dedicated to the advancement of our cause. My work at Telemark could very well turn the tide of this war in our favor, and I will not be delayed by baseless suspicions and bureaucratic red tape."

She held out her hand, her eyes locked with the officer's in a silent battle of wills. "Now, if you would be so kind as to stamp my papers, I have a long journey ahead of me and much work to be done."

For a long, tense moment, the officer hesitated, his jaw tight with reluctance. But something in Elsa's gaze, in the unwavering certainty of her words, seemed to give him pause. With a curt nod, he reached for his stamp, the sound of it striking her documents like a gunshot in the quiet of the compartment.

"Very well, Fraulein Doktor. You may proceed. But know that the eyes of the Reich are always watching, and any hint of disloyalty or deception will be dealt with swiftly and without mercy."

Elsa took her papers, her fingers brushing the officer's in a final, subtle show of dominance. "I would expect nothing less, Officer. But you need not worry about my loyalty. I know where my duties lie, and I will not fail in them."

The two soldiers left closing the door behind them. As the SS moved on to the next compartment, she settled back into her seat, feeling a sense of triumph burning in her veins. She had passed the test, but the weight of Aadland's presence still hung over her like a shroud. Elsa knew that she would have to find a way to trust in the woman's persona. But the guilt and the fear were like chains around her neck, dragging her down into the depths of her own doubts.

As the train lurched back into motion, carrying her ever closer to her destination, Elsa closed her eyes, trying to summon the strength and the courage that had brought her this far. She would need every ounce of it, every shred of determination, to face the trials that lay ahead. For the fate of the world hung in the balance, and Elsa knew that she would do whatever it took to tip the scales in favor of the light, even if it meant embracing the darkness that lurked within her.

As the train hurtled through the Norwegian countryside, Elsa gazed out the frost-lined window. The landscape was a study in contrasts, the pristine white of the snow-covered fields broken by the dark green of the towering pines that lined the tracks. In the distance, the jagged peaks of the mountains loomed, their surfaces glittering in the pale winter sunlight like diamonds against the steel-gray sky.

Elsa pressed her forehead against the cool glass, her breath fogging the pane as she tried to calm the nerves that threatened to overtake her. She was crossing into Aadland's homeland now, a lair of secrets and dangers that she would have to navigate with all the skill and cunning she could muster. The weight of her mission settled heavily on her shoulders, a burden that she would have to bear alone in this strange and hostile land.

As the train eased to a squealing halt at Oslo Sentralstasjon, Elsa smoothed imaginary creases from her stylish ensemble, a mask of confidence slipping over her features. She stepped out onto the platform, her heels clicking authoritatively against the polished stone, and took in the imposing granite terminal that bustled with activity.

Banners bearing the insignia of the Third Reich fluttered in the chill breeze, a stark reminder that Norway now marched to the beat of Germany's drum. SS officers scrutinized travel papers at every gate, their cold eyes assessing as they surveyed the weary travelers who passed before them. Families embraced under the station's high ceilings, their reunions tinged with a sense of desperation and fear, a reflection of a nation held captive by the iron grip of occupation. Nobody knew when they could be taken in for interrogation for the simplest error.

A rap at her cabin door interrupted her anxious thoughts, and Elsa slipped on her silken gloves with renewed poise as she answered the conductor's inquiry about her luggage needs. She requested full porter service, her voice cool and assured, a flawless mimicry of Aadland's haughty demeanor.

But as the conductor turned to leave, Elsa detained him, a flicker of uncertainty breaking through her carefully crafted mask. She asked for details about the train to Telemark, hoping to verify the specifics of her cover story, but the man's smile faded, his words sending a chill down her spine.

"Apologies, Fraulein, but the mountain trains have all been suspended - an avalanche caused by terrorists. While the rails are covered with debris, the road is still untouched. Buses run towards Rjukan."

Elsa managed a terse nod as she tried to process this unexpected development. She knew that Aadland would balk at the idea of common transport, that she would have to improvise convincingly and swiftly if she was to maintain her cover.

With a deep breath, Elsa buttoned her fur coat against the still air and gathered up her fortitude. It was time to brazenly walk behind enemy lines, to put her skills and her training to the ultimate test.

As she emerged from the train and crossed the platform, her heels clicking authoritatively against the stone, Elsa moved towards the taxi queue, her mind rehearsing the responses she would need to navigate the treacherous waters ahead. But before she could reach her destination, a black-clad SS lieutenant waved her over, his face a mask of suspicion and disdain.

"Papers! State your business!" he barked, his eyes raking over her with a look that made Elsa's skin crawl.

She handed him her papers and passport, summoning every ounce of hauteur she could muster as she replied in German, "I am Doktor Aadland, undertaking sensitive research at the Telemark Hydroelectric Facility."

The lieutenant's glare was like a physical weight, his gaze lingering on her documents with a mixture of skepticism and something far more insidious. "Research, you say," he mused, his tone dripping with insinuation. "And how might you pretty scientists better serve the Reich in your efforts, I wonder..."

Fury kindled in Elsa's veins at his lewd innuendo, but she tamped it down, knowing that Aadland would have leveraged her privilege rather than succumbing to indignance. She prepared a scathing retort, the words dancing on the tip of her tongue, but before she could unleash them, a voice erupted nearby, a lifeline thrown to her in her moment of need.

Myra, the young secretary from Telemark, pushed through the milling travelers, her face alight with relief and excitement as she called out to Elsa. "Doctor Aadland! Thank heavens we finally found you out here. The director sent a car as soon as your wire announcing early arrival came through."

She turned to the SS officer, her voice firm and unwavering. "Lieutenant, I request you release the good doctor to carry out her vital work at Telemark. Reichsführer Himmler awaits results eagerly."

The officer's face flushed with embarrassment, and he relented with a brusque apology, handing Elsa's papers back to her with a curt nod. Myra ushered her away, her words a soothing balm to Elsa's frayed nerves. "Apologies for the crude interruption. We'll have you at Telemark swiftly."

As they made their way through the exterior doors, Elsa felt a surge of gratitude towards the young woman who had plucked her from the wolf's jaws. She wanted to thank her, to express her appreciation for the quick thinking and clever maneuvering that had saved her. But she knew that Aadland would never show such weakness, that she would expect this kind of treatment as nothing more than her due.

And so Elsa remained silent, her arm locked with Myra's as they emerged into the bustling square of Jernbanetorget. The once-vibrant streets of Oslo were now a labyrinth of propaganda and austerity, the venerable buildings adorned with garish swastikas and stern banners that proclaimed the Nazi's iron grip on Norway's fate.

Myra led them through the crowds with a brisk efficiency, past groups of Wehrmacht soldiers smoking on the sidewalks and shops that traded in drab necessities rather than the glittering luxuries of yesteryear. Elsa couldn't help but notice the signs of Norway's economic ruin, the way the German occupation had drained the lifeblood from the nation's veins, leaving only a husk of its former glory.

As they reached the waiting town car, Elsa caught a glimpse of the elderly residents of Oslo queuing obediently before an administrative annex, their faces etched with a quiet defiance that belied the indignities they suffered at the hands of the sneering SS. It was a tribute to the resilience of the Norwegian spirit, a reminder that even in the darkest of times, hope could still flicker in the hearts of the oppressed.

Myra waved down the driver, and Elsa climbed into the warm interior of the car, pulling Aadland's lush ermine cloak tighter around her shoulders as the engine purred to life. She watched through the frosted window as the driver retrieved her luggage from the porter, her eyes taking in every detail of the exchange.

When the man returned, Elsa handed him a minimal tip, a pang of guilt twisting in her gut at the paltry sum. But she knew that she had to stay in character, that Aadland would never show such consideration for those she deemed beneath her.

As the car merged onto the open highway, Elsa pressed closer to the window, her hungry eyes devouring the details of the homeland she had only known through her mother's gauzy recollections. The snow-capped mountains loomed closer, their jagged peaks shrouded in mist and memory, a landscape that seemed to echo with the whispers of a past long gone.

Myra glanced over at her, a smile playing at the corners of her mouth as she read the wonder in Elsa's eyes. "Still takes my breath too sometimes," she remarked quietly. "We endure, still loving Norway even now."

Elsa nodded, a lump forming in her throat at the young woman's words. She knew that Myra spoke for all of Norway, for a people who had been beaten down but not broken, who still clung to their love of country even in the face of unimaginable hardship.

As the car wound its way through the dense thickets of fir and birch, past isolated steads that pierced the wilderness with thin trails of peat smoke, Elsa felt a sense of connection to this land, a longing that went beyond mere ancestry. She leaned forward eagerly as they descended the last winding pass, her heart quickening at the sight of Telemark nestled within the glacial valley. High above Telemark was the Norsk Heavy Water Research and Production facility built into a steep slope like a fortress of secrets. The towering peaks of the mountains loomed on either side, their jagged surfaces casting long shadows across the snow-covered landscape. The black Mercedes turned off the road onto a bridge that spanned a deep gorge, the concrete fortress of the Norsk Hydro plant looming on the opposing precipice like a beast of legend.

"It's an impressive sight, isn't it?" Myra said, her voice soft and reverent.

Elsa nodded, her eyes fixed on the imposing structure that rose up from the mountainside ahead. The facility was a sprawling complex of concrete and steel, its brutalist architecture a stark contrast to the natural beauty that surrounded it. High walls topped with barbed wire encircled the perimeter, and guard towers stood at regular intervals, their searchlights sweeping the grounds and the sky above with a relentless intensity. More than a dozen 128mm heavy antiaircraft gun emplacements surrounded by triple layers of sandbags kept the Ally bombers at bay.

As they approached the main gate, Elsa couldn't help but notice the heavy security presence. SS guards armed with machine guns patrolled the entrance, their faces hard and unsmiling beneath their coal-scuttle helmets. Myra handed over their papers to the guard on duty, her expression a mask of cool professionalism as he scrutinized the documents with a critical eye.

After what felt like an eternity, the guard handed back the papers and waved them through. The car passed beneath the raised barrier and into the facility. Elsa's breath caught in her throat as she took in the sheer scale of the operation, the way the buildings seemed to go on forever, their facades a patchwork of pipes and scaffolding that glittered in the weak winter sunlight.

"The facility is divided into several key areas," Myra explained, her voice taking on a lecturing tone. "Over there, you can see the power station, where the hydroelectric turbines generate the massive amounts of electricity needed for the heavy water production process."

She pointed to a long, low building with a series of massive pipes running along its length, each one as wide as a train tunnel. Elsa could hear the distant roar of the turbines, a sound that seemed to vibrate through the very ground beneath their feet.

"And there, in the center of the complex, is the main production plant," Myra continued, indicating a towering structure that rose up from the midst of the other buildings like a monolith. "That's where the heavy water is actually produced."

Elsa nodded, her mind recalling the details of the process. She knew that heavy water was essentially water that contained a higher proportion of the hydrogen isotope deuterium, and that it was a key component of nuclear reactions.

As the car pulled up to the administration building, Elsa took a deep breath, steeling herself to be on her guard at all times, that even the slightest slip could expose her true identity and compromise the entire mission.

But as she stepped out of the car and followed Myra towards the entrance, Elsa felt a flicker of determination burning within her, a resolve that could not be quenched by the chill of the mountain air or the looming specter of the Third Reich. She would find a way to succeed, to uncover the secrets of the Norsk facility and use them to strike a blow against the Nazi war machine.

As they passed through the heavy steel doors and into the sterile, brightly-lit corridors of the administration building, Elsa couldn't shake the feeling that she was walking into the belly of the beast, a place where the very air seemed to hum with the weight of the secrets that lay within. Inside these walls, the enemy was always listening, always watching.

Passing through the administration building, they entered the researchers' residence, a long building of dormitories and suites for dignitaries and high-level management like Aadland. It would be Elsa's home until the mission was completed. A gilded cage.

Unpacking Dr. Aadland's stylish clothes from her luggage, Elsa glanced around her sterile quarters when a brisk knock echoed from the steel door. She opened it to an imposing SS officer wearing a Major's insignia and two armed guards.

"Documents, Fräulein Doktor," he commanded evenly. "Standard procedure for new facility arrivals. I am Major Hoffman, Internal Security Commander."

Masking nervous tension, Elsa handed over her papers with aloof impatience. Hoffman scrutinized them closely, then eyed her features just as invasively.

"I understand you possess a distinctive scar normally obscured?" he stated.

"I do, not that it is any of your business," said Elsa.

"Everything is my business, Fräulein Doktor. Please show me the scar for the records."

With dignified reluctance she allowed Hoffman a brief glimpse of her veiled mar.

"Is your curiosity satisfied, Major?"

"Yes, thank you for your cooperation. We cannot be too careful at one of the Reich's most prized possessions."

"And here I thought it belonged to Norway."

"No longer."

"If you don't mind, I must unpack before starting my duties."

"Of course," said the major heading toward the door. He stopped short and turned. "If you would indulge me once more… How did acquire your scar?"

Elsa hesitated, then said, "Ponies."

"Excuse me?"

"I was on vacation with my family. It was raining when I saw several ponies in a meadow surrounded by a fence. I climbed the fence to pet the ponies when I lost my footing on the wet wood. I hit a fence post face-first. The resulting wound left the scar."

"Thank you. That is correct according to our records."

"Of course, it's correct."

"I shall leave you to your unpacking. Welcome back to Norway."

The major exited her room closing the door behind

her. Elsa waited a moment to ensure that the officer was indeed gone, then collapsed on her bed shuddering. She realized she would need to keep a constant guard and her character consistent. No room for flaws with Major Hoffman about.

Elsa donned her disguise touching up her scar makeup as Myra arrived. "After breakfast in the dining hall, the director asked me to give you a complete tour before you dive back into your vital research!"

Elsa was pleased. It might help in her search for key equipment in the heavy water process. "I hope they have good coffee," said Elsa.

"The best available."

"We shall see. Lead on."

The concrete canteen was a bleak and utilitarian space, its gray walls and harsh lighting a stark contrast to the breathtaking beauty of the mountains that surrounded the facility. Elsa sat in a corner, her eyes darting nervously around the room as Myra collected their breakfast, including two steaming cups of coffee that promised a brief respite from the chill that seemed to permeate every corner of this place.

As she waited, Elsa couldn't shake the feeling of unease that had settled in the pit of her stomach. She knew that some of the staff here might be acquainted with the real Aadland, that any one of them could see through her carefully crafted disguise and expose her for the imposter she was. And so, she kept to herself, her head down and her shoulders hunched, hoping to avoid any unwanted attention until she could pinpoint the potential threats among the sea of unfamiliar faces.

But her solitude was short-lived, as an elderly man

with a shock of silver hair and a smile that seemed to light up the room approached her table. "Dr. Aadland, you've returned from Finland!" he exclaimed, his voice filled with a warmth and familiarity. "What an unexpected surprise seeing you here instead of those wretched Soviets hoarding your talents!"

Elsa forced a laugh, the sound brittle and false to her own ears as she met Dr. Oleson's searching gaze. She could feel the weight of his expectations, the unspoken questions that lurked behind his friendly demeanor, and she knew that she would have to tread carefully if she was to maintain her cover.

"I hope the Reich will make far better use of my gifts than bleak Leningrad ever could," she said, the words tasting like ashes on her tongue.

As they talked, Elsa gathered bits and pieces of their shared history, the fragments of a past that she had never lived but that she would have to embody if she were to survive in this place. She learned that they had met at the University of Oslo, where Oleson had been a professor and Aadland a student, and she couldn't help but wonder if there had been more to their relationship than met the eye.

Had Aadland used her feminine wiles to curry favor with the professor, to gain an edge in the cutthroat world of academia? It was a dangerous game, one that could easily backfire if past intimacies were to come to light. But Elsa had no way of knowing the truth, no way of gauging the depth of their connection or the secrets that might lurk beneath the surface.

And so she clung to her façade, her every word and gesture a carefully choreographed dance of deception. She could only hope that Aadland had cultivated a reputation for aloofness, for a self-interest that would make it easier to maintain the illusion of distance and detachment.

Just as Oleson began to recount an event that surely held great significance for Aadland, Myra appeared at their table, a tray laden with food and coffee in her hands. Elsa seized the opportunity to make her escape, her words a hasty apology as she begged off further conversation.

"I'm sorry I have no more time to chat, my old friend, but Myra has me on a strict schedule today. Perhaps I will see you later and we can visit some more," she said, the words feeling hollow and insincere even to her own ears.

But Oleson simply smiled, his eyes crinkling at the corners as he inclined his head in a gesture of understanding. "I look forward to it," he said, his voice filled with a warmth – a friend among wolves.

As he walked away, Elsa turned to Myra, her expression in a mix of relief and frustration. "A chatterbox, that one," she said, her voice low and conspiratorial.

Myra's eyes widened in surprise, her head tilting to the side as she regarded Elsa with a curious expression. "Where do you know him from?" she asked, her words laced with a hint of suspicion.

Elsa's mind searched for an answer that would satisfy Myra's curiosity without arousing further suspicion. "The university," she said at last, her voice calm and measured. "He was a professor before joining the research team. Not a very good one. His lectures were more effective than sleeping pills and so are his conversations."

Myra nodded, a smile tugging at the corners of her

mouth. "We shall avoid him then," she said, her tone light and playful.

"That would be advisable," Elsa replied, her own lips curving into a smile that felt brittle and false. "I have far more important things to do than listen to him prattle on."

She could see the flicker of doubt in Myra's eyes, an unspoken question that lurked behind her friendly demeanor.

"I must admit, I am a bit intimidated giving you a tour of the facility," Myra said, her voice hesitant and unsure. "You know far more than I do about the production of heavy water."

Elsa waved a hand, her expression one of cool indifference. "Do not concern yourself, Myra. I know more about most things than the people I work with. Just do as you were instructed by the director, and I shall make allowances."

As Myra led her out of the canteen and into the labyrinthine corridors of the facility, Elsa couldn't shake the feeling that she was walking into the heart of darkness.

The icy winds tore at their collars as Myra led Elsa up the winding exterior stairs to the hydroelectric plant's rooftop overlook, the sprawling Norsk Hydro facility wedged deep within the soaring gorge like a festering wound upon the face of the earth. Myra's voice was barely audible over the howling gusts, her words a breathless torrent of information that washed over Elsa like a tidal wave.

"Magnificent view, isn't it, Frau Doktor?" she shouted, her eyes alight with a fervor that made Elsa's skin crawl. "I often wonder whether most onsite fully appreciate our special geography and resources making this entire endeavor possible. The Telemark region is pristine undeveloped wilderness. The mountain runoff comes from glaciers and winter snowpack rather than mineral-rich soil drainage in most valleys. This results in very soft water with low mineral content. The snow run-off feeds the Mana river which in turn feeds the facility a reliable high-volume flow of water year-round. In addition, the hydro plant provides the power needed for the process required to make heavy water. It's really an ideal location when you think about it. Nowhere else like it in the world."

Elsa nodded, her expression one of muted agreement as she focused her gaze downward, her eyes taking in the hive of concrete bunkers and pipe conduits that clung to the gorge walls like parasites, feeding off the lifeblood of the earth itself. She couldn't help but feel a sense of revulsion, a deep and abiding horror at the thought of the pristine gift of nature being churned into salts of death rather than life.

And yet, even as the disgust welled up within her, Elsa knew that she was a part of this, a cog in the wheel of creation, whether for good or for ill. She watched the thundering water cascading downward into the plant, the crush of gravity a miracle of nature that had been harnessed for the most terrible of purposes, and she felt a deep and abiding sense of melancholy settle over her like a shroud.

"We should go," Myra said, her voice cutting through the haze of Elsa's thoughts. "It's warmer inside the plant and there is still a lot you need to see."

Elsa followed Myra down the slippery stairs, her mind still reeling from the enormity of what she had seen. As they made their way towards the entrance of the hydroelectric plant, Myra's voice droned on, a ceaseless torrent of information that washed over Elsa like white noise.

"The combination of natural geologic filtering, few contaminant sources nearby, and Mana river's enormous output allows the highest achievable purities from Telemark's water feeds. Its remote location secluded in the valley provides security from Allied bombing. But it doesn't stop them from trying. We usually get a bombing raid once every couple of months. They keep us on our toes."

Elsa's head snapped up, her eyes wide with a mix of fear and curiosity. "Do they do any damage?" she asked, her voice barely above a whisper. "The bombs?"

Myra shrugged, her expression one of cool indifference. "Not really. The more the Allies try to destroy, the more underground facilities the Germans build. It's mostly the town of Telemark that suffers. The Norwegian resistance occasionally carries out a successful sabotage, but as of late even those have all but disappeared. The SS has a tight hold on Telemark. Troops are everywhere."

Elsa nodded, her mind calculating the implications of Myra's words. She knew that the SS presence could prove to be a significant obstacle to her mission, that their constant surveillance and interference could make it nearly impossible to carry out the sabotage that she had been sent to help accomplish.

"I can see that," she said, her voice tight with tension. "I hope they don't interfere with the research."

Myra smiled, a thin and brittle thing that didn't quite reach her eyes. "They can be bothersome at times, but they have instructions to allow the scientist and technicians to do their work unimpeded. The director,

Dr. Knutsen keeps them in their place."

Elsa followed Myra through a steel blast door, her senses assaulted by the harsh lights and the deafening roar of machinery that echoed through the concrete underworld of pipes, chambers, and turbine halls. The air hummed with urgency, the legions of jumpsuit technicians monitoring pressurized valves and storage cylinders with wary eyes.

As they made their way across metal gangways and down steel steps slick with condensation and chemical effluents, Elsa couldn't shake the feeling that the entire complex was a ticking time bomb, a fragile and precarious thing held together by fraying knots and silent prayers. The cold penetrated her bones despite her thick wool and fur layers, the chill of the mountain air mingling with the fear that crept up her spine.

And then, at last, they arrived at the final repository, an imposing steel-reinforced vault door recessed within the bedrock, guarded by two SS sentries who stood like silent sentinels, their eyes hard and unforgiving. Elsa watched as one of the guards spun the locking wheel and heaved open the thick hatch, revealing row upon row of glass ampoules, each one filled with the precious heavy water that had become the object of so much anxiety and desire.

The sentry's grip tightened on his machine pistol as Myra described the production metrics, his eyes boring into them with a cold and calculating intensity that made Elsa's skin crawl. She could feel his gaze upon her, the unspoken threat that lurked behind his every movement, and she knew that no feminine sentimentality would be tolerated this deep within the security perimeter.

As the steel hatch boomed closed once more, Elsa

shuddered despite herself, the imagined potential swirling within those vessels a haunting reminder of the stakes that hung in the balance. She knew that the Nazis were close, that they almost had enough heavy water to fuel their twisted ambitions, and the thought of what they might unleash upon the world made her blood run cold.

The rest of the tour passed in a blur, a maze of corridors and laboratories that seemed to stretch on forever, each one filled with teams of scientists conducting cryptic experiments and arguing equations under the harsh glare of fluorescent lights. It was a world that Elsa knew all too well, a realm of scientific academia that had once been her sole focus and passion.

But now, as she walked through the halls of the Norsk Hydro plant, Elsa couldn't shake the feeling that she was a stranger in a strange land, a woman caught between two worlds, two identities, two destinies that threatened to tear her apart at the seams.

Entering a lab, Myra and Elsa found Dr. Svein Knutsen, an impeccably-dressed gentleman in a deep discussion with a disheveled Dr. Ober wearing a crumpled tweed-jacket.

"Dr. Knutsen, if I may interrupt for a brief moment?" said Myra. "This is Dr. Paula Aadland, your new heavy water research director. Dr. Aadland this is Dr. Svein Knutsen the director of Norsk."

"Dr. Aadland, I am delighted that we have finally met. I became your most loyal fan after I read your paper on heavy water purification. Well done. I am so glad you chose to join our little community on the mountain," said Knutsen with a smile. I know your insights will catalyze our entire research program to new heights.

"Dr. Knutsen, I am afraid you've got it all wrong. I am a fan of yours. It was your research before the war that got me interested in physics," said Elsa.

"Really! You make me sound like a dinosaur."

Everyone laughs except for Dr. Ober who is annoyed at being disrupted and clears his throat.

"Of course, of course. Dr. Aadland, apologies for my abruptness - my associate Dr. Ober questions my electroanalysis efficiency models presently. And I must set him back on the path of real science."

"I understand completely."

Elsa noticed that Knutsen carried a leather-bound notebook with his initials "SK" on the front cover. She imagined that he made notes about research and production throughout his day but didn't see him carrying a pen or pencil in his shirt pocket like the rest of the scientists.

"How about this… let me take you to a charming bistro in the village where we can discuss our visions over dinner and a bottle of Brennevin?"

"Dr. Knutsen, we have just met and you are already trying to get me drunk. Of course, I accept. Research thrives through vibrant exchange and alcohol after all."

"Wunderbar! This evening, let's say 6 o'clock?"

"Let's say 7:00. A woman needs time to dress."

"Who am I to argue? I shall have my driver collect you at 7:00. I have a bit of business in Telemark, so I will meet you at the restaurant."

As Elsa and Myra moved away leaving the two men to their discussion, Elsa wondered if she has just made a huge mistake. Knutsen was pleasant enough, but she wondered about his intentions. Still, getting to know the director could be of great benefit to the mission.

And his notebook could be of great help depending on what was inside. Somehow, she needed to get a look at his notes to determine their significance.

Moving into the office area, Myra introduced Elsa to her colleagues. In each bleak cell, tired men in rumpled ties welcomed their new boss warmly, seemingly too preoccupied by machinations of protons and turbines to doubt the imposition from their Berlin overlords.

As she had been instructed by Culper, Elsa committed each researcher and specialty to memory alongside sketched diagrams of custom equipment setups. Every handshake passed without outward suspicion, the falsified credentials she had taken from Aadland apparently still intact. She was relieved when nobody made mention that they had met her before.

Myra concluded the tour in a sterile conference room with scenic Alpine murals absurdly incongruous with the concrete brutality everywhere else. Scientists filtered in offering written reviews of their specialty and verbal progress reports, but no flicker of recognition passed any face at Elsa's presence. The presentations droned on while Elsa studiously collected piles of critical documents she would examine later.

When Elsa returned to her room, she discovered a notice from the local post office had been slipped under the door. Opening the envelope, she found a receipt for a package waiting for her to pick up. She wondered why the package had not been delivered to the research facility.

She telephoned the director's office and informed the receptionist that she would meet Dr. Knutsen at the restaurant at the appointed time, but would like the driver to pick her up early so she could pick up her package before the post office closed for the evening. Hanging up the phone, she considered which of Dr. Aadland's dresses and shoes to wear. Aadland had brought a wide selection for almost every occasion.

Elsa selected her outfit carefully for the dinner, wanting to embody sophistication and style befitting Dr. Aadland's tastes. Nothing too alluring. She didn't want her conquest to be obvious. That was beneath Dr. Aadland she felt who was far more subtle in her seduction.

She decided on an elegant midnight blue evening dress made from rich velvet, nipped in at the waist before flaring out slightly over the hips into a modest A-line skirt that fell just below the knees. The squared neckline showcased her collar bones without revealing too much. Over this, she layered a matching bolero jacket with three-quarter sleeves to provide a touch more coverage for the mountain chill.

On her feet, Elsa donned a pair of dainty black heels, closed toe, and sturdy enough for snowy terrain but with a slim elegant silhouette and a modest two-inch heel. She chose to wear elegant pearl teardrop earrings and a matching multi-strand pearl necklace borrowed from Aadland's sophisticated accessories.

Looking in the mirror, the woman staring back wasn't Elsa or Dr. Aadland. She was someone else. A stranger... and yet familiar. Elsa wondered if she had gone too far in how she dressed. It seemed over the top. She thought of what Aadland would do and concluded that Aadland would make it work for her... like everything else. Elsa decided to go with what she had chosen, grabbed her purse and left her room with a confident stride.

Telemark, Norway

That evening, Elsa arrived at the post office just minutes before closing. She gave the attendant her receipt and was given a box wrapped in brown paper. There was no return address on the address label. Her curiosity peaked, until she saw Culper outside walking in front of the window.

She walked outside with the package in hand and casualty glanced at Culper rounding the corner at the end of the block. She asked the driver, Hans to take the package and said she would walk to the restaurant so she could stroll through the town. Not arguing, Hans took the box and drove off.

Elsa walked down the block and turned the corner into an alley. Culper waited at the end of alley. "You made it," said Elsa approaching.

"You doubted I would?" said Culper.

"A little. That was one heck of a jump from the train."

"Any problems?"

"None worth mentioning. I'm having dinner with the director tonight."

"That's good."

"That's what I thought, but I am not sure he sees our evening as all business."

"That's even better."

"You would prostitute me for information?"

"I would do whatever is necessary and so should you."

"That wasn't in the mission dossier."

"It never is but it's understood."

"Have you ever…"

"No. It's never come up. But I won't hesitate if I felt our country needed it."

"I see."

"You know what's at stake, Elsa."

"I do. I just never thought about what I might have to do."

"I think you did, you just didn't want to admit it to yourself."

"Perhaps. So, if the director has other plans, I should cooperate?"

"It's your call but remember the consequences if we fail."

"Of course. I just don't know if I can go that far."

"Then don't. Let Aadland do it."

Elsa knew exactly what he meant, and it wasn't a bad idea. She nodded slowly.

"Good. Have you pinpointed any of the key equipment?"

"Some of it – the generators in the power station, the electrolysis cannisters, and the heavy water storage vault. There's more. I just haven't gotten to it yet."

"And personnel?"

"I did as you said and memorized the names of the key researchers."

"Good."

"What will happened to them?"

"Those that we can convince to join us will become spies and saboteurs like you."

"And those that don't?"

"Like I said, we will do whatever is necessary to ensure the Nazis do not develop an atomic bomb before America."

"In other words, you'll kill them like Aadland?"

"Yes. But I believe most will join us if given the opportunity. The Norwegians have no love for the Nazis."

"Where are you staying?"

"It's better you don't know."

"In case I am discovered?"

"Honestly, yes. You can't reveal what you don't know."

"So, how do I get a hold of you if I need you or I have information?"

Culper handed her a slip of paper with a phone number on it and said, "Memorize this phone number, then give me back the slip of paper. If you need me, call that number and tell the person that answers you have the wrong number, then hang up. Don't leave a message. I'll meet you here at the post office within thirty minutes of your call."

Elsa nodded in agreement and memorized the phone number, then handed the slip of paper back to Culper.

"So, any more instructions?"

"No. You're doing great. Just remember not to panic no matter what happens. Think it through, then act without hesitation."

"Got it."

"One last thing…" said Culper as he pulled a small pistol from his pocket along with an extra clip of bullets. "Just in case. It should fit nicely in your purse."

"Why now?"

"I didn't want to take the chance that the SS might search you upon arrival."

"And they won't search me now?"

"No. Not unless you give them a reason."

Elsa considered for a moment, then handed the

pistol back to Culper shaking her head, "No. I don't want it."

"Elsa, be smart. You don't know what could happen. You should be prepared to defend yourself."

"I'm not going to carry a gun. I'll find some other way if I get into jam."

Culper sighed. "I don't think it's wise, but I suppose it's your call."

"I agreed to help you, Culper. But I never agreed to shoot anyone."

"No. You didn't. You still have the push dagger?"

Elsa patted her thigh, "Right where it belongs."

"It's nasty little beast as I can personally testify."

"Well, I'll be off to offer myself up to the director."

"It doesn't make you less of a woman. It makes you more of a patriot."

"Sounds like a war bond advertisement."

Elsa walked out of the alley leaving Culper to follow a few minutes later.

Elsa stood outside the intimate little bistro with a mixture of anticipation and dread. The restaurant was a charming oasis nestled between towering pines on the outskirts of Telemark village, its cheerful red door and fluttering curtains a beacon of warmth and comfort amidst the stark beauty of the mountain landscape.

She paused for a moment, her hand resting on the weathered wood of the door frame as she gathered her courage. The chill of the evening air seeped through her fur stole, a reminder of the icy world that lay beyond the cozy confines of the bistro. But Elsa knew that the real danger lurked within, that the man waiting for her inside held the key to her mission's success or failure. And she knew what he wanted… from Dr. Aadland. Could she do it? Could she turn her body over to Aadland and let her do what was necessary? She imagined she would find out soon enough.

With a deep breath, she pushed open the door and stepped inside, the rich scents of roasting meats and mulled wine enveloping her like a warm embrace. The dining room was a study in rustic elegance, all burnished wood and flickering sconces, with rich textiles in shades of ruby and gold that seemed to glow in the soft light. Twelve tables dotted the space, each one adorned with a petite arrangement of pinecones and candles that lent an air of intimacy and romance to the already cozy atmosphere.

Elsa's eyes scanned the room. She spotted Knutsen already seated at their table, holding court with a group of passersby from the research facility. As a university student, Knutsen was heavily influenced by a charismatic professor who was a secret Nazi sympathizer and fascist, shaping his ideology and loyalty. Knutsen believed that by helping the Nazis win the war, he could secure a high-ranking position in the new world order, while ensuring Norway's prosperity and survival.

Laughing and bantering, Knutsen seemed to be in his element, his charismatic presence drawing people to him like moths to a flame. And there, sitting on the table beside him, was the leather-bound notebook that never seemed to leave his side.

As the bistro's receptionist escorted Elsa to the table, Knutsen excused himself from his admirers and stood to greet her, his eyes raking over her with an appreciative gaze that made her skin crawl. "Dr. Aadland, you look exceptionally lovely tonight," he said, his voice low and smooth, a predator's purr.

Elsa forced a smile, her cheeks aching with the effort of maintaining her facade. "You're too kind, Dr. Knutsen," she replied with flattery and demurral.

Knutsen waved her to her seat with a flourish, his eyes glinting with a hunger that had nothing to do with the meal that lay ahead. "Please, sit! We must properly welcome your arrival."

As the server arrived with a bottle of Brennevin and two chilled shot glasses, Elsa sipped the potent herbal spirits cautiously. She knew that she would have to be on her guard, that any misstep could expose her true identity.

"My driver informed me that you picked up a package at the post office," Knutsen said, his tone casual but his eyes sharp and assessing.

She kept her expression carefully neutral. "Yes, I left it in your car. I hope that's okay?"

Knutsen waved a hand dismissively, his smile never quite reaching his eyes. "Of course. It's strange that they held it at the post office and didn't deliver it to the research facility."

Elsa shrugged, her mind fighting to come up with a plausible explanation. "I thought the same, but there was postage due."

Knutsen nodded, his gaze still fixed on her with an intensity that made her skin crawl. "Ah, well that explains it. I take it you ordered something through the post?"

Elsa swallowed hard, her throat suddenly dry despite the burn of the Brennevin. "Yes," she replied, her voice barely above a whisper.

"May I ask what?"

Elsa's mind went blank, a sudden panic seizing her

as she struggled to come up with a believable answer. "Of course, but I don't remember what I ordered, and I didn't get a chance to open it," she said at last, the words feeling flimsy and unconvincing even to her own ears.

But Knutsen merely smiled, his eyes glinting with a hint of amusement. "A mystery. How intriguing."

As he refilled their glasses, Elsa could feel the warmth of the liquor spreading through her veins, a slow fire that burned away the last of her inhibitions. She met Knutsen's gaze directly, praying that her next words would pass muster.

"Well, Doctor, lately I ponder whether we focus too much on incremental gains rather than grand visions," she said, her voice steady despite the fear that gnawed at her insides. "Our targets fixate on volume and efficiency logarithms, yet we neglect reframing scientific direction more fundamentally to send us to the next level where production increases and quality yields might be exponential."

Knutsen nodded eagerly, his eyes alight with a fervor. "Precisely why I lobbied command for your transfer here!" he exclaimed, his voice rising with excitement. "While our constituency tinkers within comfort zones, we require iconoclasts like yourself reshaping entire research paradigms!"

As he topped off her drink once more, Elsa could feel the room beginning to spin, the crystal blue of Knutsen's eyes blurring into a haze of color and light. She knew that she was treading on dangerous ground. But she also knew that she had no choice but to press on, to play the role of the brilliant and unconventional scientist to the hilt.

"Imagine - configuring our chromium distillation

cascade not simply for purity gains of one-tenth percent here or there but overhauling the fundamental approach to transcend reliance upon these flawed incremental models completely!" Knutsen said, his words a dizzying torrent of jargon and enthusiasm.

Elsa swallowed hard, as she tried to keep up with Knutsen's train of thought. She knew that she would have to tread carefully, to guide his passion in a direction that would serve her own ends without arousing suspicion.

But before she could formulate a response, the receptionist approached their table once more, her face a mask of polite concern. "Dr. Knutsen, there is an urgent call for you," she said, her voice soft but insistent.

Knutsen sighed, his eyes flicking to Elsa with a hint of regret. "My work is never done, not even for dinner. I shall only be a moment," he said, rising from his seat and following the receptionist towards the back of the bistro.

Elsa watched him go, her eyes darting to the leather-bound notebook that lay on the table beside his empty chair. This was her chance to steal a glimpse inside its pages and uncover the secrets that might hold the key to her mission's success.

But even as her fingers twitched with the urge to reach for the notebook, Elsa's gaze swept the room, taking in the other diners with a sudden sense of unease. Could one of them be an SS agent in disguise, waiting for her to reveal herself as a fraud? The thought made her blood run cold, and she forced herself to sit back in her chair, her hands clasped tightly in her lap.

Moments later, Knutsen returned, his face a mask of irritation as he snatched the notebook off the table and tucked it under his arm. Elsa watched him go with the realization that her chance had slipped away, that the secrets of the notebook would remain locked away for now.

As the evening wore on and the bistro began to empty, Knutsen helped Elsa don her fur stole, his fingers brushing against the soft fur in a way that made her skin crawl. "A nightcap in my suite perhaps, before we retire from this invigorating discourse?" he said, his smile a predatory thing. "I have a lovely Napoleon brandy and a warm fire awaiting..."

Elsa hesitated. This was it. Time for a decision. She tried to weigh the risks and rewards of accepting Knutsen's invitation. She knew that Aadland would have leapt at the chance to gain the favor of her superior, to use her feminine wiles to advance her own agenda. But the thought of playing the coquette, of allowing Knutsen to paw at her with his greedy hands, made her stomach turn.

And yet, even as the revulsion welled up within her, Elsa knew that she had no choice. Culper's words echoed in her mind, a reminder of the role she had been sent to play, the sacrifices she would have to make for the greater good. She did what she had to do and lets Aadland's persona take over. It was easier than she thought. Almost as if Aadland wanted to do it… to take control. And so, with a coy glance through her long lashes, she forced a smile to her lips and nodded her assent.

"Well, since you already have it uncorked and a fire sounds lovely, one toast can't hurt to warm us against the night's chill," she said, her voice a breathless purr as she pulled her fur collar tighter around her neck.

Knutsen's eyes gleamed with triumph as he helped

her into his town car, the leather-bound notebook clutched tightly in his hand. And as the car pulled away from the curb, neither of them noticed the cloaked figure lurking in the shadows of a nearby alley, a camera clutched tightly in his gloved hands.

As the car passed, he shutter clicked once, capturing the moment for posterity, a silent witness to the dangerous game that Elsa had been sent to play. And as the figure melted back into the darkness, Elsa couldn't shake the feeling that she had just crossed a threshold from which there was no turning back, that the fate of the mission - and perhaps the world itself - now rested squarely on her shoulders.

Norsk Research Facility

Elsa followed Knutsen into his sumptuous quarters with a mixture of anticipation and dread. The etched brandy glasses that awaited them beside the crackling hearth seemed to mock her, a reminder of the dangerous game she was playing. As she sank into the offered leather armchair, Elsa felt the weight of isolation's intimacy pressing down upon her, the realization that she was now truly alone with the man who held the key to her mission's success.

She forced herself to meet Knutsen's lingering gaze, her composure a fragile mask that threatened to crack at any moment. The snifter he pressed into her numb fingers felt like a lifeline, the amber liquid within promising a brief respite from the churning emotions that threatened to overwhelm her. She drank deeply, the burn of the brandy a welcome distraction.

As the evening stretched on and the liquor lowered Knutsen's inhibitions, Elsa felt her own resolve beginning to waver. His touch, once a source of revulsion, now seemed to ignite a fire within her, a desperate need for connection in a world that had become a labyrinth of secrets and lies. In that moment, with the warmth of the brandy coursing through her veins and the weight of Knutsen's gaze upon her, Elsa found herself powerless to resist.

Later, as she lay beside Knutsen's sleeping form, Elsa's mind was filled with a torrent of conflicting emotions. Shame and self-loathing warred with a desperate need for absolution, a longing to be free of the burden of her deception. She rose from the bed, wrapping herself in silk bedding as she made her way to the powder room, the worn leather journal that had caught her eye earlier clutched tightly in her trembling hands.

As Elsa locked herself within the ornately carved door of the powder room, she felt a sense of unease wash over her. She knew that what she was about to do was a violation of Knutsen's trust, but the need for answers, for some shred of meaning amidst the chaos and uncertainty of her mission, was too great to ignore.

She opened the journal's engraved cover and began to flip through the pages, her eyes scanning the handwritten notes and diagrams that filled each vellum sheet. At first, nothing seemed out of the ordinary, the technical jargon and complex equations as impenetrable as ever.

But then, as she turned to a new page, Elsa's heart stuttered in her chest, her breath catching in her throat as a wave of shock and recognition crashed over her. The handwriting that stared back at her from the yellowed pages was achingly familiar, the intricate loops and precise strokes as dear to her as her own reflection.

It was her father's hand, the same elegant script that had filled the pages of his research notes and papers. For a moment, Elsa could only stare in disbelief, her mind reeling as she tried to make sense of what she was seeing.

As the realization sank in, emotions washed over her - fierce pride in her father's brilliance, anguish at the thought of all the years she had been denied his presence, and a sickening sense of betrayal as the truth behind Knutsen's work was revealed. It was clear that Knutsen had stolen her father's work, had taken the brilliant ideas and theories that Sebastian had poured his mind and soul into and claimed them as his own. The entire foundation of the heavy water research program, the very reason for Elsa's presence in this godforsaken place, was built on a lie, a twisted perversion of her father's vision.

Elsa sank to the cold marble floor, her legs no longer able to support the weight of her grief and rage. Hot tears spilled down her cheeks, splashing onto the faded ink strokes that had once held such promise, such hope for a better world.

The realization that her own research, the work that she had believed to be a pure pursuit of knowledge and understanding, was nothing more than a cog in the machine that threatened to unleash untold destruction upon the world.

Elsa's shoulders shook with silent sobs, her heart breaking for the man who had been taken from her so cruelly, for the dream of a better future that had been twisted into a nightmare.

A sudden knock at the powder room door jolted Elsa from her thoughts as Knutsen's muffled voice reached her ears.

"Everything okay in there?" he called, his tone laced with concern.

Elsa jumped to her feet, hastily dabbing at her tears with a towel as she tried to compose herself. "Yes, I'm fine!" she called back, wincing at the tremor in her voice. "Just freshening up."

She tucked the journal under the silk bedsheet wrapped around her body, her mind struggling to come up with a plan. She knew that she couldn't let Knutsen find the journal, couldn't risk exposing her true identity.

With a deep breath, Elsa opened the door, forcing a smile to her lips as she met Knutsen's searching gaze. "A lady never reveals her entire beauty regimen too swiftly, Doctor," she purred, hoping that her coquettish tone would be enough to distract him from the redness rimming her eyes. "I couldn't spoil all my mystery immediately!"

Knutsen studied her face for a long moment, his sharp eyes seeming to pierce through her façade. But Elsa held fast, her smile never wavering as she led him back towards the bed, the journal burning against her chest.

As she slipped beneath the silken sheets, Elsa discreetly tucked the journal between the linen folds near the carved headboard, already spinning with plans for how she would retrieve it later. But for now, she had to focus on the task at hand, on keeping Knutsen distracted and unaware of the storm raging within her.

"Now, where were we before I slipped off to pamper myself?" she murmured, pulling Knutsen close and guiding his eager mouth to hers.

As his hands roamed her curves and his passion

ignited once more, Elsa's eyes shone with a fierce determination over his shoulder. With every touch and every sigh, Elsa reaffirmed her silent vow, her mind fixed on the battles yet to come and the hope that someday, the sacrifices she had made would not be in vain. For in the end, she knew, it would all be worth it, if only she could find a way to reshape the destiny that had been laid out before her, to guide the power of the atom towards a brighter future, free from the darker impulses of the human heart.

The Hunted

Telemark, Norway

The bell jangled merrily as Alf Ingvaldsen, the portly baker, pulled a fresh tray of limpa loaves from the blistering oven, the warm aroma of savory seeds and molasses glaze enveloping his quaint shop like a comforting embrace. The bakery, a small haven nestled among the cobblestone streets of Telemark, had been in Alf's family for generations, a reflection of the enduring spirit of the Norwegian people.

The interior of the shop was a cozy amalgamation of worn wooden floors, lace-trimmed curtains, and shelves lined with an array of freshly baked goods. The walls, painted a soft butter yellow, were adorned with black and white photographs depicting the bakery's history, from its humble beginnings to the present day. A rustic chandelier hung from the ceiling, its soft light casting a warm glow over the display cases filled with an assortment of pastries, breads, and cookies.

The air was thick with the scent of cinnamon, cardamom, and freshly brewed coffee, a tantalizing aroma that drew in customers from far and wide. The bakery's specialty, the limpa bread, was a favorite among the locals, its distinct flavor a reminder of the comfort and tradition that had been passed down through the ages.

With practiced ease, Alf quickly served Mrs. Klemetsen her weekly ration, a small gesture of normalcy in a world turned upside down. The elderly woman's face, lined with the cares and sorrows of a lifetime, softened as she accepted the still-warm loaf, her eyes brimming with gratitude.

As the pale violet dusk descended upon the quiet cobblestone streets, Alf latched the fogged bay windows, his movements measured and cautious. He glanced through the threadbare curtains, his eyes searching for any signs of patrol silhouettes, a constant reminder of the oppressive presence that haunted their once-peaceful town.

Satisfied that he was alone, Alf turned the sign to CLOSED, locked the door, and made his way to the back of the shop where metal racks held the cooling rounds of bread and pastries. With a deft touch, he opened a concealed doorway to the basement, the gateway to a world of secrets and resistance.

The creaking steps groaned beneath his weight as Alf descended into the root-veined chamber, the lone bulb casting an eerie glow upon the shelves of amber glass jars filled with glowing preserves. The basement, a stark contrast to the warmth and comfort of the bakery above, mirrored the dual nature of Alf's existence - the jovial baker by day, and the clandestine member of the resistance by night.

In the far back brick alcove, insulated from the prying eyes of the outside world, six gaunt faces looked up expectantly from their makeshift table of cable spools and planks - the faces of the Norwegian

Resistance.

Alf approached the group, his arms laden with fresh loaves and cheese from his cousin's farm, a small offering of sustenance in a time of scarcity. He distributed the bundles wordlessly, the men accepting them with a nod of gratitude, their eyes never leaving the photograph that Johannes, their leader, had slid across the table. A former Norwegian Army officer who refused to surrender when the Nazis invaded, Johannes went underground to form a resistance movement in Telemark, his unwavering commitment to his country's freedom driving him to risk everything in the fight against the occupying forces.

The woman in the image on the table was striking, her platinum-blond hair a beacon of beauty in a world of darkness. But the men knew better than to be fooled by her appearance, she was Elsa, disguised as Dr. Paula Aadland.

Johannes tapped a typewritten cable, his voice low and urgent. "Our lookout intercepted this telegram yesterday," he said, his words heavy with implication. "Seems Telemark has attracted another collaborator with the Nazis - Dr. Paula Aadland. An elite nuclear physicist now roosting at Norsk facility. Turns out the director chose her himself to help them ramp up their heavy water production."

Alf frowned. "Aadland? Can't say I've heard of her. Where'd she come from?"

Johannes shrugged. "Doesn't matter. What matters is that the director handpicked her for the job. And if he's brought her all the way out here to Telemark, you can bet she's no friend of ours."

The men exchanged glances, their faces etched with a mixture of anger and unease. They knew all too well the devastating potential of the work being done at the Norsk facility, and the thought of the Nazis bringing in new experts to accelerate their progress was a chilling one.

"So, what do we do?" asked one of the younger members, his voice tight with tension. "We can't just sit back and let them keep churning that stuff out."

Johannes nodded. "You're damned right we can't. But we need to be smart about this. Aadland's not going to be an easy target, holed up in that fortress. We need more information, and we need a plan."

Alf cleared his throat, his expression thoughtful. "What about the townspeople? If she's working with the Nazis, they'll know about it soon enough. Maybe we can use that to our advantage, turn some of that anger and resentment against her."

Johannes considered this for a moment, then nodded slowly. "It's a good thought, Alf. We'll need all the help we can get on this one. But we have to be careful. We can't risk innocent lives, and we can't let the Nazis catch wind of what we're planning."

"We should kill her, before she does more harm," one of the men said, his voice a low growl.

Johannes nodded, his eyes flashing with a fierce resolve. "I agree, but how? She's locked up in that facility, surrounded by SS guards."

"Then we wait until the good doctor comes back to town," another man chimed in, his fingers drumming on the table in a nervous rhythm.

"We could be waiting a long time," a third man said, his voice heavy with frustration.

Johannes leaned forward, his elbows resting on the table as he fixed each man with a steely gaze. "What other choice do we have?" he asked, his words a challenge and a rallying cry. "None. So, we wait for the right moment. But when we strike, we need to send a clear signal to the SS and the scientists at Norsk that nobody is untouchable."

The men around the table nodded. They knew the risks, the price they might pay for their resistance, but they also knew that they could not sit idly by while their country was slowly destroyed from within.

"A bomb?" one man suggested, his voice a tentative whisper.

Johannes shook his head, his expression thoughtful. "Maybe, but I don't want any civilians hurt. We can choose the method when we understand the situation better." He looked around the table, his gaze settling on each man in turn. "I want eyes and ears on the ground. Talk to your contacts, see what you can find out about this Aadland woman. Her movements, her schedule, anything that might give us an opening."

As the men sat in silence, each lost in their own thoughts, Johannes couldn't help but feel a sense of pride and purpose wash over him. He knew that they were just a small part of a much larger struggle, a fight for freedom and justice that would require sacrifices from them all.

But as he looked around the table at the faces of the unsung heroes who risked everything for the sake of their country, Johannes knew that they would not rest until Norway was free once more, until the darkness that had descended upon their land was finally lifted, and the light of hope could shine again.

Norsk Heavy Water Facility

Elsa stood before her new research team, her crisp

white lab coat that hung from her shoulders like a mantle of authority. The room, a claustrophobic chamber carved deep into the Norwegian mountainside, seemed to pulse with a nervous energy, the bare rock walls dimly illuminated by caged bulbs and webbed with twisting electrical conduits.

She could feel the weight of their gazes upon her, a dozen of the sharpest scientific minds of the occupied nation, each one wrestling with the most primal forces of human knowledge, bending them towards a horrifyingly destructive potential. In their eyes, she saw a glimmer of suspicion, a wariness born of the uncertainty that hung over her Norwegian breeding and the counterfeit background she had so carefully crafted.

As Elsa navigated the complex web of deception, her conscience ached for the Norwegian scientists she was forced to mislead, knowing that the lies she wove could seal their fate as collaborators in the eyes of their countrymen, even as she fought to tip the scales against the Germans and bring an end to the war.

But Elsa refused to let their doubt unsettle her. She straightened her shoulders and summoned every ounce of confidence she could muster. "Now then, let's begin status updates, shall we?" she said, her voice ringing out clear and strong above the drone and whoosh of the ancient ventilation ducts. "Dr. Magnusson, highlight your centrifuge purification advances first."

The distinguished chemist shuffled his papers, his movements officious and precise. "We have achieved an almost three percent increase in extracted deuterium concentration with my vortex separation revisions," he began, his voice tinged with a hint of pride. "However, production quotas—"

But Elsa was quick to interrupt, her finger raised in a gesture of calculated insight. She had scanned his notes briefly, as she searched for the flaw in his logic, the crack in his armor that she could exploit to establish her own credibility. "Are you compensating derived analysis for temperature flux at the collection membrane phase?" she asked, her tone sharp and probing. "I'm concerned covariance not centered along the..."

She outlined a more rigorous statistical method, her words flowing with an ease and confidence that belied the churning uncertainty in her gut. But even as she spoke, she could feel the tension in the room mounting, the skepticism of her colleagues growing with each passing moment.

It was Frode, a junior physicist with a keen mind and a hungry ambition, who finally broke the silence. "That appears an innovative deviation from standard German guidance though?" he said, his voice tinged with a hint of challenge.

Elsa refused to let her unease show on her face. Instead, she continued evenly, her words measured and precise. "As research directors, we must apply discretion to tailor global best practices towards local opportunities, would you agree, Frode?"

The younger man frowned in a gesture of defiance. But he held his tongue, his challenge checked for now by the force of Elsa's gaze and the weight of her authority.

Elsa hid a relieved exhale behind a shuffle of papers, as she tried to navigate the razor-sharp expertise of her colleagues. She knew that one misstep, one moment of hesitation or uncertainty, could expose her for the fraud she was, could bring her carefully constructed facade crashing down around her ears.

But she refused to let that happen. She had come too far, had sacrificed too much, to let her mission fail now. And so she pressed on, her voice steady and her gaze unwavering, even as the doubts and fears churned within her.

As the meeting drew to a close and the other scientists filed out of the room, Elsa couldn't help but feel a sense of unease settling over her. She could feel Frode's gaze boring into her back, his suspicion smoldering like embers in the darkness.

And when he approached her, his words a thinly veiled challenge to her expertise and authority, Elsa felt a spike of anger rising within her. But she tamped it down, summoning every ounce of icy hauteur she could muster.

"And since you apparently skipped Professor Lindgren's statistical analytics course," she said, her voice dripping with disdain, "I will summarize simply - dynamic covariance matrices prevent such risks. But by all means verify through proper peer-reviewed literature... unless you question my qualifications further without cause?"

The silence that hung between them was thick and heavy, a palpable weight that seemed to press down upon them both. But Elsa refused to back down, her gaze locked with Frode's in a silent battle of wills.

Finally, the young physicist looked away, his defiance crumbling beneath the force of her scrutiny. "My apologies, Doctor," he said, his voice tight with barely contained resentment. "Your pedigree certainly exceeds most peers. Simple academic rigor, nothing personal intended."

He gathered his papers and hurried from the room,

his retreat a tacit acknowledgment of her victory. But even as the door swung shut behind him, Elsa could feel the weight of his suspicion lingering in the air, a constant reminder of the precariousness of her position.

She sagged against the chalkboard, her breath coming in short, sharp gasps as the adrenaline of the confrontation slowly ebbed from her veins. She knew that she had won this battle, that she had established her credibility and authority in the eyes of her colleagues.

But the war was far from over. And as she stood there, her mind reeling, Elsa couldn't shake the feeling that the true test of her mettle, the ultimate trial of her courage and conviction, was still to come.

For in this world of secrets and lies, of hidden agendas and deadly stakes, there could be no room for weakness, no quarter given to the doubts and fears that threatened to consume her. And so Elsa steeled herself, her jaw set and her eyes blazing with a fierce determination. For the weight of history rested squarely upon her shoulders.

Norsk Scientist Residence

The clock struck half past eleven as Elsa cracked open her door, peering into the sterile concrete corridors that stretched out before her like a labyrinth. The air was thick with tension, broken only by the occasional echoing bootfalls of the SS patrols that stalked the halls, their eyes sharp and their weapons at the ready.

Elsa pulled her black layers tighter around her slender frame, tucking loose blonde wisps under a knit cap as she prepared to venture out into the unknown.

She clutched her faint red-lens flashlight like a lifeline, its dim glow a feeble defense against the absolute darkness that awaited her.

As she slipped into the shadows, hugging the barren walls like a ghost, Elsa couldn't shake the feeling of unease. She was a scientist, not a spy, and the weight of her mission hung heavily on her shoulders, a burden that threatened to crush her beneath its weight.

She thought back to her training, to the endless hours spent memorizing codes and practicing her cover story. But even now, as she descended into the buried mechanical chambers, Elsa couldn't help but feel a creeping sense of doubt.

The distant reverberation of massive turbines pulsed beneath her feet, a restless, invisible monster that seemed to mock her very presence. Elsa knew that these machines, these marvels of modern engineering, held the key to the Nazi's plans. It was her job to stop them. And yet, as she crept past unlocked laboratories and darkened offices, she couldn't shake the feeling that she was in over her head.

The facility itself was a declaration of the Reich's ruthless efficiency, a sprawling complex of laboratories, workshops, and power stations that burrowed deep into the mountain's core, out of the American bombers reach. Every surface was polished to a high sheen, every piece of equipment gleaming with a clinical precision that belied the dark purpose that lurked beneath.

As Elsa made her way deeper into the bowels of the facility, she couldn't help but marvel at the sheer scale of the operation. Miles of pipes and cables snaked through the walls and ceilings, carrying the lifeblood of the heavy water production process to every corner of the complex. Massive tanks and pressure vessels loomed in the shadows, their surfaces etched with a complex web of valves and gauges that seemed to defy comprehension.

And everywhere she looked, Elsa saw the signs of the SS presence that permeated every aspect of life at the facility. Grim-faced soldiers patrolled the corridors in pairs, their boots clicking against the concrete with a metronome-like precision. Fearsome German Shepherds strained at their leashes, their eyes glinting with a feral intensity that made Elsa's blood run cold.

Even the scientists and technicians who staffed the laboratories seemed to move with a hunted, furtive air, as though they too were aware of the constant surveillance and the ever-present threat of violence that hung over their heads.

Creeping past an unlocked laboratory, Elsa overheard two muffled guards speaking.

"This damned night shift will drive me to drink, Hans - either from boredom or these hellish drafts!"

A hacking cough answered faintly. "Save your flask then, Dieter! Maybe if we ask our brilliant physicists to invent indoor weather next, eh?"

Their laughter faded as Elsa continued her secretive search undisturbed. Lab after lab could be easily sabotaged once she decoded inner workings along with map layouts. What was important and what wasn't, it all had to be located and adjudicated. And then there were the scientists. Culper wanted them too – join the Allies or die. Not much of a choice.

Flattening against cold concrete, she allowed darting beams to fully recede clockwise, then plunged her faint ruby glow counter, deeper into darkness. Elsa descended through the humming mountain nerve center.

As Elsa ducked into a darkened office to avoid a passing patrol, she couldn't help but feel a pang of homesickness wash over her. She thought of her tiny apartment back in Chicago, of the familiar streets and faces that had been her whole world for so long. What she wouldn't give to be back there now, curled up with a good book and a cup of tea, far from the madness and danger of this place.

But even as the longing threatened to overwhelm her, Elsa knew that she had no choice but to press on. She had a job to do that could change the course of the war and save countless lives. And so, with a deep breath and a silent prayer, she stepped back out into the corridor, her senses on high alert as she continued her secretive search.

As Elsa approached a set of metal doors stenciled with a dire warning of HIGH VOLTAGE, she felt a shiver run down her spine. She knew that the massive dynamo chambers that lay beyond those doors were the pulsing, electrified core that fed the voracious demands of the heavy water processing. She could feel the electricity in the air passing through her. She raised her hand and used her flashlight to watch the hair on the back of her hand rise like some kind of magician's trick. Her mind said she was in no danger, but her instincts said otherwise.

Part of her wanted to turn back, to flee this place and never look back. But Elsa knew that she had come too far to give up now. And so, she reached for her lock pick kit, determined to unravel the secrets that lay beyond those forbidding doors.

But before she could even begin, the sound of

approaching footsteps sent a jolt of pure panic through her. Elsa pressed herself tighter against the cold steel doors as she watched the bobbing halos of the guards' flashlights grow closer and closer.

There was nowhere to hide. Elsa was trapped, cornered like a rat in a maze of her own making. As the heavy bootfalls grew louder, echoing off the smooth tunnel walls, she felt a wave of desperation engulf her.

She thought of her father, of the legacy of brilliance and courage that he had left behind. She thought of her mother, of the quiet strength that had sustained her through so many years of hardship and loss. And she thought of her own dreams, of the bright future that she had once imagined for herself, a world of discovery and wonder that now seemed so impossibly far away.

But even as the tears pricked at the corners of her eyes, Elsa knew that she could not let her emotions cloud her judgment. She had to think, had to find a way out of this impossible situation before it was too late.

In a last, desperate gamble, she reached for the heavy breaker switches that lined the wall beside her, praying that one of them would plunge the corridor into darkness and give her the cover she needed to escape.

The first switch yielded nothing, the lights remained stubbornly on. The second switch too proved useless. As panic threatened to consume her as the guards rounded the bend, their flashlight beams cutting through the gloom like knives, Elsa's fingers found the third switch.

With a desperate cry, she threw the lever, sparks flying as the heavy contacts cleared their housing. And then, miraculously, the lights went out, plunging the corridor into a blessed, impenetrable darkness.

"Gottverdammt!" The guards rushed down the corridor straight at her to investigate the abrupt blackout. To avoid the guards' flashlight beams, she moved to the opposite side of the corridor from where the breakers were located.

Elsa held her breath, pressing herself into the shadows as the guards approached. She could feel the electricity crackling behind her, the raw power of the dynamos humming through the walls like a living thing.

The guards stopped at the junction box and breaker switches just a few feet from where Elsa stood and focused on resetting the tripped circuits. They too were fearful of the awesome power within in the cables and wary to touch the switch handles. As a klaxon began blaring, she inched down the corridor on their blind side.

Once she reached several yards away from the guards busy deciding who would throw the switches, Elsa sprinted full speed down the dark corridor praying that her footfalls would not be heard by the bickering guards.

As she neared the first junction at the end of the corridor, there was a loud CRACK and the ceiling lights came back on. Fortunately, the guards were too busy congratulating themselves to notice her rounding the corner.

She moved quickly back the way she had come. She had enough for the night. But the danger wasn't over...

Muffled barking gave her seconds to duck inside a dark office before clicks of animal nails rapidly approached. Peering out cracked blinds, Elsa glimpsed two Belgian Malinois straining past, followed by another sentry patrol.

When the corridor was once again clear, she ran

until her lungs burned and her legs ached, until she found herself standing once again in the dubious safety of her own room, the stolen schematics and carefully-sketched maps scattered across her desk like pieces of a puzzle that only she could solve.

And as she sat there, her pencil flying across the pages as she committed every last detail to paper, Elsa felt a sense of pride settle over her like a mantle. She had pulled it off. She was alive and doing what Culper had instructed her to do. Although she still had a lot to learn, she was a spy. There was no denying it. She chuckled thinking about how it might look on her resume – nuclear physicist, intelligence operative, and savior of the free world. She liked the ring of it.

She enjoyed the moment until she remembered that the price of failure would be measured in the lives of the innocent. But she also knew that she would use every last ounce of her courage and her cunning to bring an end to the evil that had taken root in this place and the Nazi's dreams of conquest were reduced to ashes and dust.

And so, with a final, determined snap of her pencil, Elsa pushed the papers aside and blew out the flickering candle that had been her only source of light.

After all, she thought with a wry smile as she settled into her narrow bed, pulling the thin blanket up to her chin, *she had always been a woman who thrived on challenge, who found strength in adversity and purpose in the face of the impossible.*

Faceless

Tocksfors, Sweden

Blanketed in deep drifts, ice-covered birch trees, and etched fields, the Swedish lowlands lay frosted. A muted gray sky hung over the village of Tosksfors. Every last surface smoothed by wind piling snow into sculptural waves. Chimney wisps from hunched cottages across the white wastes were the only signs of life visible.

Trudging through the snow drifts with his rifle slung over his shoulder, Rolf cursed under his frosted breath. The sinking afternoon sun offered little time to bag an elk before the night's squall descended and the thought of eating porridge for another evening turned his stomach. Behind him, his loyal bloodhound Freki sniffed urgently between buried stands of alder and birch. Rolf looked to the dark clouds approaching. A storm was coming… a big one.

"Easy boy! Visibility will vanish out here fast. We best be getting back," Rolf shouted over the shrieking wind. Distant thunder promised the coming blizzard's vanguard as light dissolved cobalt.

Suddenly Freki bayed wildly just below the meadow

crest ahead. With a frustrated sigh Rolf slogged uphill nearing the hound's circling point. Cresting the ridge, his breath froze into limp crystals on his beard. Where Freki pawed deliberately, Rolf glimpsed white silk draped over a rigid, feminine form like some macabre ghost. He staggered closer shouting disbelief into the surrounding trees. Gently lifting fabric, sanity itself unraveled - crusted gore surrounded shredded tissues of a woman's face with glinting sinew clinging to muscle. Rolf fell back, horrified at the ghastly sight. He clambered at the snow trying to gain traction, trying to get away.

Hours later, Rolf with Freki by his side, sat retelling horrors to Captain Nemec at the town's police station. But no details could capture the sight seared in his brain - afterimages of bone and fraying nerve. All humanity's barbarism blinked back behind frozen lashes.

"Rolf, I know you have had a hard time. But I need you and Freki to go back with me and find this woman before snow covers her completely and we lose her 'till spring thaw," said Nemec.

"I ain't going back and neither is Freki. We've seen enough to haunt us a lifetime and then some," said Rolf.

"It's not an option, Rolf. You are part of this investigation. A key part."

"Who is she?"

"I don't know, but we need to find out."

"Is anyone in the village missing?"

"Not that I know of, but she may not be from the village."

"Well, where then?"

"She could be from anywhere. But one thing for sure… we won't be able find answers unless we go now."

Rolf sighed, "Alright, but just me. Freki can stay here where it's safe."

"Are you sure you can find the body without Freki?"

"Yeah, I'm sure. You don't forget something like that, ya know?"

"Yeah, I know."

Grabbing their snowshoes and a long aluminum sleigh, Nemec and Rolf headed out. Left behind, Freki whined for a moment, then curled up by the warm stove.

As the night descended upon the Swedish lowlands, Captain Nemec and Rolf found themselves enveloped in a darkness that seemed to seep into their very bones. The wind howled through the trees, a mournful sound that echoed across the frozen landscape, and the snow swirled around them in a blinding white dance.

With only the thin beams of their flashlights to guide them, the two men trudged through the deep drifts, their breath coming in ragged gasps as they fought against the biting cold. Rolf led the way as he retraced the steps that had brought him to the horrifying discovery just hours before.

As they neared the ridge, a sense of dread washed over them, a palpable force that seemed to hang in the air like a suffocating blanket. Rolf's hand shook as he directed the beam of his flashlight towards the crest of the hill, his mind reeling with the memory of what lay ahead.

And then, as they topped the rise, the harsh glare of

their lights fell upon the woman's body, a ghostly figure sprawled across the snow. Rolf felt bile rise in his throat, his stomach churning as he took in the sight of her disfigured face, the once-delicate features now a grotesque mask.

As they moved closer, Nemec drew in a sharp breath as he stared down at the carnage and sheer savagery of what lay before them. He had seen death before, had witnessed the aftermath of violence and brutality, but it never got easier for him. Nemec, a man of deep faith who believed that his work as a police officer was a calling from God, approached each case with a sense of moral urgency and a commitment to uncovering the truth.

Nemec reached out and gently lifted the woman's shoulder, his fingers sinking into the icy flesh. As he did so, the beam of his flashlight caught the glint of something metallic, and he leaned in closer.

It was a charm bracelet, the clasp caught on the fabric of her dress, the delicate links twisted and broken. And there, nestled among the glittering baubles, was a small silver locket, its surface tarnished and dull in the harsh light.

With numb fingers, Nemec pried open the locket, his breath catching in his throat as he saw the two small photographs inside. They were faded and worn, the images barely visible in the dim light, but the inscription on the back was still legible, the Norwegian words etched into the metal with a steady hand - "May your light always shine. Love Mon & Dad."

Rolf leaned in closer, his own flashlight playing across the locket as he read the words aloud, his voice barely a whisper in the howling wind. Jewel mementos were all that was left for this woman to cling to. For a moment, the two men stood in silence, the weight of the woman's life, of the love and joy that had once filled her days, pressing down upon them like a physical force.

But even as they stood there, lost in their own thoughts and memories, the harsh reality of the crime scene intruded once more. Nemec's flashlight played across the woman's hands, the beam illuminating the terrible damage that had been done, the bones and tendons exposed in a grisly display.

It was clear that no animal had inflicted these wounds, that the killer had taken great pains to strip away every last trace of their victim's identity. The faint odor of lye still lingered in the air, a sickening reminder of the lengths to which the murderer had gone to conceal their crime.

Examining the body further, Nemec discovered the garrote that had been used to cinch up one end of the silk bedsheets. As he untied the wire, he doubted that the killer had left any fingerprints on the wooden handles, but he might be able to determine the weapon's origin. Careful not to touch the handles, he wrapped a handkerchief around the garrote and it in his coat.

As Nemec searched the surrounding snow for any more sign of evidence, his flashlight casting eerie shadows across the frozen ground, he couldn't shake the feeling that they were being watched, that the killer was still out there somewhere, lurking in the darkness.

But even as the thought sent a shiver down his spine, Nemec knew that he could not let fear or uncertainty cloud his judgment. He had a job to do, a duty to the woman and to the law.

And so, with a final sweep of his flashlight and a

nod to Rolf, Nemec began the long, slow process of documenting the scene, his mind already mulling with the possibilities.

Back in the warmth of his office, Nemec sat in his chair thinking as he stared out the frosted window at the blizzard covering the town in a thick white blanket. Calls would come in about villagers stranded and in need of help. He would let his two officers handle the calls. He had a murder that needed to be solved.

As he watched the flakes dance and twist in the wind, Nemec couldn't help but think of his own past, of the experiences that had shaped him into the man he was today. He had seen his fair share of darkness over the years, first as a soldier in the Great War and later as a police officer in Stockholm.

But it was his time as a detective in the city's homicide division that had truly left its mark on him. Nemec had seen firsthand the depths of human cruelty, had looked into the eyes of killers, and seen the emptiness that lurked within. It was a burden he carried with him always, a reminder of the evil that men were capable of.

And now, as he sat in the quiet of his office, that same sense of unease settled over him like a cloak. There was something about this case, something about the brutal nature of the crime, that set his instincts on edge. He knew that he would have to use every ounce of his skill and experience to unravel the mystery of the woman's death and bring her killer to justice.

Nemec had set the wheels in motion, had made the necessary calls and inquiries that would help him piece together the puzzle of the woman's identity. But even as he waited for the answers to come, Nemec couldn't shake the feeling that there was more to this case than met the eye. The charm bracelet that had been found on the woman's body lingered in his mind, a talisman of the life that had been so brutally cut short.

Why had the killer left it behind, when they had been so meticulous in their efforts to strip away every last trace of their victim's identity? It was a question that gnawed at him, a riddle that he knew he must solve.

As the hours turned into days and the leads began to trickle in, Nemec found himself consumed by the case, his every waking moment devoted to the pursuit of justice. He pored over the autopsy report, searching for any clue that might have been overlooked, and he followed up on every lead, no matter how small or seemingly insignificant.

It was a lonely and often thankless task, but Nemec was no stranger to hard work and dedication. His time as a soldier and a police officer had taught him the value of perseverance, of pushing through even when the odds seemed insurmountable.

And so he pressed on, his determination unshakable and his resolve unwavering. He would find the killer, would bring them to justice and give the woman the peace she so deserved. It was a promise he had made to himself, and one that he intended to keep. For he was a man of honor, a seeker of truth in a world that often seemed to value lies and deceit.

As he turned away from the window, he considered where the woman might have come from. The railway passed through the town but rarely stopped unless requested by a passenger or one of the town's people. The train ran through Norway, Sweden, Finland, and Russia. It was a lot of territory connecting millions of people. She could have come from anywhere. Still, it was his duty to try and located the women's origin.

He fingered the charm bracelet sitting on desk waiting to be stored in a manilla evidence envelope. The inscription on the locket was Norwegian and the photos were of her parents, but she could have been going or coming from Norway.

He called the border crossings of Norway and Finland inquiring if anyone on the train passenger manifests had failed to cross the border in the last month. Both said it would take time to check. So, again, he waited. That seemed like much of his job lately... waiting for answers.

A few days later, the autopsy report came in as expected. Teeth marks were a surprise. It seemed an animal, probably a wolf, had dug up the corpse but refused to eat any of the flesh because of the lye. It wasn't enough just to bury the victim, the killer didn't want her identity to be discovered. He was probably connected to the woman in some way. Maybe a former boyfriend or husband. Hard to say. A clue, but not much of one. Nemec had so little to go on.

Later that afternoon, an officer from the Norwegian border crossing called. There was one female passenger and one male passenger on a train manifest that had failed to cross the border a few weeks ago. A married couple - Mr. and Mrs. Nilsen. Their luggage was found abandoned on the train when it arrived in Oslo. As part of standard procedure, Nemec requested a copy of Mr. and Mrs. Nilsen's passports and marriage certificate from Oslo to verify their identities. He did not tell the border officer that Mrs. Nilsen was dead and her husband was the prime suspect.

Hanging up the phone, Nemec considered how simple it was – the newlyweds had fought on the train, Mr. Nilsen killed his wife in a moment of passion, jumped off the train with her body, took all her jewelry so it looked like a robbery gone bad, buried her in the meadow, then simply disappeared. Everything wrapped up with a nice bow. Nemec didn't like it. It was the locket on the charm bracelet that bothered him. Why didn't Mr. Nilsen take it along with everything else of value? Had he simply missed it?

Telemark, Norway

The narrow mountain pass winding along the river gorge was prone to loose falling rocks cracking windshields and shattering headlights despite cautious speeds. The single-lane gravel track allowing only glimpses of Telemark's valley roofs between soaring lichen-covered cliffs switch-backed treacherously, overhung by pine boughs that left icy patches lingering in cold shadows.

Hans knew every hidden fork intimately from years of driving diplomats and scientists. As the road leveled near town, the river slowed and the whitewater all but disappeared.

Fidgeting in unfamiliar silken stockings in the rear seat of Dr. Knutsen's polished town car, Elsa glanced up to see Hans' gaze skate her legs in the mirror despite himself. She flushed, reaching hurriedly for her fur coat. Flustered from being caught, Hans straightened the mirror and locked his eyes on the road.

Elsa was incensed but then calmed as she considered the situation. A man like Hans, always in control was flustered by her no less. She realized the power inadvertently at her fingertips now. She could disarm masculine discipline trained to ignore distraction if she honed allure just right. Emboldened, Elsa resumed adjusting gossamer seams at an agonizingly slow pace. When Hans' eyes dragged inevitably back, she granted the smallest smirk then turned casually away, glimpsing how little men's fortress walls stood immune to well-placed temptation.

She understood why creatures like Aadland reveled in such theatrics. No door was secure or dark secret kept safe to femininity's delicate touch it seemed. Elsa hid a sly smile settling back. She must remember well that advantage hid even behind silk or rouge pots.

Hans pulled up to the quaint lingerie shop squeezed between stone-hewn cafes, its gilt window revealing a cozy amber glow within promising warmth and fineries. He rushed to open the car door and assist Dr. Aadland inside. Tempted to follow her in, Hans returned to the car, retrieved a rag from under the front seat, and cleaned the road dust off the polished sheet metal and glass. That was his place, not inside with his master's mistress.

Inside the shop, a matronly shop owner bustled over asking preferences as Dr. Aadland browsed delicately embroidered items with seeming uncertainty. Wasn't she intimate with the latest continental underthings fashion?

"Perhaps Mademoiselle desires something sheer for special evenings out?" The owner leaned in smiling conspiratorially. "This French silk chemise or exclusive garter belt..."

"Ah, of course..." Aadland managed eyeing items hesitantly. "Though such daring luxury hardly finds cause up at Hydroelectric's rustic quarters I'm afraid..."

"Your perfume… Chanel?"

"Yes. How kind of you to notice. A Christmas gift I treasure during long dreary conferences within rock walls that smell like wet dogs."

"I imagine the scientists have trouble focusing with you in the room."

"I don't know. I don't think they see me that way."

"If they are men, I assure you… they see you that way."

Aadland giggled incredulous, "Really?"

"Definitely."

Unsure how to reply, Aadland pulled a demure lace negligee without flourish off a rack. "I should like to try this on."

"Of course. Right this way," said the owner leading Aadland behind a white linen dressing screen.

Outside, Hans glanced through the shop window and saw Aadland's silhouette as she undressed behind the slightly translucent screen. He sighed, "I'm a dead man."

Elsa sat outside the quaint café, bundled up in her coat, her hands wrapped around a steaming cup of coffee. As she took a bite of the delicate krumkake, the brittle cookie crumbling on her tongue, she was transported back to her childhood, to the warm, comforting memories of her mother baking syv slags kaker in their cozy kitchen.

The flavors and scents of the cookie stirred something deep within Elsa, a sense of connection to her Norwegian heritage that she had never fully explored. Growing up, her mother had shared stories of their homeland, painting vivid pictures of the rugged, beautiful landscape, the resilient spirit of its people, and the rich cultural traditions that had been passed down through generations.

Elsa had always felt a certain pride in her Norwegian roots, a sense of belonging to something greater than herself. But it wasn't until this moment, sitting in Telemark, that she truly understood the depth of that connection.

As she gazed out at the snow-capped mountains that loomed in the distance, Elsa felt a sense of peace wash over her, a feeling of being exactly where she was meant to be. The crisp, clean air filled her lungs, invigorating her senses, and the gentle bustle of the town around her seemed to pulse with a quiet, steady rhythm that echoed the resilience and strength of the Norwegian people.

For a moment, Elsa allowed herself to imagine what her life might have been like if her family had never left Norway, if she had grown up among these mountains and valleys, immersed in the language and customs of her ancestors. Would she have found the same passion for science, the same burning desire to uncover the secrets of the universe? Or would her path have taken a different turn, leading her to a life of quiet contentment, surrounded by the beauty and simplicity of the Norwegian countryside?

Elsa took a sip of her coffee, savoring the rich, earthy flavor, and let her thoughts drift. She knew that she could never truly go back, that the choices and experiences that had shaped her life had set her on a course that should not be altered. But sitting there, in her mother's homeland, she felt a sense of belonging that gave her strength and purpose.

Suddenly, the sound of footsteps echoing on the pavement jolted Elsa from her reverie. She looked up to see a man in a heavy overcoat approaching, his hands buried deep in his pockets, his gaze fixed on her with an intensity that sent a shiver down her spine.

Elsa's peaceful thoughts gave way to a sudden, gripping fear. Could this man be someone who knew Dr. Aadland? Someone who might see through her carefully crafted disguise and expose her for the imposter she was? The thought filled her with a sickening sense of dread, and she rose from her seat, her voice trembling as she called out to Hans as the man closed the distance between them.

"Hans, I think I'm ready to go," she said, her words clipped and urgent.

But before Hans could respond, the man in the overcoat pulled his hand from his pocket, revealing the glinting metal of a machine pistol. Elsa froze, her breath catching in her throat as she stared down the barrel of the gun, her mind reeling with the realization that she was about to die.

The crack of gunshots filled the air, and Elsa watched in stunned disbelief as the man crumpled to the ground, his blood staining the snow a vivid crimson. She turned to see Hans standing by the open door of the car, a smoking pistol in his hand, his eyes scanning the area for any further threats.

"Please get in the car, Fraulein," he said, his voice calm and steady.

Elsa obeyed without a word, her legs shaking as she climbed into the backseat. As Hans slid behind the wheel and put the car in gear, Elsa's mind raced with questions as she tried to make sense of what had just happened.

"Who was he?" she asked, her voice barely above a whisper.

"I don't know. Probably Norwegian resistance," Hans replied, checking the mirrors for any sign of pursuit.

"Why would the resistance want to kill me?"

"You're a prominent scientist working at Telemark. Of course, they want to kill you."

Elsa's stomach churned at the realization that her presence in Telemark had put her in the crosshairs of those who sought to resist the Nazi occupation. But even as fear and uncertainty gripped her, she forced herself to take a deep breath, to focus on the mission at hand.

"Thank you for saving my life," she said softly, catching Hans's gaze in the rearview mirror.

He nodded, a flicker of warmth in his eyes. "It's a life worth saving."

Elsa felt a rush of gratitude wash over her, a sense of kinship with this man who had risked his own life to protect hers. And as the car wound its way through the narrow, twisting streets of Telemark, Elsa smiled gratefully as they exchanged a look in the rearview mirror.

She was frazzled by events but had calmed herself. Just as Culper had instructed her, she had to keep a cool head about her and stay on mission. With luck and a bit of manipulation, she might be able to turn this into an opportunity.

Norsk Research Facility

Elsa stepped into the lobby of the Norsk Research Facility, her fashionable heels clicking unsteadily on the polished floor. She scanned the room for any signs of security leaks, her nerves frayed from the chaos of the day's events. She had barely taken a few steps when she caught sight of Dr. Svein Knutsen rushing towards her, his face deeply creased with concern.

"Dr. Aadland! Good God, what happened in town?" His hands fluttered around her, unsure whether to offer comfort or check for injuries. "The SS commander said some lunatic publicly attacked you on sight?"

Elsa allowed herself to shudder, a calculated display of frail distress. "Oh, Svein, that awful brute of a man approached so suddenly. Were it not for Hans's quick reactions..." She trailed off, her chin quivering as she let the unspoken horrors hang in the air between them.

Knutsen drew her in protectively, his Teutonic possessiveness palpable as his ego swelled at the prospect of consoling the rattled beauty now dependent on his strength. "There there, Paula, you're safe back with me, away from further danger." He waved over the SS security chief impatiently. "Colonel Bauer! This is the Reich's most important research project, and we almost lost one of our lead scientists. I want the group that did this hunted down and disposed of immediately. If you must, pull squadrons from the valley and get riflemen stationed on overwatch. I'll have no further security embarrassments, is that clear?!"

Bauer snapped a sharp salute, his voice crisp and efficient. "We'll bolster defenses two-fold immediately, Director Knutsen. No need for concern!" As he marched off, barking orders at his subordinates, Knutsen turned back to Elsa, who dabbed at her eyes delicately.

"I am so distraught. I am not sure I can work today, Svein. But I don't want to be alone," she whispered, her voice trembling with a carefully crafted vulnerability.

"I understand completely. Let's get you upstairs and comfortable, away from these bothersome grunts and distressing business." He lifted her fingers to his lips, brushing a reassuring kiss over her knuckles. "I have a lovely brandy and a warm hearth that can soothe away such awful memories, if you'll allow it."

Elsa managed a waifish nod, letting him guide her protectively along into his private quarters.

Dr. Knutsen's walnut-paneled study exuded old-world luxury, tucked behind the lavish curving stairwell. The dark wood and intricately carved crown moldings spoke of power and ambition, while the rare scientific manuscripts and obscure curios displayed in the glass bookshelves hinted at a keen and curious mind. The massive clawfoot desk, strewn with classified diagrams, anchored the space, well-worn from generations of powerful men leveraging their influence over careers made or broken within these walls.

Yet for all its grandeur, the room lacked warmth, the flickering fireplace casting irregular shadows across the hearthstones where Elsa and the latest master of this realm had recently intertwined. Beside the fire, Elsa lay beneath fur throws, listening for Knutsen's breaths to slow into the rhythm of post-coital slumber. His earlier fervent exertions had required much gentle reassurance that her shock was mending, an easy deception for her to play the vulnerable maiden to his Alpha male.

Unlike their previous encounter, she had made sure his glass of brandy was refilled several times before their zealous tryst, wanting him relaxed and heavy-eyed when they were finished. Soon, his hand loosened its proprietary grip on her bare shoulder, and unconsciousness overtook his disciplined resistance.

Elsa measured his rhythmic wheezing carefully, then slipped from the passionate disarray. She picked up the well-worn notebook from his leather reading chair and glided down the staircase to the bedroom, locking the door behind her. She turned on the amber light on the nightstand and opened the engraved leather journal, her heart surging as she traced the elegant equations that revealed her father's brilliance.

Each page was a window into his mind, the pioneering theories that had defined his life's work. Yet as she delved deeper into the theorems of neutron acceleration and heavy particle bombardment, her excitement gave way to melancholy. In the mere decades since her father's death, atomic science had vaulted ambitiously beyond his postulations, harnessing the power of starfire itself.

Elsa wept silently, grieving the profound loss that time's lens had brought into sharp focus. Her father's designs, once deemed timeless by a worshipping girl, were now antiquated relics, eclipsed by the very machinations she herself had pioneered at the University of Chicago.

But as she closed the notebook and stared into the darkness, Elsa found a glimmer of purpose amidst her sorrow. If Knutsen had built the foundation of the Nazis' heavy water research program on her father's obsolete insights, with none of his own original concepts, then he was out of ideas on which to transform the program.

The dazzling Dr. Aadland was meant to be his savior, to prevent the Reich from discovering that he was a fraud. And if that were true, then Elsa's seductions could lead Knutsen wherever she wanted, like a bull with a ring in its nose.

She thought back to her work in Chicago, to the fruitless paths she and her team had explored in their quest for knowledge. Perhaps those same dead ends could be used to lead Knutsen astray, to undo the Third Reich's atomic ambitions from within.

With sorrow, Elsa returned the notebook to the reading chair and curled up beside the slumbering Knutsen once more. She knew that sleep would be elusive that night, her mind calculating strategies and schemes to unravel the very fabric of the Nazi war machine.

But even as the weight of her mission pressed down upon her, Elsa felt a flicker of hope. For if she could succeed, if she could turn Knutsen's own ambitions against him, then perhaps no one else would have to die. Perhaps, in the end, the power of her intellect and the strength of her conviction would be enough to change the course of history itself.

And so, as the night wore on and the shadows lengthened, Elsa lay beside the man who held the key to her mission's success, her mind awhirl with possibilities and the fire of purpose.

Telemark, Norway

The snow continued to fall from a morning storm as Johannes pushed open the warped door of Ingvaldsen's Bakery. The overhead bell jingled. Stomping his boots to rid the snow and dirt, Johannes approached the counter. Alf was nowhere in sight, but the aroma of Alf's renowned pepperkaker spice cookies revealed his presence. Johannes inhaled greedily - rare moments before another covert strategy meeting.

The broad shopkeep appeared in the doorway from the bakery kitchen wiping floured hands upon his apron with familiar cheer. But Johannes immediately noted worry creasing Alf's ruddy features. His own instincts bristled. Something was wrong.

"Are the others here yet?" said Johannes.

"No. But you have a guest waiting below."

"A guest?" said Johannes.

Alf nodded.

Descending into the root cellar beneath baker Alf's shop, Johannes froze seeing Culper waiting grimly at the cable spool table. The OSS officer had coordinated this Norwegian resistance cell since the early occupation years.

"You were reckless," said Culper.

"There is risk in everything we do," said Johannes.

"An assassination in broad daylight in the center of town no less?"

"Dr. Aadland is a lead scientist and a key research manager."

"I know who she is. But gunning down Aadland in broad daylight risks everything we've built! You're lucky your man was killed and not captured, or you and your group would be sitting in an SS cell right now."

"I don't think one of my men's death should be categorized as luck."

"You know what I mean."

"If we eliminate key research heads, it hinders the Reich. Isn't that our shared mission, Culper?"

"Yes, but there is more at play here that your actions affect."

"Like what?"

"Like none of your damned business."

"We are supposed to be allies."

"And you think we share everything with our allies?"

"Why wouldn't you?"

"The same reason you didn't tell me about the assassination before you bungled it – trust."

"You're right. I should have told you."

Culper softens, "I'm sorry about your man."

"He was an idiot. He should have known that Knutsen's driver would have a weapon."

"Yeah, he should have. But still… I know the risks all of you are taking for your country."

"It's our home. What else could we do?"

"Let's just agree, that you check with me before attempting any new actions against key personnel. I may have information that could affect your outcome."

"All right. And you will do the same?"

"You know I can't promise that. I would have to clear it with command and that can take time."

"Why is it that I feel you see us as your subordinates?"

"You're not my subordinates. We are partners as we agreed. But we are not just fighting in Norway. We have a lot of irons in the fire that constantly need tending. You understand that, right?"

"I do. But that doesn't make it feel any less patronizing."

"I promise to let you know when I can. That's the best I can do, Johannes."

"Then that's what we will accept… your best."

"By the way, we have a supply drop scheduled for early next week. I'll give you the drop coordinates as soon as I have them."

"What's in the package?"

"Satchel charges."

"Sounds like Christmas is coming early."

"I suppose it is."

"Come upstairs and have some cookies and coffee. I'll have Alf put on a fresh pot."

"I'd like that, but I think it's better if I slip out the back. The SS is everywhere since your little mishap."

"Okay. No cookies for you, Culper."

Culper laughed.

Securing his collar against the bitter wind, Culper slipped out the bakery's rear exit into the shadowed alleyways, scanning for patrolling threats. He cursed under frosted breath - the amateur assassination bid had nearly killed Elsa. Had it not been for Knutsen's driver, the assassination would have succeeded. Elsa and the mission would be dead. He wasn't sure which was more tragic.

His boots echoed as rage simmered. The entire Norwegian initiative had hung by gossamer threads simply because determined fools had acted without thinking. Even the heavy water sabotage seemed hollow consolation weighed against Elsa's silenced genius lost permanently to impulsive reaction.

Despite her pacifist leanings, Elsa was a determined fighter and Culper admired that. He knew his feelings for her put the mission and Elsa at risk. But he couldn't help it. They were beyond his control and that pissed him off. Jaw clenched, he disappeared into darkness.

Norsk Research Facility

Elsa retreated to the sanctuary of her Telemark office, shedding the persona of Dr. Aadland like a heavy coat. The weight of her deception, the constant need to maintain the illusion, had left her feeling drained and raw, her nerves frayed to the breaking point. With a sigh, she massaged the tension from her neck, her fingers kneading the knots of stress and worry that had taken up permanent residence in her muscles.

Retrieving the hidden notes and maps from their secret compartment, Elsa began to detail all that she had witnessed in the laboratory and prototype chambers, her pen flying across the pages in a desperate attempt to make sense of the madness that surrounded her. If she could just steer the Axis scientists off course, even a little, it could set the Reich's research efforts back months or even years.

Her mind drifted back to her time in Chicago, to the months her team had wasted pursuing various dead ends. Each setback had been excruciating, a painful reminder of the stakes they were playing for. But in the end, those failures had provided critical data, steering them towards eventual success.

Elsa pondered how to plant similar seeds of wasted effort at Telemark. It would have to be subtle, nothing catastrophic that might raise suspicions. And then, like a bolt of lightning, it hit her - the electrolysis rotor assemblies. If she could suggest tweaks that would lead to instabilities below the threshold of detection, it might significantly hamper heavy water output.

With a newfound sense of purpose, Elsa scribbled down the chemical molecular changes. Tomorrow at lunch, she would artfully lead Knutsen down this false trail, a breadcrumb path to nowhere.

But as she sat across from him the next day, picking

at the woefully under-seasoned potato and leek soup, Elsa felt a sinking feeling in the pit of her stomach. Knutsen, for all his bluster and bravado, seemed unmoved by her suggestions, his rugged features thoughtful as he savored a long swallow of contraband scotch.

"I'm pleased the adjusted distillation coefficients helped inform acceleration variances," Elsa said, setting the bait. "If we incorporate selectivity filters in the next centrifuge prototype, I believe heavy water production rates could improve exponentially."

Knutsen lifted one thick brow, a hint of amusement playing at the corners of his mouth. "An innovative proposal as always, Doctor," he said, his tone patronizing. "However, I believe staying the current course will yield more rapid results given present constraints."

Masking her surprise, Elsa gently pressed on. "Of course, each process refinement carries development risks. But just imagine - effectively 10X yields in the same footprint! We could power substantial expansion."

But Knutsen merely chuckled, refilling his tumbler with a dismissive wave of his hand. "Your talents show immense promise, my dear. Someday you may direct great institutions if you learn well from our achievements. But leave logistics concerns to the veteran administrators. Your focus should be on research. That's where you are needed most."

Elsa felt a surge of frustration, a bitter taste in her mouth. "I understand, Dr. Knutsen," she said, forcing a smile. "I appreciate your guidance and mentorship. I'll keep my focus where it belongs."

Elsa felt a surge of frustration, a bitter taste in her

mouth. Something was wrong, a nagging sense of unease that she couldn't quite shake. Knutsen had been so open to new ideas when she had first arrived, so eager to explore every avenue of possibility. But now, he seemed content to keep her in her place, to relegate her to the sidelines while he played at being the grand visionary.

As she paced her cramped office later that night, eyes burning with unshed tears, Elsa felt a wave of despair wash over her. Two fruitless weeks of trying to misdirect Knutsen, only to be patted on the head like a child. She was failing, the mission was failing, and it was all her fault.

Choking back a sob, Elsa knew that she wasn't up to the task. Damn Culper for imagining that she, an untrained civilian, could carry out such an important mission. It was true that she had successfully fooled Knutsen and the Nazis into believing she was Aadland, had even convinced the resistance fighters that she was their enemy. But pretending to be someone else was one thing - manipulating brilliant minds was another entirely.

And yet, even as the doubt and self-recrimination threatened to consume her, Elsa knew that giving up was not an option. Too many lives were at stake, too much hung in the balance. She had to keep trying, had to find a way to make this work.

As the clock struck midnight, Elsa, dressed in black slipped out of her room once more, her footsteps echoing in the empty corridors of the research facility. She had explored this place a dozen times before, had mapped out every locked door and hidden corner in her mind. But tonight, she had a specific destination in mind - the Norsk document archives.

She picked the lock and slipped inside, the musty scent of old paper and dust filling her nostrils. Using her red-lensed flashlight, she moved down the aisles of shelves, her eyes scanning the faded labels until she found what she was looking for - a box marked "University of Chicago."

Elsa pulled out the leather folder and spread the pages under the dim light. She recognized the drawings and data sheets immediately - they were the basis for the nuclear reactor she and her colleagues had built and tested. But as she pored over the papers, her eyes widening with each new revelation, she felt a wave of nausea wash over her.

Mixed in with the work of others, she found her own calculations and designs, mockingly annotated for Nazi assimilation. It was a straight shot to a fission reaction, without any of the mishaps and setbacks that had plagued her own team's efforts.

Anger flared white-hot as the realization hit her - Knutsen had been using her work at the university, her brilliant ideas, to further his own ambitious career, no matter the ethical costs. He had hunted down this precious knowledge through cutthroat espionage, had stolen it from under her very nose.

With trembling fingers, Elsa retrieved the miniature Minox Riga spy camera from her shoe. She began to snap photos of the incriminating documents. She knew she would run out of film before she was finished, but she had to try, had to gather as much evidence as she could.

As the camera clicked and whirred as she advanced the film, Elsa's thoughts turned to her colleagues back in Chicago, to the idealistic scientists and engineers who had poured themselves into this work. One of them was a traitor, a mole who had been feeding information to the enemy. The very thought made her sick to her stomach.

And then, like a lightning bolt, another realization hit her - what if she herself had been careless with her own work? What if, in her naive belief that science belonged to all mankind, she had inadvertently handed the keys to the kingdom to the very people who sought to destroy it?

The question haunted her, a specter of guilt and recrimination that would not be silenced. But even as the doubts and fears threatened to overwhelm her, Elsa knew that she could not let them win. She had to keep fighting, had to find a way to stop the Nazis from achieving their twisted goals.

And so, with a grim determination, she tucked the camera back into her shoe and slipped out of the archives, her mind designing plans and possibilities.

Telemark, Norway

The early morning mist clung to the streets of the sleepy Norwegian town as Elsa traveled in the bus to Telemark, her soul heavy with the weight of the secrets she carried. She had tossed and turned all night, her mind filled with the implications of what she had discovered in the Norsk archives. The knowledge that her own research, her life's work, was being used to further the twisted ambitions of the Nazi regime had left her feeling depressed.

Elsa couldn't shake the feeling of eyes boring into her back, of unseen enemies lurking in every shadow. She knew that the SS had eyes and ears everywhere, that even the most innocent conversation could be twisted into something sinister. There was also the resistance fighters that could be watching her and even send another assassin to hunt her down, believing that she was the traitorous Dr. Aadland. The longer she was in public, the higher the risk.

She questioned her decision to take the bus rather than have Hans drive her into town. But she didn't want Knutsen to know what she was doing and Hans was loyal to the director. Even without Hans's protection, Elsa believed she would be safer alone.

And so, as she stepped from the bus, she made her way to the small shop where she had purchased her lingerie, Elsa kept her head down and her voice low, as she asked the owner if she might place a local call.

The woman nodded, her eyes kind and understanding, and led Elsa to the back room where the phone sat, a silent sentinel in the midst of the shop's faded elegance. Elsa dialed the number that Culper had given her, her breath catching in her throat as the operator answered.

"Oh, is this the Gyldenløve Butcher Shop?" she asked, her voice barely above a whisper.

"No, it's the Sverre Hostel," came the reply, and Elsa felt a wave of relief wash over her.

"Sorry. I must have been given the wrong number," she said, and hung up the phone with the knowledge that the message had been delivered, that Culper would know to meet her at the post office.

But as the minutes ticked by and Culper failed to appear, Elsa felt a growing sense of unease settle over her. She sat on the bench outside the post office, her eyes scanning the faces of the passersby, searching for any sign of her handler. But the longer she waited, the more certain she became that something was wrong, that the SS had somehow intercepted their communication and that she was now in grave danger.

Elsa rose from the bench and began to walk down the sidewalk, considering what she should do next. And then, like a bolt from the blue, a man's voice called out to her from the shadows of a nearby alley.

"This way," he said, his voice low and urgent.

Unable to see the face behind the voice, Elsa was unsure. It could be Culper, or an SS trap or a resistance assassin. There was no way to know except to follow the instructions of the faceless voice.

She glanced around, making sure that no one was watching, and then slipped into the alley, perspiration beading on her forehead.

And then, like a ghost materializing from the mist, Culper appeared from behind a stack of empty vegetable crates, his face etched with concern and relief.

"I'm glad to see you're okay," he said, his voice low and steady. "That incident the other day was unfortunate."

"You've been watching?" said Elsa accusing.

"Of course."

"Why didn't you do anything?"

"Your driver acted before I had a chance."

"I could have been killed."

"Yes, but you weren't. I've spoken with the underground. There will be no more attempts on your life."

"You know the men that tried to kill me?"

"Yes. They acted without authorization. It won't happen again."

"I should hope so."

"So, why the message?"

"There's a mole at the University of Chicago."

"Really? How do you know?"

Elsa took a deep breath, the words tumbling from her lips in a rush of anxiety. She told him about the documents she had found in the archives, about the damning evidence that someone at the University of Chicago was funneling research to the Nazis, aiding their efforts to build an atomic bomb.

"This would explain a lot of how the Reich has advanced their research with such speed."

"I photographed everything I could," she said, her voice trembling as she removed her shoe and handed Culper the concealed camera. "But finding the infiltrator won't be easy. The list of scientists and engineers working on the reactor program is long."

Culper frowned, turning the camera over in his hands, his mind disturbed by the implications of what Elsa had discovered. "You're right," he said, his voice heavy with concern. "But we have to try."

Elsa nodded. "I've narrowed it down," she said, her voice low and urgent. "And I have a plan to expose the traitor."

"I'm all ears."

She outlined her idea, explaining how she had come up with a new design for heavy water separation, a process that had proven to be a dead end, but one that only she knew about. If she could send a letter to her mentor at the university, asking him to reveal the design to a select group of scientists, they might be able to catch the mole in the act.

Culper listened intently. "It could work," he said, his voice tinged with doubt. "But we need to move fast. Every moment we wait is another chance for the Nazis to get their hands on our technology. Any lead our team might have will quickly disappear."

Elsa nodded, knowing what was at stake. She handed Culper the letter to her mentor.

"I've got to ask," Culper said, his voice low and serious. "Can you trust your mentor?"

Elsa met his gaze, her eyes unwavering. "With my life," she said, her voice firm and resolute.

Culper nodded, his expression grim. "Good," he said, "because that's the bet you're making. If your scheme doesn't work, there's not much I can do to protect you, except end the mission and send you home. Even then, you'll be in danger. But you need to understand… there is no one else that can do this. You're all we have."

Elsa felt the weight of his words settle over her, the realization of just how much was riding on her success in uncovering the mole. She had known that the stakes were high, that the fate of countless lives hung in the balance. But to hear it laid out so starkly, to know that she was the last hope, it was almost too much to bear.

But even as the fear and doubt threatened to overwhelm her, Elsa thought of her father, of the legacy of brilliant achievement and selfless sacrifice that he had left behind. She thought of the innocent lives that would be lost if the Nazis succeeded in their twisted ambitions, of the cities that would burn and the families that would be torn apart.

And she knew, with a certainty that went beyond mere conviction, that she could not let that happen. That she would fight with every ounce of strength and courage she possessed to stop the Reich, to protect the world from the horrors that it sought to unleash even if it cost her her life.

"It'll work," she said, her voice steady and strong. "I'm sure of it. Post the letter as soon as possible. I'll watch from my end."

Culper nodded, impressed by the steely resolve he saw in her eyes. He had always known that Elsa was brilliant, that her mind was a force to be reckoned with. But now, seeing her stand tall in the face of such insurmountable odds, he realized that she was so much more than just a scientist.

As he watched her disappear into the misty streets of the town, Culper never imagined the shy scientist he met in Chicago could be this strong and determined. He didn't know how much of her courage and confidence came from impersonating Aadland, but to him it didn't matter. Every warrior must find their inspiration from somewhere or someone. If it was Aadland for Elsa, so be it. She had become a lion… like him.

University of Chicago

Winter's icy grip still held the University of Chicago campus firmly in its grasp, the bare branches of the trees standing stark against the gray sky. Inside the mathematics department, Dr. Sanders stood at his blackboard, his mind consumed by an intricate equation, when a knock at the door interrupted his musings.

A special courier, his face a mask of professionalism, entered and presented Dr. Sanders with a letter from abroad. As the doctor signed for the delivery, the courier handed him a slip of paper bearing a phone number. "Please call this number when you are ready to reply to the letter," the courier explained before departing, the door clicking shut behind him.

Sanders lit a cigarette, curiosity piqued as he unfolded the letter. It was from Elsa, his protégé, whose journey through the rigors of doctoral studies he had guided with a steady hand. Their bond was deep and enduring, yet her recent absence had left him worried that he had inadvertently offended her or, worse still, that she had forgotten him entirely.

As he read on, his interest grew. Elsa divulged that she was collaborating with the military on a confidential project but could not reveal more. During her work, she had uncovered evidence suggesting the presence of a mole at the university, surreptitiously funneling documents to the Germans. She implored Sanders to aid her in exposing the traitor, using the enclosed designs as bait.

Sanders, like Elsa, was a pacifist, and the notion of working with the military gave him pause. Yet, he grasped the grave implications of a spy operating within the university's physics department. The thought of design documents falling into German hands, potentially accelerating their research into nuclear energy and the creation of an atomic bomb, sent a chill down his spine. He and Elsa now faced a decision that could alter the course of humanity.

He pondered the weight of Elsa's request, trusting in her intentions but knowing her youth and propensity for leaping into situations she did not fully comprehend. Still, if she claimed to be collaborating with the military, he had faith in her word. The whispers of Nazi atrocities in Europe and the terrifying prospect of Hitler wielding an atomic bomb weighed heavily on his mind. With the success of the Pile-1 project and the current state of research, Sanders recognized that the development of atomic weapons was not only possible but merely a matter of time. Feeling a profound sense of duty to delay their creation for as long as possible, he resolved to follow Elsa's path, but not at the expense of his moral compass. He would not compromise his ethics by harming another human being.

Elsa had provided a list of potential suspects, all familiar names to Sanders, but in these perilous times, everyone guarded their true thoughts and opinions closely, especially when they deviated from the mainstream. While he could confidently eliminate some from suspicion, others remained viable candidates for treachery. The idea of accusing an innocent colleague of betraying their country filled him with dread. He opted to begin with the scientists he deemed most likely to be in league with the Germans, and added one more name to the list—an individual Elsa had overlooked but whom Sanders suspected. If they sought his assistance, he would provide it, but on his own terms.

Sanders reached out to each of the suspects by phone, requesting a meeting in his office to discuss recent mathematical advancements that might benefit their work.

Days later, a knock at the door revealed Arlo McMahon from the engineering department, standing in the corridor. "Good to see you again, Arlo," said Sanders, shaking his hand and inviting him into his office. "I think I have some new mathematical methods that could help you with your modeling turbulent hydrodynamics."

"That would be great. I could use all the help I can get," said Arlo, looking for a place to sit in the cluttered office.

Arlo's gaze fell upon an unfamiliar technical folder, its contents exposed atop a stack of graded coursework. The drawings within resembled a novel design for electrostatic chambers. "Sorry for the mess," Sanders chuckled, quickly closing the folder. "Just reviewing some old student proposals."

Arlo moved a precarious textbook stack off a guest chair, re-anchoring his curiosity firmly on fluid mechanics while stealing occasional glances toward the nondescript folder. "So, I was reading up on recent advances in computational fluid dynamics," said Sanders. "The sophistication of the differential equation solvers and volumetric modeling methods is really getting remarkable."

Later that night, when Arlo was sure Sanders had left, he returned to the office, his lock-picking skills making short work of the door. Riffling through a locked file cabinet, he located the folder and studied the groundbreaking designs within, his basic understanding of nuclear physics and heavy water processing sufficient to grasp their significance.

The creak of floorboards behind him shattered the silence. Arlo turned to find Sanders blocking the doorway, their eyes locked in a moment of revelation.

"Why?" said Sanders with sadness in his voice.

Arlo, caught red-handed, shrugged. "Money. Why else?"

"But your family is wealthy."

"That's true, but when I lost my scholarship, my father refused to help. I had to find another way and the Germans paid well for the right information."

"Jesus, Arlo. You betrayed your country and your

fellow scientists."

"Yeah. I felt bad about that for weeks, then I bought a new car and I didn't feel so bad. A Chrysler Saratoga. She's a real looker," said Arlo as he slowly reached for Sander's heavy ashtray. "I'll take you for a ride sometime."

"This isn't a joke, Arlo. You're in serious trouble. I have no choice but to report you," said Sanders, reaching for the phone.

"Gee. Is that really necessary?"

As Sanders started to dial, Arlo lunged for the ashtray, bludgeoning the professor to death in a brutal, desperate act. Sanders's blood pooled on the floor, and Arlo carefully stepped around it as he closed the office door. With the threat of exposure eliminated, he meticulously gathered the files he believed the Nazis would pay handsomely for, the electrostatic chamber design folder crowning the stack.

The Hydra

Norsk Research Facility

The Norsk Hydro plant, nestled deep in the Rjukan mountain valley, was originally constructed in the early twentieth century to produce chemicals and explosives that required enormous amounts of electrical energy. Its remote location allowed the large complex to be powered by multiple hydroelectric dams built along the river gorges feeding into the rugged Telemark region.

When German forces occupied Norway during the war, they expanded production at the hardened Norsk factory to supply the Third Reich's arms programs. However, built-in capacity exceeded munitions output alone. So, the commandant overseeing daily plant operations arranged for hundreds of tons of commercial nitrate fertilizers to also be manufactured using the abundant electricity.

This excess agricultural production was then shipped to reinforce Nazi supply lines. The sprawling Norsk workings churned day and night, its turbines fed endless waterpower to generate both destruction and growth for the German war machine simultaneously from occupied Norway's icy peaks and plunging ravines.

As she continued her nightly clandestine searches of the facility, Elsa had to keep up with her daily routine. There was no time off. It was a constant grind. She was tired and drank large amounts of coffee to keep her mind crisp. On an ongoing basis, refined heavy water output needed to be audited to ensure stability and viability. Fortunately, the audit didn't require much thought. Simple tests, noting the results for future review should a problem develop. It was the walk to the vault in high heels that wore her out. She longed for a foot soak in Epson salts.

The checkpoints grew increasingly fortified the deeper Elsa descended into the remote mountain facility. As the canned air grew chilled and thin, so did her stomach knot tighten. There were more guards than usual on patrol and at the checkpoints. Had something happened? Was there a security breach she didn't know about?

Elsa's heels clicked steadily across the cavernous heavy water production chamber. Passing giant collection tanks and piping, she flashed her security badge to enter the heavily guarded vault chamber where ampules of processed deuterium were secured. Even with headscarf and lab coat, the sense of profound forces being leashed here still left her breathless.

As the guard wheeled the steel-reinforced door open, Elsa grasped its frame shocked as endless empty racks gaped back at her, where tens of thousands glowing ampules should lie cradled according to her inventory scrolls. Less than a dozen tubes now glinted coolly under the lights.

Voice strained thin before the terrifying void, Elsa called to a technician inspecting gauge tolerances nearby, "Where are the ampules?"

Pausing reluctantly in his adjustments, the technician's eyes dropped sheepishly. "I meant no presumption, Doctor. But Director Knutsen received orders this morning for emergency transport of all refined product to Berlin's research laboratories." He swallowed anxiously. "Surely one so highly ranked as yourself would be... informed of shifting priorities?"

Casting her icy glare to hide her dismay, Elsa continued the deception. "But of course. I must have missed the relocation notice on my daily logistics report. I need an exact count of the ampules removed and their serial numbers to update my inventory."

"Right away, Doctor," said the technician moving off to find the transport list. Moving inside the vault, Elsa scoured row after row of empty racks for any sign of overlooked ampules. There were none. It was a true nightmare in the making. If the Reich had ordered such a large amount of processed deuterium, it could only mean two things – either the SS was concerned about security at the facility or the research teams in Berlin had progressed to the point where they were ready to test an experimental reactor as the Americans had done in Chicago. Increased security would make her nighttime excursions more difficult, while a successful experimental reactor would establish that the Germans were much farther along in their research than originally estimated.

When the technician returned with the transportation list, Elsa asked, "When did they finish transporting the ampules?"

"Only an hour ago. They've been loading the train

most of the night," said the technician.

"The train?"

"The armored coach used for transport of the ampules to Oslo, then by ship to Berlin."

"Of course. This the first time they've transferred the ampules since I arrived. I'm unfamiliar with the process."

"Quite understandable. The SS use a dedicated locomotive and armored coach for transport of heavy water. No civilians allowed aboard the train. The train travels to Tinnsjo Rail Ferry on Lake Tinn where the armored coach under heavy guard is loaded onto the SF Hydro which transports rail cars along with passengers."

"I see. And how long does it take to cross Lake Tinn?"

"Only a few hours if there are no delays. The armored train ferry has priority when it's traveling."

"Excellent. I'm curious… how many people does the ferry hold?"

"I'm not sure when it's fully loaded, but there are usually thirty to forty passengers that travel across the lake."

"Well, that's all I need to know for now. You may resume your duties."

Elsa took the transport list from the technician who returned to work. Moments later, she was hurrying out of the processing chamber and through the mountain facility. She did not run which would have drawn unneeded attention, but her pace was brisk.

Elsa rushed to the courtyard where Hans always parked the town car waiting for Knutsen's use. She had to reach Culper swiftly if they stood any chance disrupting the Wehrmacht's latest obstacle. Finding

Hans polishing the vehicle's wheels, Elsa composure strained beneath veneer of icy command, "Hans, I need to go into town right away."

Hans answered her hail, surprise clear, "Doctor, is everything alright?"

"Yes, quite. Except I realized I'm out of migraine tablets after that tedious inventory affair." Elsa injected weary tension, praying it read as authentic. "Would you be able to drive me to the village pharmacy? I know Director Knutsen dislikes disruptions, but I fear a splitting headache coming."

"Of course! No trouble whatsoever. I'll just leave Director Knutsen a message at the checkpoint as we leave."

"Thank you, Hans. You're a dear."

Once secured in the sleek staff vehicle, Elsa feigned fatigue, watching pine peaks furrow then smooth as they careened down slick roads, Hans cheerily recounting boyhood misadventures by each familiar tunnel and crag. She manufactured weak laughter while scanning ahead for signs of the armored train. There were none. She looked in the rearview mirror to make eye contact with Hans. "While your memories are amusing, I would appreciate any speed you might generate. I can feel my migraine beginning. Such horrible things."

"My apologies for droning on, Doctor. Of course, I will make haste," said Hans hitting the gas pedal, pushing the vehicle to its limits.

Pulling to a stop in the middle of town a few blocks from the post office, Hans dropped Elsa in front of the small pharmacy where she rushed through the front door.

The proprietor glanced up alarmed as this frantic blond woman bursting inside his shop demanding his telephone. "Please, sir, your phone. It's an emergency." The pharmacist pointed to the phone on the wall. Elsa's fingers trembled as she dialed.

Once again, Elsa played out the rouse of dialing a wrong number that would secretly leave a message for Culper. She hung up the phone and once again turned to the pharmacist, "Thank you. Do you have a back door?"

Again, the pharmacist pointed. Elsa glanced out the front window at Hans reading his newspaper while waiting in the car. Elsa slipped out the back door and into the alley.

Not wanting to be spotted, Elsa waited in the alley for Culper to show up and enter the post office. She quietly called him before he entered the front door. He moved to the alley and said, "What's up?"

"The German's have moved the delirium ampules from the vault. They're transferring them to Berlin."

"Any idea how many?"

"All of them. Six months' worth of production."

"Jesus."

"They were transported by armored train to the railway ferry on Lake Tinn this morning. We need to stop them."

"I need to stop them. You need to get back to Norsk before Knutsen realizes that you are gone."

"Right. Can you do it? Can you stop them?"

"Yeah… I think."

"That's not a good answer."

"It's the only one I have until I figure this thing out.

Look, you did your job. You need to leave this to me."

"You're right. I just…"

"Just what?"

"I don't want them to win… the Nazis"

"Have you finally decided to take sides?"

"No. I mean… yes. Just stop them, okay?"

"Sure. Piece of cake."

As they both began to move off in different directions, Culper turned and said, "Good job, Elsa. You're getting the hang of this clandestine work."

"Doesn't feel much like it," said Elsa as she disappeared around the alley's corner.

As she walked back to the pharmacy, Elsa wondered if her work on the Pile 1 project at the University of Chicago had proven to the Reich that fission was possible and encouraged them to charge ahead with their own efforts to achieve a self-sustaining reactor. Her intentions had been pure, but it seemed it didn't matter. More and more she realized that Culper was right. She needed to commit and stop pulling her punches, if she was going to stop the Nazis' progress toward a technology that could very well obliterate mankind.

Culper entered the bakery and headed for the basement without announcing himself to Alf pulling a sheet of fresh pretzels from the oven. Culper climbed down the stairs where he found Johannes and his rebel soldiers gathered around a table with a satchel charge sitting in the middle. Johannes was instructing his men on how to use the explosive packet.

"Johannes, we need to talk," said Culper.

"I'll be done in a few minutes," said Johannes continuing his lecture.

"Now, Johannes… and alone."

Johannes didn't like receiving orders from Culper, but he didn't want another argument so soon as his man had muffed the assassination attempt on Dr. Aadland. "Go get yourself a pretzel, boys. Culper's buying."

As the men climbed the stairs and shut the door, Johannes turned to Culper and said, "You have my attention, Culper. What is so damned important?"

"The Germans have moved the heavy water from Norsk."

"All of it?"

"All of it."

"So, what shall we do about it?"

"We're gonna sink the railway ferry SF Hydro on Lake Tinn. Right in the middle where it's deepest."

"There are civilians that use that ferry."

"I know."

"You're just going to kill them?"

"We'll try not to, but if push comes to shove, we can't let the Germans transport the heavy water to Berlin."

"I'm not killing innocent Norwegians, Culper."

Culper thought long and hard about what to say next. "If we place the charges correctly, we can minimize the risk to the passengers and crew. The ferry should sink slowly, giving them enough time to get off the ship."

"And swim where? That lake is almost freezing. They'll never make it to shore."

"There are two lifeboats on the Hydro."

"That's not nearly enough for all passengers and crew."

"They're gonna to have to be enough, Johannes. We

can't let the Germans move the heavy water. Not now, not ever. There is too much at stake."

Johannes knew that Culper was right, but he couldn't just let his fellow countrymen die, especially the innocents. "What if we sail a barge near the Hydro when it explodes? We could offload the passengers and crew."

"That might work, but we'd need to make sure we don't tip off the SS guarding the shipment."

"We can do that. I know Lake Tinn as well as anyone. I've been fishing there before I could walk. There are plenty of places to hide a barge along the shore. If we wait until the last minute to sail into the middle of the lake, the SS won't expect anything until it's too late."

"Alright. I'm gonna need some of your satchel charges to build the bombs we're gonna need."

"We can do that."

Johannes and Culper went to work.

Lake Tinn, Norway

Lake Tinn was a long, narrow lake situated high among the Telemark hills of central Norway. Its steep walls plunged over 3,300 feet to the crystalline turquoise waters below. Over eighteen miles from end to end, the fjord-like lake twisted snake-like through the rugged alpine landscape, fed by meltwaters that granted the water remarkable clarity and purity. Most of the perimeter consisted of dramatic granite cliffs and sparse birch forests clinging precariously to their heights.

It was already dark by the time Akzel - a young rebel, Johannes, and Culper arrived at the Tinnsjo

Railway Ferry on the southern end of the lake. The armored coach was already on board the SF Hydro and surrounded by SS guards. "Akzel will create a diversion. I'll plant the bomb on the keel. Johannes will plant the bomb in the bow," said Culper quietly. "Once the bombs are set, we meet back here, then steal ourselves a barge and head out into the lake."

"Agreed," said Johannes.

The team split up. Culper made his way down by the lake's shore where he had hidden the bomb he was going to place and his scuba gear – a closed-circuit oxygen rebreather system developed for covert naval operations. It consisted of a large rectangular backpack crafted from riveted aluminum that contained a compact oxygen tank, scrubber canister to refresh spent breathing gas, and absorbent cartridges to manage carbon dioxide.

Two sturdy rubber hoses connected the supply backpack to the full-face diving mask covering his nose and mouth. The special contraption utilized valves and tubes that recycled exhaled gas rather than releasing bubbles that could give away underwater position. The rest of Culper's gear was likewise streamlined for stealth and freedom of movement. Form-fitting gray-black vulcanized rubber covered him neck to ankle. Fins on his feet, lead weights at his belt, and gloves with traction pads on the palms enabled power and maneuverability underwater.

Checking the rebreather's supply gauges and backup pony bottle, Culper gripped his satchel of demolition charges, ready to plunge into the dark fjord. The experimental rig's limited oxygen capacity meant every minute counted locating then crippling the ferry's propellers and rudder mechanisms.

He waded into the lake shallows, then submerged into the dark water. A moment later, he was gone without a trace. The water was bitter cold stinging him like hundreds of needles. Underwater Culper could not see, but he could feel his way along the bottom of the lake. He knew which way the SF Hydra was located. Every couple of minutes he pushed his way to the surface and poked his head out of the water to quickly gather his bearings.

As he crawled closer to the ferry, he could see the SS guards with their submachine guns patrolling along the shore and around the ship. He knew he would be an easy target if he was discovered. He limited his movements when on the surface so as not to splash. It wasn't easy. The gear was awkward as he treaded water. It was easier to control when he was underwater. Keeping below water the last hundred yards he found he could see slightly from the lights around the dock and on the ferry.

Culper gripped the satchel charge tight, powerful kicks propelling him toward the darkened ferry hull. Reaching the ferry, he maneuvered his way along the hull to the stern of the SF Hydra and found the rudder and propellors. The explosive charge was sealed tight in the satchel to prevent water from entering. For the device to work properly, Culper would need to affix the satchel holding the charge and set the redundant timing devices above the waterline. He had to take into the account the wake and froth that the propellors would create once out on the lake.

Culper grasped the slime-covered anchor chain, hoisting himself just high enough to scan the darkened deck. Finding a cleat on the stern of the ferry, he wrapped the satchel's strap several times around the metal casting's wings, then set the timers. It was far from perfect, and he questioned whether the whole thing would fall into the lake once the ferry got underway, but it was the best he could do without being seen. At times, luck was required for sabotage to work. This was one of those times.

His tense breaths sent frost billowing as he slid back into concealing dark waters, the ripples ebbing swiftly. Taking a breath, he submerged and kicked his fins toward the distant shoreline where he began.

From behind the fishing barrels stacked together at the side of the dock the young rebel Akzel peered out nervously at the looming SF Hydro ferry and the SS soldiers guarding it. Johannes, kneeling with him behind the barrels could see the doubt in his eyes. "Easy, son. Just get their eyes off that ramp a few moments," said Johannes.

Akzel nodded.

"It's time," said Johannes glancing at his watch.

Taking a deep breath, Akzel rose and walked toward the ferry and the SS. He emerged onto the creaking pier, passing under each pool of light feeling instantly exposed. Two sentries quickly spotted him. "You, boy! Why are you about so late?" they demanded.

Voice quivering, Akzel improvised about his horse throwing a shoe near mountain passes and needing help before the beast froze to death. As the guards debated the unlikely tale, Akzel spotted Johannes slip past unseen behind them. Akzel stalled the guards with wide helpless eyes until Johannes flashed a quick salute from the ferry entrance. The SS soldiers turned Akzel away and he obeyed walking back into the darkness toward the mountains.

Johannes crept low across the ferry deck, guts knotting tighter with each exposed stretch between cranes and covered loads. Frosty breath held tight, he slipped aftward on soundless feet.

Passing the aft cabins, he froze at approaching echoes - an off-duty engineer fumbling out for a smoke. Crouching lower in shadows as the man lit a cigarette, Johannes wrestled with urgency and stealth. When the engineer extinguished the remains of his cigarette and return to work, Johannes moved once again deeper into the ship.

Ensconced in engine throb and humming pipes, the resistance fighter wormed his broad frame toward the mechanical bellows deep within the vessel. At the peaked bow, he found a space between a stack of cargo and the ship's hull. He set the charge's dual timers, then hid the rucksack holding the charge behind the cargo covering it with excess tarp.

Task complete, Johannes made his way back to the deck and slipped to a seaward rail. None marked his splash amid lapping inky waves. Powerful strokes propelled him beyond the pier's harsh lamps safely into the night's embrace.

The three saboteurs met at their rendezvous point. Johannes guided them to a barge he had selected earlier. Akzel picked the ignition and started the engine. Backing the barge up, then shifting to forward Johannes directed Akzel where to steer into the lake. There was no way to determine where the SF Hydra would be when the bombs went off, so Johannes picked a hiding spot near the middle of the lake along the shoreline. Their hope was the ferry would sink in the deepest part of the lake making recovery of the ampules difficult, if not impossible. Anchoring the barge a few yards offshore, they waited and watched for the lights of the ferry as it made its way across the lake.

Johannes became concerned when his watch approached midnight and they still hadn't seen the SF Hydra. If the bombs went off while the ferry was still at the pier or in shallow waters, the Germans would be able to quickly recover the heavy water ampules and transport them to Berlin.

As if on cue to relieve their angst, twinkling lights appeared in the distance. It was the ferry. Culper pulled the anchor as Akzel restarted the engine. "Two minutes," said Johannes exchanging glances at his watch and the distant ferry.

"We're too far out," said Akzel.

"We shouldn't move. It will tip off the guards," said Culper.

"More Norwegians could die if we don't reach the ferry quickly," said Johannes.

"Then so be it," said Culper. "The mission comes first."

"You really are a heartless prick," said Johannes.

Culper shrugged off the insult and stayed focused on the SF Hydra. Johannes glanced at his wristwatch as the second hand swept past midnight. Still no explosions. "Somethings wrong," said Johannes.

"Wait for it…" said Culper continuing to watch the ferry, his eyes unmoving.

Then… a flash pierced the darkness.

Inside the ferry, a thunderous blast tore out from the ferry's front flank, shredding through steel plates. The shaped charge unleashed its force straight toward the hull with devastating effect. Icy water flooded inward.

On the barge, Culper yelled, "Go, go, go…" as Akzel pushed the throttle to full. The barge was driven by powerful but slow diesel engines. It gradually picked up speed as it headed toward the sinking ferry.

Inside the Hydra's ruptured front compartments, panicked passengers and crew were hurled about violently as everything listed starboard. The ferry's engineer smashed against his pilothouse shattered window and knew no more.

On deck, screaming travelers were dragged by their luggage across steeply tilting floors toward the frigid lake. Before horror could fully register, the groaning ferry plunged forward at a sharp pitch, bow compartments filling with swirling black water. Fear burst through training and discipline - every man racing aft toward higher ground and hope of the lifeboats.

Amidships, stunned crew and soldiers were just finding their feet from the first explosion when a second violent eruption in the rear of the ship threw them into bulkheads again.

The ship's rudder was completely torn from its mounts and disappeared into the dark water below. One of the propellors was sheared from its shaft while the other hung frozen mid rotation. The vessel was crippled and unable to steer.

As the doomed Hydra began to sink, those aboard the fast-approaching barge already knew there was little time for most to escape the disabled leviathan's final death-throes. Precious silhouettes were glimpsed stumbling against the tilting outline before darkness reclaimed all.

Flames etched the night orange and black as Akzel steered the barge alongside the fast-foundering ferry, its mangled aft half raised skyward. They glimpsed soot-streaked crew and dazed passengers cramming the one remaining lifeboat.

"Get lines over!" Johannes bellowed, throwing grapples aboard the listing rails. The rebel watercraft slammed into the battered metal hull as the straining ropes pulled taut. Culper and Akzel grabbed life-rings, preparing to sling them into swirling black waters after those already leaping overboard.

While Johannes fixated on saving the few souls still on the sinking ferry, Culper and Akzel leaned over the side of the barge reaching down to the survivors in the water. "Here, take my hand!" Culper shouted as terrified faces emerged spluttering before him only to vanish again beneath the bone-chilling waves. He locked wrists with a wailing teen girl, heaving her shivering form to Akzel. Unable to reach those treading water, Culper jumped over the side. He swam toward vague forms still struggling closer through the lake's icy maw. Some fell beneath the surface before he could reach them. He dove into the blackness in hopes of bringing them back to the surface, but it was too late. They were gone. Better to save the living, he swam to a woman gasping for breath as her body seized up from frigid water. He pulled her close to the barge and Akzel's outreach, then swam back to retrieve another.

Next to the ferry, Johannes hauled up frigid bodies, laying them wrapped in musty wool blankets. No distinction now between Norwegian crew or German masters - only common fragile souls wrested temporary from the abyss. Seeing that the ferry was sinking fast, Johannes cut the lines to save the barge and those on board. The night rang with cries for mercy or absent kin, ferry hissing defeat as it finally slipped completely under, no more to surrender to salvation.

When Culper crawled last over the sodden side, leaden arms barely lifting him clear of the dark waters, he realized numbly their tragic bounty. Too many indeed still entombed in the Hydra, buried alongside the heavy water ampules. Two dozen refugees lived who would witness against the madness. It hardly felt enough.

Johannes locked eyes with Culper. It was a victory for the Allies, but at a tremendous cost. Akzel turned the barge to shore and gunned the engines. More would die if their warmth could not be restored before their hearts stopped. They would save who they could. It was the best they could do.

In all, they pulled twenty-eight survivors from the Lake Tinn. Fourteen civilians and four German soldiers died in the manmade disaster. Except for a few half-empty barrels that bobbed to the surface over the next few days, all the heavy water ampules were buried beneath the waves at depths beyond retrieval. The loss of the heavy water was massive to the Reich's nuclear research program. But it wasn't enough to stop it. More heavy water would be refined as production at the Norsk Research facility continued.

Norsk Research Facility

The next morning, Elsa entered the facility's cantina for coffee and a simple breakfast. No sooner has she sat down when she overheard the rumors flying around her within earshot. Word traveled fast about the sinking of the ferry and the fourteen Norwegians killed.

The news hit Elsa hard. She immediately lost her appetite. Was she to blame for the deaths? She was the one that had revealed the information about the shipment of heavy water. How could Culper be so careless? How could she not think about the consequences of her actions? Culper never said how he would destroy the shipment. Had she known, would she have tried to stop him? Would he has let her? How much control did she have over the information she shared?

She wanted answers but knew better than to contact Culper so soon after an operation when the SS would be combing the town to find the culprits. She would have to wait a day, maybe two. Until then, she still had work to do. Her mission hadn't changed. It was just more complicated. All things needed to measure against one another, especially human lives. It was impossible for her to figure out, to judge. She wasn't God. There was no way around it... more people would die to prevent the development of the atomic bomb. She couldn't stop. She couldn't go back. The only way was forward.

Later that day, Elsa went to visit Knutsen in hopes of once again convincing him to change the course of the team's research. Knutsen was in his office, eyes downcast.

"Why the sad face, Svein?" said Elsa.

"The entire shipment of heavy water was destroyed in transport. Six months' worth of production gone," said Knutsen.

"How?"

"They think it was the resistance fighters in Telemark."

"How did they know about the shipment?"

"They're not sure, but counterintelligence suspects we have a leak in security."

"I suppose that's possible."

"Anything is possible at this point. Our problem is that Berlin is demanding we vastly increase our heavy water production to make up for the losses."

"We're at ninety-five percent efficiency now. It's difficult to do better than that without technology advancements."

"We need to do whatever is required to meet their demands. I've been told the führer himself is monitoring our production reports."

"What an honor!"

"If we succeed, then yes."

"And if we don't?"

"I don't want to think about disappointing Hitler if you don't mind. You had some ideas about increasing production. I'd like to revisit them plus anything else you or your team can come up with."

"Of course. I will get right on it."

"In the meantime, I'll see that the new equipment is installed in the heavy water production line."

"New equipment?"

"Yes. More efficient electrostatic chambers. I designed them personally. They should help us catch up with Berlin's increased production demands."

"I was not aware you had approved such changes."

"I don't tell you everything, Doctor," said Knutsen putting Elsa in her place. "Was there anything else you needed?"

"No. I was just checking on you. We haven't had

many late-night visits as of late."

"I apologize. I am distracted, but I will find time for you, Paula. I know it's important to maintain our affair."

"Affair?"

"What would you call it?"

"A relationship."

"Semantics. But have it your way. Relationship."

"Thank you, Director."

Elsa put in an extra sway in her hips as she exited - a reminder of what Knutsen had been missing. The effort was not lost as his eyes followed her behind through the doorway.

As Elsa closed the door behind her, she considered the new equipment being installed. Knutsen's own design. It was highly unlikely. While he had a good grasp of the overall manufacturing process, she had not been impressed with his engineering skills. She decided to have a look at the new equipment for herself.

Elsa felt the weight of her obligation press upon her as she made her way to Knutsen's suite, summoned by his command. The information he held was crucial, and she steeled herself for the inevitable embrace, her body a mere token in the grand scheme of lives sacrificed to thwart the Reich's nuclear ambitions.

Knutsen, still visibly distraught by the news of the lost heavy water shipment, paced the room like a caged animal. The specter of Berlin's blame loomed over him, despite the inventory having passed from his hands to those of the SS. In the Reich's eyes, it was far more prudent to lay the blame at the feet of a civilian, especially a Norwegian, than to risk the wrath of the powerful and ruthless SS commanders.

As they lay entwined, Knutsen's anxiety rendered him distracted, his lovemaking a futile endeavor. Elsa played the role of the concerned paramour, her words of reassurance belying her true intentions. She needed him pliant and malleable, not wound tight like a coiled spring ready to unleash its energy.

When sleep finally claimed him, Elsa slipped from his arms and the confines of his suite, her nightly investigation of Norsk beckoning. With a sense of urgency, she headed directly for the heavy water processing chambers, her usual cautious exploration abandoned.

The distant glow of work lights illuminated the tunnel, certification of Knutsen's orders for round-the-clock shifts until the new equipment was operational. Elsa's daytime freedom of movement was a stark contrast to the restricted access at night, where only those with passes were permitted. She had neither pass nor desire to raise suspicions.

Shadows became her allies as she ventured deeper into the tunnel, the sight of engineers carrying new electrolysis chambers into the production area spurring her forward. The need to assess the Reich's progress and the implications for their atomic weapons program burned within her.

Concealed behind wooden crates, Elsa waited with bated breath for the engineers to retrieve another chamber before making her move. With swift, silent steps, she approached one of the devices, her red-filtered flashlight revealing a truth that drained the color from her face. The designs were her own, bastardized by the Reich to further their destructive agenda.

The sound of returning footsteps sent Elsa diving

for cover, her choice of hiding spot behind a forklift proving ill-fated as an engineer climbed aboard and started the engine. With mere moments before discovery, she wedged herself between two empty crates, shafts of light from the work lamps threatening to betray her presence. Fortune smiled upon her as the overworked engineers remained oblivious.

Calculating the remaining crates and the installation timeline, Elsa realized the Reich's heavy water production would resume within days, her own designs enabling them to replace their losses in weeks rather than months. As she melted back into the safety of darkness, a sense of futility gnawed at her, the battle seeming increasingly insurmountable.

The following morning, a notice of a waiting package at the post office greeted Elsa, Culper's reaching out a welcome lifeline. Questions swirled in her mind, the news of the new devices a burden she knew would weigh heavily on him. It fell to Culper now to devise a strategy to counter the Reich's advances, and Elsa could only hope that their efforts would not be in vain.

Telemark, Norway

Culper was already waiting when Elsa arrived at the post office. He slipped into the nearby alleyway. Elsa followed.

"What in the hell happened to the ferry?" said Elsa.

"It couldn't be helped," said Culper in no mood for her criticism.

"It couldn't be helped? Fourteen civilians died."

"I know. I was there fishing them out of the water. I did my best to save those that I could."

"That's not good enough, Culper. You never should have sunk the ferry. You should have found another way to destroy the heavy water."

"There was no other way. It's not like I have endless resources, Elsa. We were lucky to sink that ferry."

"Lucky?"

"Have you asked yourself how many people could have died if the Germans received that shipment? We are not playing for peanuts here."

"I didn't know we were playing at all."

"You know what I mean."

"There's more bad news."

"Great. What is it?"

"The engineers at Norsk are replacing the obsolete equipment far more advanced devices that will great increase the efficiency of the processing plant. They'll be able to replace the lost heavy water in weeks once it is up and running."

"Jesus. Can it be sabotaged?"

"Yes, but not without being detected. Knutsen will run the plant twenty-four hours a day until the heavy water has been replaced. You won't be able to get near it without being seen."

"What about you?"

"I don't blow things up, remember?"

"Things have changed."

"Even if I was willing, I have the same problem. I won't be allowed near that equip once it's installed."

"Alright. I'll find another way. I have news for you too."

"What's that?"

"Your mentor, Dr. Sanders was killed."

Elsa was in shock and wept, "Oh, God, no."

"They haven't found the killer, but I imagine it's the

mole we were looking for. He must have figured out it was a trap and killed Sanders to prevent from being revealed."

"He was like a father to me. And I killed him."

"No, you didn't. A traitor killed him. Remember that."

Elsa stopped for a moment deep in thought.

"What is it?" said Culper.

"The equipment being installed is my design."

"That's not your fault."

"No. That's not the point. I never showed those designs to anyone except the engineer that helped me with the mechanics."

"What was his name?"

"Arlo McMahon."

"He wasn't on the list you gave me."

"No. He wasn't. Sanders must have suspected that he might be the mole and confronted him."

"How sure are you that it's him?"

"I don't know how anyone else could have gotten their hands on the designs. Not even Sanders knew about the project. You should question Arlo as soon as possible."

"Of course. I'll see to it."

University of Chicago

Arlo pulled up to the residence building and parked his new car. He climbed the stairs to his room and saw that the door was open. He entered with caution and found an attractive woman sitting on his bed. He smiled, "Can I help you?"

"I don't know, can you?" she said.

"Depends on what you need."

"At the moment, I need you to close the door," she said with a coy smile.

"Of course," said Arlo closing the door.

When he turned back, he saw that the woman was holding a silenced pistol. The folders he had stolen were in a stack beside her on the bed. His face went ashen as he said, "No, wait—" were his last words as two bullets – one in his heart and the other in his right eye entered his body. He crumbled to the floor. She unscrewed the silencer and slid the pistol and the silencer into her purse along with the stolen folders. Stepping over the blood seeping into the rug, she left the room, closing the door behind her.

Persons of Interest

Tocksfors, Sweden

Nemec sat at his desk, the weight of an unsolved case bearing down on him, when the mail courier interrupted his musings. The officer at the front desk handed him a large envelope, the one from Oslo he had been eagerly awaiting.

With a sense of anticipation, Nemec tore open the envelope, its contents spilling onto his desk—a train passenger manifest, copies of two passports, and a marriage certificate for Mr. and Mrs. Nilsen. He reached for Mr. Nilsen's passport first, studying the photograph with a critical eye. The man appeared unremarkable, but Nemec knew all too well that killers often hid behind the most ordinary of facades.

It was the second passport that sent a jolt of surprise through him. The woman in the photograph bore little resemblance to the one Rolf and Freke had discovered in the snow. Her eyes, a rich brown instead of piercing green, and her hair, a fiery red, were striking contrasts. But it was the shape of her face, square and freckled, that truly set her apart from the alabaster-skinned, unblemished beauty they had found. Mrs.

Nilsen was clearly not their mystery woman, leaving Nemec with a myriad of questions. Who was she, and who had gone to the trouble of forging her passport?

Frustration gnawed at him as he realized he was no closer to the truth, but the thought of a killer roaming free was far more unsettling. Mr. Nilsen, he suspected, was likely not the culprit, his own passport a potential forgery as well. But the reason behind it all eluded him.

Nemec took stock of the few certainties he possessed—a woman's lifeless body and a charm bracelet adorned with tiny photographs of an elderly couple, possibly her parents, though even that connection was tenuous at best. It was a starting point, however meager.

His gaze fell upon the train manifest, over 200 names strong. Somewhere among them, he was certain, were the identities of the dead woman and her killer. But extracting that information would prove challenging, given the German SS's reluctance to cooperate with Swedish authorities.

Sweden's neutrality, a point of contention for the German military, left them at odds. Germany relied on Swedish iron ore for their weapons factories but had refrained from invading, opting instead to blockade the passage into the North Sea between Denmark and Norway, effectively strangling Swedish exports. Sweden, left with little recourse, begrudgingly sold their ore and other goods to Germany. The tension between the two nations was palpable, a mere tolerance born of necessity.

Nemec knew that his only hope of identifying the woman lay in accessing the passport records in Oslo himself. The Norwegian passport office, though overseen by the SS, was largely staffed by Norwegians who maintained a civil relationship with the Swedes, their shared enmity towards the Germans a unifying force. If he could find his way inside, Nemec was confident he could uncover the woman's identity and, perhaps, that of her killer. It was a risk, but one he was willing to take.

The following morning found Nemec hurrying along the snowy platform, his leather case clutched tightly as he boarded the third-class carriage of the Oslo express. He settled into the worn velvet seats near the grimy window, his scarlet uniform jacket neatly folded beside him. The locomotive began its arduous fifty-mile journey north, towards the border crossing and the answers he sought.

As the frozen landscape rushed by, barren birches and granite ridges bathed in weak light, Nemec's thoughts turned to the moment he first laid eyes on the dead woman. Faceless. Frozen. He wondered if uncovering her identity would dispel the macabre images that haunted him, or if only bringing her killer to justice would grant him peace.

The train lurched to a stop at the heavily fortified Norwegian border, SS officers moving methodically from compartment to compartment, scrutinizing each passenger's documents. Nemec waited patiently for his turn, surrendering his passport and travel papers to the stern-faced lieutenant.

The officer's disapproval was evident as he noted the English entry stamps. "You've been to England?" he questioned.

"Yes, before the war. Forensic training at Scotland Yard," Nemec explained.

"And your contacts there?"

"None remaining. It was quite some time ago."

The officer's suspicion grew. "Why does Sweden send police across my border?"

"A murder case requiring investigation in Oslo," Nemec replied, producing a photograph of the faceless woman from his satchel.

The officer studied the image, taking in her glazed expression and tattered condition. "What happened to her face?"

"Wolves and lye."

With a dismissive slap, the officer set the photo down. "You demand much to pass here without more cause," he warned.

Nemec met his gaze unflinchingly. "Wouldn't you want to find the killer if she were your wife or daughter? That's cause enough."

A grunt of acknowledgment, and the officer brusquely approved the papers. "Execute your business, then return home without delay."

"I have no desire to stay in Norway any longer than needed," Nemec assured him.

The officer departed with a scowl, and Nemec carefully tucked the photograph back into his satchel. Twenty minutes later, the SS had disembarked, and the train resumed its journey, carrying Nemec ever closer to the truth he so desperately sought.

Twenty minutes later, the SS had deboarded and the train was moving once again.

Oslo, Norway

As the Oslo express slowed through ramshackle outskirts, Nemec noted SS patrols scanning passengers at snapped attention even here. He averted his gaze from angry red banners declaring curfew hours and penalties which marred so many familiar buildings behind snaking tram cables. Iron fisted occupation permeated all veins since Norway's searing defeat only two years previous.

The cavernous station interior felt equally garish now to his senses after lonely mountain ranges - harsh fluorescent strips casting shadows from imposing portraits of Führer and collaborators lined above scarred timetables altered for Reich routed priorities. Wheels screeched dispatching trains only southward towards greater wars rather than coastal family communities.

Nemec shuffled past murmuring groups of workers with tags identifying night pass permissions towards the squat administrative building housing immigration processing and police liaisons. Inside the gloomy hall reeked thickly of stale sweat and cigarette smoke lingering for days. He wrestled gut impulse seeing the long line for arriving foreigners and stateless under hard gazes. An exiled countryman himself just hours earlier without warm hearth awaiting return. He joined the mass of petitioners clutching satchels and affidavits, some forged.

Eager to escape the crowded facility, Nemec crossed snow-lined Karl Johan Boulevard to a modest cafe adrift locomotive steam. He shouldered inside the warm nutty air, breathing easier away from the queues and barked orders. A cheese sandwich and hot tea provided simple escape sitting alone at the copper-topped bar, watching bundled crowds rush between sooty slush piles outside. No furtive glances noted his alien police uniform amid the noon rush, perhaps a speck of normalcy persisted if circumspect.

Fortified, Nemec reentered the bustling government annex, winding towards a broad office marked PASSPORT ARCHIVES. A matronly records clerk peered over owlish spectacles as he politely explained the investigation and handed her a list of Norwegian citizens from the train manifest. "I would like to examine the passport documents for this list of individuals."

Examining the list, the clerk said, "Captain, there are over eighty names here. That is a big request and will take some time."

"I understand. But I assure you it is of immense importance."

"Is there any way to shorten the list? Maybe weed out some of the more improbable candidates?"

"I cannot. I must be thorough in my search."

"Very well. Have a seat while I start pulling the documents."

Nemec sat as the clerk disappeared into the valley of shelves with boxes on each. The SS archivist moved up beside him and said, "This woman you are searching for, does she have some significance?"

"Every woman has some significance, don't you think?"

"Some more than others, I think."

"She is the daughter of her parents. They have a right to know what happened to her."

"I see. How did she die?"

"Murdered," said Nemec pulling the photo of the dead woman and handing it to the SS soldier hoping to shock him away.

"I see your problem. She has no face."

"Nor fingertips. The killer used lye to hide her identity."

"Interesting…"

Nemec realized he had said too much to the man and had unintentionally peaked his interest. It was the opposite of what Nemec wanted… the attention of the Reich.

"You are looking for women and men, are you not?"

"Yes."

"Why men?"

"I might find her killer. He was most likely on the train with her."

"How will you recognize him?"

"I don't know. I am hoping there is some connection between them."

"I see. Grasping at straws?"

"I prefer to think of it as narrowing the possibilities."

The clerk brought the first three folders containing copies of the passengers' passports, then returned to the stacks to find more. The SS archivist, Lieutenant Weber watched over Nemec's shoulder as he opened the folders. It pissed Nemec off, but there was little he could do about it. He was in the Reich's territory and had to play by their rules.

The first passport was of a brunette woman. Weber compared her photo to the photo of the dead woman and said, "Wrong hair color."

"Maybe. People can dye their hair. But the shape of her face is wrong. Too long."

"I can see that. You will rule her out?"

"Yes," said Nemec closing the file and setting it

aside to form a pile of rejected passports.

He opened the file – a man with a dark beard and hair.

"Her lover, perhaps?" said Weber examining the man's photo.

"Or ex-husband, or a crazy killer, or just another passenger. There is no way to tell without finding a connection."

"A long shot, I think."

"I agree. But I have to start somewhere."

Nemec read through the file, then closed the folder and set it aside making a pile of men. He opened the third file – a heavyset woman with blond hair.

"A blonde, but fat," said Weber.

"People can lose weight. Maybe she was pregnant and looks different now."

"Hard to know without a face to compare."

"It's her eyes that give her away. Too far apart."

"You can see that?"

"Yes."

"How?"

"I measure from where the eye sockets would begin on the inside of the skull. She is not my victim."

"Another reject?"

"Yes," said Nemec placing the folder on the women's reject pile.

Tired of standing, the SS archivist pulled up a chair beside Nemec and said, "How long have you been a police officer?"

"In my current posting, seven years. Before that, Stockholm for eight years. You ask a lot of questions."

"Why? Do you have something to hide?"

"No."

Weber shrugged and said, "Questions comes with

the job."

"The Reich is very nosey," said Nemec, immediately wondering if he had gone to far.

Weber waited a long moment before he responded, "The Reich will last a thousand years. You best get used to it."

"I don't need to get used to it. I am a Swede. We're neutral."

"So was Norway. Things change. Only time will tell."

The implied threat sent a chill down Nemec's spine. He would never submit to the Reich's authority no matter what happened. Better to become a resistance fighter than a slave. He realized he had antagonized this Nazi enough and held his tongue in response.

After six hours of sitting on a hardwood chair, Nemec finished reviewing the last of the folders. His ass hurt. Weber looked at the stacks of folders and said, "Only four possible candidates for the dead woman, I see."

"Yeah. I suppose that's a good thing."

"How will you narrow your search from here?"

Nemec considered not telling the soldier about the locket he had found on the dead woman, but decided he might need the help of the SS in the near future. He pulled out the charm bracelet and opened the locket revealing the tiny photos, "According to the inscription on the back - mom and dad."

"Interesting... If you find the parents, you verify the identity of the dead woman?"

"Exactly."

"And how will you find the parents?"

"Parish records in each of the person of interest's hometown."

Nemec had made written copies of the passport files of each person of interest, including the men. It took him over two hours with Weber's help.

"You're good at this – investigation."

"I was trained by the best."

"I think it may be more than that. You have an analytical mind."

"So, I've been told."

"…and you're cocky. You would have made a good Nazi."

Nemec held his tongue once again. He finished copying the last of the files and tucked his handwritten notes in his satchel.

"You will let me know how your investigation turns out?" said Weber.

"If you wish," said Nemec. "How can I contact you?"

"Through this office. I have a feeling I won't be going anywhere soon."

"Okay," said Nemec rising to leave after the thanked the clerk for her help. As he approached the door to exit, Weber called out, "Good luck, Captain."

Nemec nodded and left. It was late in the afternoon, and it had been a long day. Nemec wanted to visit the parishes of the four persons of interest before he returned to Norway. He would stay the night in Oslo.

Nemec pulled his coat tighter against the biting wind as he made his way down the darkened Oslo street. It was barely 5pm, but the heavy blanket of clouds and steadily falling snow made it feel much later. He just wanted to find a room for the night and get some sleep before his meetings tomorrow.

The Grand Hotel Bristol loomed out of the swirling flakes ahead, the impressive four-story stone edifice still imposing despite now serving mostly as an officers quarters. As Nemec climbed the steps, a sentry demanded in German, "State your business!"

Nemec replied calmly in the same language, "I am Captain Nemec of the Swedish police. I have meetings with your authorities tomorrow. I need a room for the night."

The guard scrutinized his papers in the light of a flickering lantern before waving Nemec inside. The ornate lobby glowed from a great stone fireplace, well-dressed German officers and officials mingling before it with drinks in hand. They eyed Nemec curiously as he checked in at the long oak front desk.

The hotel manager, an older Norwegian named Henrick, told Nemec politely, "I'm very sorry, but we only have rooms left on the third floor. I hope that will be suitable."

Nemec nodded, taking the proffered heavy key. "That will be fine. I am sure you are very busy here now." His eyes took in the lobby's occupants meaningfully and Henrick glanced away.

"Yes indeed. Let me know if you need anything else."

Climbing the stairs, Nemec soon unlocked the plain door to room 302. Despite the hotel's commandeering by German elite, few alterations had been made besides removing ornate drapes and artwork. The simple bed, nightstand, and dresser were all classic Nordic designs of golden birch wood. Nemec set his satchel on the bed and checked his watch – just enough time to eat before getting some badly needed rest. He gazed out the narrow window into the winter darkness now fully enveloping the city.

Having asked the desk clerk for a recommendation, Nemec braved the cold leaving the warmth of the hotel behind. Hunger was a higher priority than warmth.

The brash laughter of German soldiers filled the small cafe, the only patrons seemingly unaffected by the dreary rationed fare of thin potato soup and salted cod. Their boisterous corner table piled high with sausages and beer stood in stark contrast to the silent Norwegian diners scattered around the room.

When the door opened, all eyes turned to scrutinize Nemec in his Swedish police uniform marking him apart from the work-worn locals. He surveyed the room briefly before choosing a table with a clear view of both the front entrance and the Germans.

After removing his leather gloves and laying them neatly by his satchel, he ordered in careful Norwegian, "Coffee, black, and today's dinner special, please."

The cafe owner nodded, relief flooding his face at the proper dialect and politeness from the Swedish police officer, not the usual German overlord. He rushed off to fulfill the order, nearly stumbling in his haste.

The Swede took no notice, opening his newspaper and perusing the headlines with a slight frown before turning the page. Though his neutral expression remained focused on reading, his gaze periodically flitted up to scrutinize the boisterous Germans mocking the cowed patrons.

When the owner returned with his coffee, Nemec thanked him quietly and wrapped his large hands around the chipped mug, seeming to soak in its warmth. Nemec had the watchful countenance of a policeman rather than a merchant, taking in details while giving little away.

The Germans finally noticed the new arrival and called over roughly in poorly-pronounced Norwegian, "You there! Swede! What brings you to our little Norway today?"

Nemec looked up calmly and replied, "Police business, nothing that need trouble your meal."

The Germans laughed. "Hear that? The Swedes have sent a lapdog to check on us!" They lost interest when the potato soup arrived, making rude gestures at the waitstaff instead.

Nemec's eyes narrowed, but he said nothing, returning attention to his newspaper and coffee until the simple meal of pork stew appeared with a small loaf of freshly baked bread. He ate steadily, without complaint over its meagerness.

When ready to depart, he laid payment on the table and pulled his gloves back on. With a polite nod to the owner and ignoring the increasingly drunken Germans, he stepped out into the cold evening air.

The owner sighed gratefully. The man's silent, thoughtful presence had felt more disruptive than any uniform. He was simply thankful the visit had passed without incident.

The next morning was like most winter mornings in Norway – biting cold and grey. Weak light filtered into the Grand Bristol lobby as Nemec descended the staircase. Only a few German soldiers were up this early, gathered by the fireplace with coffee and cigarettes. Nemec nodded polite greetings before entering the hotel's ornate dining room in search of his own breakfast.

The tables were empty save one where the old Norwegian hotel manager Henrick sat with a tall stack of paperwork and a pot of coffee. He looked up with a friendly smile as Nemec approached, the kind expression erasing the etched lines of worry from his face.

"Good morning, Captain Nemec. Please join me for some coffee and spise boller rolls - I saved a few extra for you."

"Takk, that would be wonderful," Nemec replied in Norwegian as he took the indicated seat. The sweet cardamom-laced buns and dark coffee perfectly offset the gloomy cold morning outside the towering windows.

As they chatted about harmless topics like the weather and how Henrick's family was faring, Nemec sensed the manager's burning curiosity about his business here. But wise man that he was, Henrick did not pry into such dangerous matters. He simply offered what small hospitality he could to ease the burden on a fellow Scandinavian so far from home.

After expressing his sincere thanks and wishing the best for Henrick's family, Nemec buttoned his long wool coat and stepped outside into the muffled white streets.

Four women to investigate: Haldis Kofoed, Marit Walberg, Paula Aadland, and Trine Eriksson. All in their late twenties or early thirties. All bearing a passing resemblance to the dead blond woman found frozen in the deserted Swedish meadow, only the charm bracelet locket with tiny portraits of her mother and father hinted at her identity. A quick check of passport records had given Nemec a short list of possibles who had traveled from Stockholm to Oslo or Oslo to Stockholm near the estimated time of death. Now to find their families and hopefully uncover which poor soul had met an untimely tragic end so far from home. Consulting a map and address scribbled in his notebook, he navigated the winding lanes to a venerable stone Lutheran church.

At the first church, Nemec verified the baptismal records of Haldis Kofoed with the parish secretary. He showed the secretary the delicate charm bracelet and its miniature portraits. Not recognizing the older couple in the locket, the secretary confirmed that they were not the parents of Haldis Kofoed whom she had known for many years. Nemec thanked her and moved on. One down. Three to go.

His search for Walberg's records at the second parish also met with a dead end when he showed the photos in the locket. No, they hadn't seen that particular young woman in years, not since her parents had moved further south to be nearer other relatives. Nemec paused outside to jot notes in his black notebook before tucking it securely within his coat. He stamped some warmth back into his numb feet and walked at an unhurried pace to flag down a taxi.

Finally at the small village church, Nemec confirmed Paula Aadland's baptismal records, the carefully opened the tiny locket again for the parish secretary. Her eyes widened behind her spectacles and she clapped her hands. "Why yes, I know these faces - the elder Aadlands! Frode and Marie. Such devoted members of our congregation. Is Paula in some sort of trouble? She'd be full grown now I suppose—"

Nemec raised a hand to gently stem the flow of speculation and questions. He felt he owed the woman an explanation. "My deepest condolences, but it seems

Paula has met with misfortune, I'm afraid. I am trying to determine the facts for certain and notify her remaining family. Please, if you recall anything more about her or her parents, I would be most grateful to hear."

With a sympathetic cluck of her tongue, the secretary told Nemec all she could about the Aadlands' history in the small tight-knit village. It seemed his tragic mystery woman had a name and a family at last. Though it pained him to have to later bring such terrible news, the truth would set them free from endless wondering about their poor lost Paula.

As Nemec prepared to leave, the secretary said as an afterthought, "It's strange. I had heard she was doing well at her new job at Norsk."

"Norsk?"

"Yes. The research facility on the mountain in Telemark. She was a manager, I think."

"Do you happen to know how long she might have been working there?"

"A few months maybe… three at the most."

Nemec nodded and thanked her again before climbing back into the cab. On the journey back to Oslo, Nemec considered Paula Aadland and her new job. He was now fairly certain that the dead woman he had found in the meadow was Dr. Paula Aadland. But if that was the case… who was the woman working at the Norsk Research Facility? Is she was impersonating Dr. Aadland for whatever reason, could she be Paula's killer?

After purchasing his train ticket back to Sweden, Nemec trudged down the snowy Oslo sidewalks, numbness seeping into his toes inside worn leather boots. His main purpose of identifying the dead woman had been solved, the tragic news soon to reach grieving relatives, but her murderer was still out there avoiding justice. The case was only half solved and here he was returning to his home. He knew the answers were here in Norway, not Sweden. He still had over an hour before his train. He could eat some breakfast and drink hot coffee, or he could continue to attempt to solve the case. Not much time for a such a complex task, but still… an opportunity not to be wasted. He turned toward the Passport Archive office next to the train terminal. Norsk's locked mountain laboratories were the key. He was sure of it.

Squaring his shoulders, Nemec climbed the passport office steps once more. The matronly clerk was perched behind the front desk, scribbling notes in spidery script. At Nemec's approach, she glanced up and said, "Back so soon? Did you find your faceless woman?"

"I believe so, yes," said Nemec.

"Good. Then how may I help you?"

"I was hoping to talk with Lieutenant Weber."

"He went for coffee. He should be back shortly if you care to wait."

Nemec nodded and sat on a bench.

"So,… the dead woman… does she have a name?"

"Dr. Paula Aadland."

"A doctor. All that education wasted. A shame really."

"I suppose you're right."

"So, you're done then?"

"Not exactly. Her murderer is still at large."

"And do you know who that might be?"

"No. Still a mystery to be solved."

"Well, you solved the first one. I'm sure you will solve the second."

"I appreciate the confidence, but I believe it will be far more difficult."

"Why is that?"

"In a way, Dr. Aadland wanted to be found. I suspect her killer does not."

The SS archivist walked in holding two hot coffees with a sweet roll balanced on top of one. He placed the coffee without the sweet roll in front of the clerk who said, "You have a guest."

Weber turned to see Nemec sitting on the bench and said, "I thought you were back in Sweden."

"That was my intent. But there were complications."

"You didn't find your dead woman?"

"No, I did - Dr. Paula Aadland."

"Good. So, what is the problem?"

"Two problems actually. Her murderer is still free from justice and well hidden."

"And the second problem?"

"That's what I came to talk to you about... in private."

The clerk wrinkled her face at the slight, then rose... "You forgot the milk in my coffee," she said carrying her coffee and exiting the office to leave the two alone with their secret.

"You have the floor, Swede," said Weber.

"Dr. Paula Aadland is dead. Her body rests in a Swedish cooler."

"Okay. So?"

"Someone has taken over Aadland's job at the Norsk Research Facility."

The SS archivist considers for a moment, then "An

imposter?"

"It seems that way."

"You understand that the research facility at Telemark is top secret?"

"I have heard such."

"Security for the facility and its staff is under direct control of the SS. If there is an imposter, it is up to the SS to route her out, not a police captain from Sweden."

"I understand that. My intent is not to hunt down an imposter, but Dr. Aadland's killer."

"The problem is one in the same, is it not?"

"Perhaps, but we won't know until the imposter is uncovered."

"…and interrogated."

"Yes. …and interrogated."

"So, why do you need my help?"

"I want to enter Norsk and question the imposter."

Weber laughed and said, "Oh. Is that all?"

"Can you arrange it?"

"Are you serious? I'm a small cog in a giant wheel. I have no power."

"You have the truth that the SS at Norsk don't know yet. That should be worth something."

"You obviously don't know how the SS works."

"No. I don't. But I do know that if the security at Hitler's prized research facility has been breached, there are many in charge of said security that would not want the truth to be known."

"You want me to blackmail the SS?"

"I want you to help me find the murderer of Dr. Paula Aadland."

"Why should I do that? If I stick my neck out, the SS commander will almost assuredly lop off my head."

"I doubt that."

"I don't."

"If we couch our argument correctly, he could see us as confederates trying to help him."

"That is a big 'if,' Captain."

"I find it hard to believe that an intelligent man like yourself wants to remain in a Norwegian archive overlooking the shoulder of a clerk."

"…and this is my way out?"

"It could be if you play it correctly."

"And you know how to do that… play it correctly?"

"Yes."

Weber considered Nemec's words carefully…

A Hunter's Cabin

Norsk Research Facility

Nemec gripped his seat as the military staff car jostled along the winding mountain highway. Snow-covered pines towered like silent sentinels watching their approach. His SS companion had barely spoken since they left Oslo, anxiety etched on his gaunt features.

Approaching a bridge spanning a deep ravine, the driver slowed to a halt, awaiting the sentry's signal to proceed. The guard scrutinized their papers before waving them across. Nemec spotted two more armed men patrolling the snowy banks, breath frosting the air.

Further up the incline, the paved road gave way to gravel and a second checkpoint loomed. More scrutiny of documents, a thorough sweep of the vehicle, then finally the barrier gate lifted for them to pass.

As the research complex at last came into view, Nemec caught his breath. The concrete brutalist architecture seemed at odds with its location nestled between towering pines and dramatic ravines. Steam issued from vents in the multi-story central edifice. Several outbuildings and pipe tunnels spread out from its base.

The staff car followed the multi-layered barbed wire perimeter fence to a final guarded entrance where the SS lieutenant presented his credentials. After a delay, the steel door rasped open on ponderous hinges to admit them into a small receiving area.

"The facility has unconceivable amount of security," Nemec remarked.

Weber nodded tersely. "And yet possibly not enough given the breach you may have uncovered."

Their escort, an armed corporal, led the way through a maze of sterile corridors to a nondescript office. Inside Colonel Bauer glanced up sharply from his desk.

"What brings you up from Oslo, Lieutenant? And with a foreign guest in tow no less?" The colonel's gravelly voice held thinly veiled annoyance as he scrutinized Nemec.

Drawing himself up, Weber replied, "Apologies for the disruption Colonel Bauer, but this Swedish captain has uncovered a serious breach of security regarding one of our Norwegian physicists."

Bauer's face reddened. "Preposterous! We screen every worker and staff member thoroughly. No imposter could simply waltz in."

"That is why I brought Captain Nemec directly, so you could hear his conclusions and determine its veracity yourself."

"Alright. But I must warn you – the accusations you make are serious and may come with consequences should they be proven false."

"I understand," said Nemec. "and I still wish to proceed."

"Then you have my attention, Captain."

Nemec started his report at the beginning when he first found the body of the woman in the snow near his village. He described finding the charm bracelet with the locket snagged on the woman's dress and the tiny photos along with the inscription on back. He handed the colonel the bracelet for his inspection. Nemec continued with the passenger manifests of trains passing near the corpse around the time of death and how he narrowed the list from over 200 to eighty individuals. He described traveling to the passport archives in Oslo where he met Weber and further narrowed down the list to just four women. Visiting each parish where they were baptized and showing the tiny photos of the dead woman's parents for verification, Nemec concluded that the dead woman was Dr. Paula Aadland.

"Your story held my interest right up to that point, captain. Dr. Paula Aadland is alive and well working at our facility. Her leadership has already proven invaluable."

"If she is Dr. Aadland."

"Even if she had a similar physical appearance, how could anyone impersonate the brilliant mind of a scientist like Dr. Aadland? It's impossible."

"Is it?"

"What would be her purpose?"

"Spying, disinformation, sabotage… I don't know. Counterintelligence is not my field. What I do know is the woman that I found in a snow-covered meadow was Dr. Paula Aadland."

"What is your game, Captain?" said Bauer aggravated.

"I assure you, I have no dog in this hunt beyond finding Dr. Aadland's killer, Colonel."

"And you think this imposter is her... the killer?"

"Perhaps. But at the very least, I think she probably knows who the killer was and could identify him or her when they are uncovered."

Bauer was infuriated, but he wasn't an idiot. He couldn't ignore a possible security breach at this level no matter how far-fetched. Bauer called his assistant in and asked for all the personnel files on Dr. Paula Aadland be brought to his desk for review.

Nemec and Weber exchanged subtle but satisfied glances. Perhaps the barest crack now opened into Norsk's forbidden intrigues.

Colonel Bauer strode down the brightly lit corridor, his boots clicking sharply on the polished floors. The Swedish policeman's questions about Aadland still troubled him. While an outsider could not grasp the vital importance of their work here, security was paramount, especially with suspected resistance agents lurking. As a university student, Bauer had been seduced by the writings of Nietzsche and the idea of the "superman," and he saw the Nazis as the embodiment of this ideal and himself as a member of the chosen few destined to rule over the "lesser" races.

Reaching the heavy oaken door bearing a brass nameplate reading "Director S. Knutsen," Bauer gave two quick raps with his knuckles and entered without awaiting a reply.

Knutsen sat writing amidst a chaos of journals, technical diagrams, and scale models. He glanced up impatiently, his rugged features set in a scowl.

"This had better be important to interrupt my work, Colonel."

Bauer adopted a respectful yet serious tone. "My

apologies, Director Knutsen, but a very alarming report was just brought to my attention by one of our Oslo archivists, Lieutenant Weber."

He proceeded to explain how Weber had arrived unexpectedly with a Swedish police captain named Nemec. This Nemec had evidence that Dr. Paula Aadland was deceased, and an imposter had somehow taken her place here at the facility.

Knutsen's scowl darkened at the mention of his lover's name. He rose abruptly, papers cascading. "Such accusations are completely insufferable! I would know if some fraud had infiltrated our ranks. What proof does this ridiculous Swede offer?"

"Disturbingly solid evidence I'm afraid. Documents and evidence identifying a woman's frozen corpse as the real Dr. Aadland. Our informant Lieutenant Weber verifies it's undoubtedly her." Bauer paused before continuing gravely. "At first, I too found it incredulous. But after reviewing the evidence I believe it is prudent to at least investigate the possibility."

Knutsen began pacing, running a hand through his hair. "This is outrageous! Paula has been my most trusted partner for months now. The advances we've achieved..." He turned on Bauer angrily. "Why was I not informed immediately about these incidents? Just how long has this supposed 'imposter' had access to restricted materials?"

Bauer raised his hands placatingly. "It appears the deception has gone on for some time. But now that we know, I assure you I will root out the truth swiftly and discreetly before real damage occurs."

"Damage has already occurred, Colonel. Your reputation and career are on the line."

"As well as yours, my dear Doctor. You recruited

her if I remember correctly."

Pouring himself a bracing drink, Knutsen slumped into his desk chair. Dark suspicions clearly warred across his face.

Bauer pressed gently, "With your permission, I would like to interview Dr. Aadland regarding her recent movements. Purely routine to establish her activities and identity beyond doubt."

Knutsen's head jerked up, eyes narrowing sharply. "You will do no such thing, Colonel! Dr. Aadland's work is at a critical juncture. I won't have her disturbed without my express knowledge and approval."

Sensing he had pushed as far as he could for now, Bauer smothered his rising frustration. "Of course. We will proceed however you think best." If the imposter theory proved true though, Knutsen would have harsh questions of his own to answer.

Nemec glanced up expectantly from scrutinizing a technical diagram as Colonel Bauer reentered his spartan office. Bauer's tight expression warned the meeting with Knutsen had not gone smoothly.

Shutting the door firmly against potential eavesdroppers, Bauer addressed the men grimly. "I regret to inform you that Director Knutsen is...reluctant to have Dr. Aadland disturbed at present. Her project reaches a critical phase apparently."

Nemec exchanged a subtle look with Weber. Clearing his throat, he replied carefully, "I understand the director not wishing any disruption. However, surely to put such troubling claims to rest swiftly, interviewing the woman would be prudent?"

Bauer moved behind his desk, weariness showing. "Believe me, Captain, I agree completely.

Unfortunately, Knutsen refuses to even inform Aadland of these concerns. And even though he is Norwegian, he outranks me here at the research facility."

Seeing Nemec's frustration, he continued, "However, my authority extends fully outside these fences. If we could lure this 'Aadland' offsite, even briefly, I could detain her for thorough questioning."

Pacing the rug thoughtfully, Nemec proposed, "Perhaps we simply send a message that a package awaits her at the post office in Telemark."

The colonel considered, then nodded. "That could work. But Knutsen will be furious if he discovers our ruse."

Nemec offered a taut smile. "Then we must ensure he does not realize until too late."

It had been well over two weeks since Elsa had been in contact with Culper. She was concerned that something had happen. He was her only contact and without him, she had no escape from Norway.

When the notice from the post office arrived of a waiting package, she was relieved. Culper was alive and wanted to meet with her. Grabbing her coat and purse, she headed out of her office to find Hans.

Telemark Downtown

Hans pulled Knutsen's town car to the curb at Elsa's request. "I have several errands I need to run. I will meet you back here in two hours, Hans."

"I don't think director Knutsen would agree with you traveling about town without an escort."

"I appreciate your concern, but I'm not a child,

Hans."

She stepped from the backseat without waiting for Hans to open her door. Marching down the sidewalk, she turned the corner and disappeared. Helpless, Hans sighed.

Arriving at the post office, Elsa took a seat on a bench out front and looked for signs of Culper. There were none, but that didn't mean anything. Culper was a master at staying hidden until he chose otherwise.

After twenty minutes, enough time that she was sure Culper had seen her, she rose from the bench and went inside the post office.

Behind the counter, the matronly mistress retrieved a slim letter-sized packet from a back shelf in response to Elsa's clipped inquiry. The older woman smiled, accustomed to the occasional mysterious parcel arriving for the mountain facility staff. She had Elsa sign the receipt for the registered package releasing the post office from liability. Murmuring her thanks, Elsa exited the post office while cautiously checking for any trailing shadows.

Elsa slipped into the first alleyway near the post office and walked to the dead end for privacy. Her hands started to tremble as she opened the envelope. Sliding a single sheet of paper free, confusion clouded her face. The paper was a vague typewritten report about ore shipments seemingly unrelated to her mission. She wondered if it was some kind of code, but Culper hadn't trained her to decipher such a message. She didn't notice the SS soldiers entering the mouth of the alley.

Footsteps echoed sharply down the alley's narrow ingress as Elsa still stared baffled at cryptic mining data.

Spinning at the sound, alarm spiked to see three black uniforms blocking the way ahead. Colonel Bauer's weathered visage stood flanked by two armed guards, eyes glinting coldly like the snow around them.

"Dr. Aadland... or whoever you are, you will come with us," said Bauer.

Elsa's eyes darted for a way out. There was none.

"Retain her."

Before Elsa could even attempt to flee, the two SS soldiers seized her arms in with vicelike grips. She glimpsed one guard snatch away the mysterious papers and drop them to the ground. Realization crashing down - Bauer had orchestrated this deception and Culper had no idea she had been apprehended. She was on her own!

Gretchen, a street vendor selling roasted hazelnuts from a cart, watched from across the street as the SS loaded Elsa into Bauer's staff car and sped away.

Thirty minutes later, Culper entered the Ingvaldsen's Bakery and descended the narrow stairwell concealed behind the bakery's storage shelves, senses alert for trouble. A coded runner had summoned him here for an urgent meeting with Johannes regarding "a sensitive development."

In the dim cinderblock basement, Johannes looked up from weathered maps spread on the lone table.

"Why the urgent meeting? What happened?" Culper probed without preamble. Each minute wasted could prove disastrous if Nazis infiltrated their ring.

Johannes gestured Culper closer as he reported softly. "Our lookout Gretchen witnessed soldiers detain Dr. Aadland today."

"She's sure it was Aadland?"

"Absolutely."

"Did she see where they took her?"

"No. They were in a car and our lookout was on foot."

Culper tensed. If SS Colonel Bauer uncovered Elsa's impersonation... "Dr. Aadland must be located before they extract information."

"Why? What do we care what they do to traitors?"

Culper considered for a moment, then replied, "Aadland is not a traitor. She's working undercover for us trying to gum up the Nazi's atomic research."

"She's an intelligence operative?"

"Of sorts. She was a physicist that looked like Aadland. We trained, then swapped her for Aadland while she was on her way to Norsk."

"And where is the original Aadland?"

"Dead and buried."

"So, Bauer must have figured out the new Aadland was an imposter."

"It looks that way. And I doubt she will last long under torture."

"Does she know anything that can hurt us?"

"I don't know, maybe… but we can't take any chances. We need to find her."

"I'm not sure we have a lot of options. They could have taken her anywhere."

"Can you send out your people to search for her?"

"Of course. But it is a needle in a haystack."

"I know, but we need to try."

"I'll see to it immediately."

Norsk Research Facility

Hans rapped sharply on the laboratory door, filled with anxiety. Knutsen had left strict orders he was not to be disturbed once engrossed in his latest intricate experiment. But Knutsen needed to hear the news whether he welcomed it or not.

At Knutsen's brisk summons, Hans entered hurriedly. "Forgive the intrusion, sir. But we've had an incident."

"An incident?"

"Dr. Aadland is missing."

Knutsen's head jerked up, features clouding. "What do you mean missing?"

Hans withered under his superior's piercing gaze. "Well, sir, after driving the doctor to town per her request, she failed to meet our rendezvous. The SS cannot locate her anywhere in Telemark currently."

Color rising in anger, Knutsen grabbed for the telephone. "Get me Colonel Bauer immediately!" he barked down the line.

Moments later he slammed the handset violently into its cradle. "Bauer has inexplicably left grounds without notice. I suspect some connection. I told that son of a bitch to leave Paula alone. If she is harmed in any way, he will pay tenfold." Striding for his greatcoat, Knutsen ordered sharply, "Hans, bring the car round now!"

Telemark Downtown

Knutsen's town car sped into downtown with little regard for pedestrians or other vehicles.

Gretchen, tending grill on her street cart, looked up as Hans and Knutsen zoomed past. Scrapping the half roasted nuts to the edge of the grill where the fire was lower, she walked across the street and into the post office. Moving to a pay phone on the wall, she inserted several coins, and dialed a number.

Hans pulled the town car to the curb in front of SS regional command. Wasting no time, Knutsen jumped from the backseat of the car and marched into the building. Knutsen stormed past startled secretaries, throwing open the local SS commander's door without preamble.

"Where is Colonel Bauer?" said Knutsen.

"I don't know, Director Knutsen. I haven't seen him in several hours."

"He was here?"

"Yes. He picked up two SS troops and left."

"You need to find him swiftly. He has detained one of my key physicists and I demand to know why?"

The officer stammered, "I assure you I have no knowledge of—"

Knutsen cut him off. "Then acquire such knowledge! Or shall I request the führer himself clarify proper authority at Telemark?"

He held the terrified officer's gaze with thinly veiled warning until finally the man raised a placating hand to make nervous inquiries.

Hunting Cabin Outside of Telemark

Elsa glared silently across the battered farm table, defiant despite fear churning inside. Her SS captors had transferred her to an isolated cabin after Bauer's ambush.

Now Colonel Bauer paced before her, boots loud on warped floorboards between drab barren walls. A single bare bulb cast harsh light and shadows over his weathered features. Elsa tensed as the remote cabin door creaked open, admitting two more figures. Bauer introduced the two men. The first was a severe-looking SS Lieutenant - Weber. The second wore a Swedish uniform, but his assessing gaze held a distinct weight - Captain Nemec.

"It was Captain Nemec that found Dr. Aadland's body in the snow. Did you kill her?" said Bauer.

"No," was Elsa's entire response.

"Then who did?"

Elsa changed the direction of the conversation, "You will pay dearly for this, Colonel. I swear it."

"You're assuming you will regain your freedom. That is doubtful as much as it is pitiful... to cling to false hope when there is none."

Telemark Downtown

An SS guard stood at the entrance of the SS headquarters with its long red flags rippling in a gentle wind. Across the street, Culper, Johannes, and five resistance fighters moved up behind a lookout at the end of an alley and watched Hans sitting in the driver's seat of Knutsen's town car.

"Where's Knutsen?" said Johannes.

"I'm not sure. He wasn't in the car when I arrived. I would guess he's inside," said the lookout.

Moments later, Knutsen exited the building and climbed into the town car. The car sped off. Culper, Johannes, and the five resistance fighters climbed into the baker's delivery truck and followed at a distance.

Hunting Cabin Outside of Telemark

Colonel Bauer slapped Elsa across the face and said, "Answer my question."

Looking at his hand, he saw smudged makeup. He pushed back her hair to reveal the smeared scar on her cheek. He held up his hand to show Elsa the makeup and said, "I believe we have found the truth. Who are you?"

"Your worst nightmare," said Elsa defiantly.

Bauer smiled, slipped his glove on his right hand, and slugged her in the face hard. She groaned, blood flowing from her lips and nose.

"The time for lies and deceit is over. I will grind you to a pulp if you do not tell me the truth, Fraulein."

Outside the cabin, the town car sped toward the cabin. Tires spitting gravel, Hans skidded the vehicle to a stop in front of the remote structure. Before Hans finished braking, Knutsen erupted from the rear door, barreling for the entrance in a fury.

Farther down the gravel road, the delivery truck pulled to a stop. Culper and the resistance fighters piled out and formed a skirmish line as they advanced on the cabin as Hans and Knutsen disappeared through the front door. "Nobody fire without my signal and only when you have a clear target. I do not want my agent shot," said Culper holding a hunting rifle with scope.

Inside the cabin, Knutsen confronted Bauer, "Are you insane, Colonel?! How dare you disobey a direct order?" said Knutsen. "Release Dr. Aadland at once!"

"I think not, Director," said Bauer moving to Elsa's side and showing her smeared scar.

Knutsen was confused by what he was seeing and

moved closer to examine the evidence on Elsa's cheek.

"She's an Allied spy. And I will have some questions for you, once I am finished with her," said Bauer with satisfaction.

"Is this true, Paula?" said Knutsen.

"Her name is not Paula," said Bauer.

"Who are you?" said Knutsen locking eyes with Elsa.

"Svein, he's lying. I am your Paula. Save me from this brute," said Elsa channeling Aadland.

And then it hit Knutsen like a speeding locomotive. He had been duped by this woman. He rushed to Hans and pried the pistol from his hand and raised toward Elsa. Bauer moved between them and said, "No. Not until we know what she was searching for."

Outside the cabin, Culper sighted Knutsen, pistol raised, through the window. He centered the scope's crosshairs on Knutsen's head and squeezed the trigger.

Inside the cabin, a shot rang out and glass shattered as Knutsen was hit in the shoulder and spun around. He fell to the floor of the cabin groaning in pain as the pistol slipped from his hand. Hans grabbed the pistol and moved to the broken window using the cabin wall as cover. The two SS guards, Bauer, and Lieutenant Weber did the same, each taking up positions aside windows.

Crouching low, Nemec was only a few feet from Elsa tied to the chair and in the line of fire. He could see hope, not terror in her eyes. His mind raced, putting the pieces of what had occurred together – the woman before him was an Allied operative impersonating the dead woman, Dr. Paula Aadland.

Aadland had clearly been an important scientist. But why kill Aadland? And what did the imposter want from the research facility? Sabotage? He had so many questions but only one was important in that moment – would he side with the Nazis, side with the Allies, or remain neutral?

One of the SS guards at a window, used his MP41 submachine gun's barrel to shatter the glass, then sprayed half of the bullets in his gun's magazine out the broken window, firing randomly without aim while keeping cover below the window's frame.

Outside the cabin, Knutsen's town car was pierced with a half dozen bullets, piercing the sheet metal panels, shattering the passenger window and flattening the front tire. The resistance fighters returned fire with their rifles and machine guns.

Inside the cabin, Nemec watched as bullets shattered more windows and pierced walls, some coming dangerously close to Elsa still tied to the chair and unable to move. He had little doubt one or more bullets would find her quickly if the barrage kept up. The time to think was over, he acted kicking Elsa and the chair over. She landed with a thud, now low to the cabin floor but still not out of harm's way.

Removing a pocketknife from his trousers, Nemec crawled over and cut the ropes binding her. She was free. Nemec crawled over and peeked around the corner to see a back door. He motioned to Elsa to go out the back. Taking his directions, she crawled across the floor and slipped around the corner. As she reached the door, she looked back at Nemec and nodded thanks. He nodded back. Elsa slipped out the back door.

The other SS guard grabbed the knob, opened the front door and fired a burst from his submachine gun. Moments later, his body was riddled with bullets, and he fell dead. Kneeling nearby, Hans kicked the front door closed.

Outside the cabin, Culper yelled at the resistance fighters to "ceasefire," but none of the undisciplined rebels were interested in obeying his orders while the Nazis were continuing to fire from within the cabin.

Movement at the back of the cabin caught Culper's eye. Somebody was trying to flank the resistance fighter's position. Culper moved off through the woods hoping to cutoff the maneuver.

Elsa raced through the trees and undergrowth trying to reach the Allied lines. Her eyes widened and she froze when she saw a man aiming his rifle straight at her. Recognizing her through the trees, Culper lowered his weapon. Elsa smiled and ran to him. Hugging him, she said, "I thought I would never see you again."

"Same here," said Culper hugging her back. "We need to go before reinforcements arrive."

The moment was shattered, but she knew he was right. He led her back to the bakery delivery truck and placed her safely inside. He moved back to the resistance fighters and told Johannes he had Elsa. Performing a fighting retreat with their wounded in tow, the fighters moved back to the truck and climbed in. Moments later, they escaped.

Inside the cabin, as the firing ceased, Hans tended to Knutsen's wound. Bauer turned to see his prisoner gone. He spun to Nemec and said, "Where is the woman?"

Nemec replied, "I have no idea, but Sweden is neutral in this matter."

Bauer was infuriated, but there was nothing he could do.

Telemark Downtown

In the Ingvaldsen's Bakery's basement, the rebels tended to their wounded while Culper cleaned up the cuts on Elsa's face. "That damned fake scar gave me away," said Elsa.

"You would have talked anyway. Nobody withstands SS interrogations for long," said Culper.

"I was holding my own," said Elsa boldly.

"I bet you were."

"So, what happens now that my cover is blown?"

"Time for you to go home. Your duty has been fulfilled."

"I didn't do much."

Culper laughed, "You've done far more than most. I'm proud of you."

"Really?"

"With the intelligence you gathered, we should be able to destroy the key components of the facility."

"Who is we?"

"When you went missing, I called my OSS superiors in London and we agreed. The British are sending in a team of commandos to destroy the facility."

Elsa fell silent. She had come so far, risked so much, and now, with the end in sight, she was being told to walk away. The thought of abandoning the mission, of leaving before the job was done, felt like a betrayal of everything she had fought for. She couldn't just return home, not when she knew she could still make a difference.

"I should stay," she said, her voice steady and resolute.

"What? Why?"

"Nobody on our side knows that facility better than me. I know what needs to be destroyed and where it is located. Those commandos stand a much better chance of success if I guide them."

Elsa's words tumbling out in a rush of conviction. She had seen firsthand the horrors the Nazis were capable of, had witnessed the devastation their research could unleash upon the world. She couldn't turn her back on that, couldn't walk away knowing that she had the power to help stop them.

"That's not going to happen, Elsa. You've done enough."

"No, I haven't. That's the point. The mission is not over until we stop the Nazi's research."

Elsa's determination grew with each passing moment. She had come too far to be sidelined now, to be told that her role was over. She had transformed from the timid, naive girl she had once been into a woman of strength and purpose. She had a duty, not just to her country, but to the world, to see this through to the end.

"Culper, you're being pigheaded. You know I'm right. I should stay."

Culper fell silent, deep in thought. Elsa held her breath, hoping that he would see the truth in her words, that he would understand the depths of her resolve.

Finally, he spoke. "Alright, but you stay close to me

and you do exactly what I say. Deal?"

Elsa grinned as she nodded in agreement, feeling a mix of relief and determination. She knew the path ahead would be fraught with danger, but she also understood that her knowledge and experience were crucial to the mission's success. The risks were undeniable, but so was her resolve to see this through. She had come this far, and now, with the end in sight, she knew she had to stay.

God's Rollercoaster

Central Mountains, Norway

The wind howled through the snow-laden pines, carrying with it a biting chill that cut through even the thickest of winter garments. The sky, a leaden gray, seemed to press down upon the mountain, the clouds heavy with the promise of more snow to come. It was a world transformed, the once-familiar landscape now a treacherous, unforgiving expanse of white.

Culper and Elsa fought their way through the knee-deep snow, their cross-country skis leaving deep tracks in the pristine powder as they ascended the secluded mountain hollow. The frigid air bit at their exposed skin, and chunks of snow clung to their wool coats, weighing them down. Suddenly, Culper spotted movement and threw out an arm to halt Elsa's progress. A lone mountain goat peered at them from behind a snow-covered outcropping, its wary eyes watching their every move. Just beyond the animal, a small log cabin nestled against a backdrop of towering evergreens.

With a cautious hand on his pistol, Culper gestured for Elsa to keep watch as he approached the humble timber structure. No smoke rose from the chimney, and the snow around the cabin remained untouched, suggesting it had been abandoned for the season. Culper tried the frozen latch and, finding it stuck, forced the door open with a grunt. He waved Elsa inside, eager to escape the bitter chill.

The single-room refuge provided a welcome respite from the knifing wind, though it offered little in the way of creature comforts. Elsa's eyes darted around the space, hopeful. "Do we have time for a fire or maybe some coffee?" she asked, her voice tinged with exhaustion.

Culper shook his head. "No. Someone could spot the smoke from a fire. Besides, we've got to keep moving to the rendezvous point once you catch your breath."

As Elsa rested, Culper consulted his map, acutely aware of her shivering form and the weariness etched on her face. He wanted to give her as much time as they could afford out of the storm, but he knew their window was limited.

With a heavy sigh, they secured the rustic door and set out once more, the snow growing thicker as they climbed higher up the mountain. Elsa struggled to keep pace, her lighter frame allowing her skis to glide more easily over the deep snow, but the burning in her thighs and calves was a constant reminder of the grueling journey.

At the ridge crest, Elsa paused, grateful for a moment to catch her breath. The thin air seared her lungs as she gulped it down, her eyes squinting against the wind-driven snow. In the distance, she could just make out their destination—a small clearing tucked between snow-capped firs. Beside her, Culper scanned the darkening horizon with concern as he sensed the storm's growing unrest.

Elsa's goggles were frosted over, obscuring her vision, but she mentally counted the kilometers that lay ahead, her heart sinking at the thought of the distance still to be covered. Culper's gloved hand clasped her shoulder, a silent acknowledgment of her weariness. "We best not linger," he warned, his voice gruff. "The cold will sap what little strength we have left."

With a grim nod, Elsa dug her poles into the snow, steeling herself for the arduous trek that still lay ahead. Together, they pushed on.

In the sky…

The amber glow of the cockpit instruments lit the pilots' taut faces as their Handley Page Halifax bomber bucked through the building headwinds. High ridgelines and snow-draped peaks reared. Though Intelligence had briefed them thoroughly on traversing Norway's elevations, seeing the harsh landscape still gave Squadron Leader Briggs a grave sense of unease as he worked the throttle for more speed.

"Bloody turbulence worse than I imagined," said his co-pilot Petty. "Those peak reports can't do justice to getting slammed head-on by the damned things!"

Beyond the vibrating windscreen of the cockpit, the pilots struggled to even discern edges of the looming cliffs piercing the darkening skies around them. Clouds and fog swallowed most traces of light, while only intermittent glimpses of dim peaks and ridges blinked in and out of sight through the oppressive gray mist enshrouding their flight path.

Briggs scowled at the shuddering cliffs piercing the

clouds outside as the wings were battered by updrafts. Gripping the controls, he cast an anxious look out the starboard windows where their sister Halifax bomber flew in tight formation. Beyond it bucked the slim outline of its towed glider, an Airspeed Horsa cutting a wild zig-zag in the violent air with its eighty-eight-foot wingspan.

"Just have to ride it out best as we're able," Briggs muttered, steeling himself against the instrument panel as his own craft groaned under the assault of the wind. "We just need to keep our aircraft in one piece and get the men delivered."

Designed for stealth insertions, the engineless plywood gliders rode powerful updrafts emanating from the jagged peaks below. The turbulence pitched and yawed the lightweight vessels violently on their long tethers trailing behind the two bombers. The plywood gliders bounced on invisible air pockets and narrowly missing the sheer cliff faces.

Inside Glider 2, the fifteen Royal Engineers of the 9th Field Company, 1st British Airborne Division braced themselves in the sparse metal frame seats bolted to the floor as the aircraft was battered from all directions. Even behind their scowling expressions, hints of green-gilled nausea could be detected in more than one battle-hardened face. Jammed tightly together in full kit, the unit checked and re-checked gear in nervous tradition - submachine guns, pistols, grenades, satchel charges, and mountaineering equipment secured for transit then inspected yet again.

Inside Halifax Bomber 1, Petty peered at the distressed glider following the bomber next to him with worry. "Let's pray those poor bastards make it through intact," he said grimly.

"I'd better radio them," said Briggs. "Raptor 1 this is Shepherd Lead, how's it looking back there? Over."

Glider Pilot: "God's own rollercoaster ride, Shepherd Lead! Whole lot of white knuckles aboard this crate I'd wager. Over."

"Apologies Raptor 1, these headwinds aren't making holding course any easier between the high ridges even without the long leash. Over and out."

Even the battle-hardened troops felt their stomachs lurch with each buffeting air pocket their gliders hit. More than one hardened SAS soldier swallowed hard against the bile rising in their throats or reached for an air sickness bag tucked in the fuselage netting. They were accustomed to parachute drops into hot landing zones, but riding as helpless cargo with no control amplified their discomfort.

From the lead glider's crew cabin, the squadron commander could glimpse their sister ship plunging and rising on violent wind shear off the starboard wing. Inside both fragile shells, he envisioned white-knuckled hands gripping bench seats as the commandos braced themselves amidst the rattling of heavy gear slamming back and forth with each shudder.

On ground below…

Elsa and Culper traversed through the rugged mountain range, their skis carving through the shin-deep powder blanketing the slopes. Jagged grey peaks jutted towards the sky all around them, their cliffsides etched with ridges and gullies. Though the late afternoon sun still hung above the horizons, fast-moving clouds swirling around the summit cast looming shadows across their path.

Elsa was bundled up against the frigid mountain conditions in a thick woolen overcoat layered over heavy canvas trousers and wool vest. Yet the relentless winds skipped across the frozen tundra to chill her to the bone. Her leather snow boots did little to keep out the numbness that prickled her feet. Every inch of exposed skin stung from windburn and potential frostbite. She cinched her scarf tighter across her face while her labored breaths fogged her primitive snow goggles.

Exhaustion weighed heavy in her pack-laden shoulders and in the strained muscles of her legs. The repeated motion of planting her wooden skis and poles through endless snowfields sapped what warmth and vigor she retained. Her gloved hands gripped her poles with determination against the resistance of each snowy mound. She feared her shaking limbs might fail her before they made their destination.

Beside Elsa, Culper was wrapped in a white fur-lined anorak, his chiseled features darkened by days in the wilderness. Only the glare of his scanning eyes showed beneath the anti-glare slits cut into strips of birch bark circles tied to his head. Years of Arctic training and previous missions in Norway had hardened him, but she noticed him clench his jaw against the barrage of wind-borne ice shards that threatened their balance and visibility. Rudimentary map in hand, he checked their bearing against the compass before relief showed in his gaze. The landing zone coordinates were close...if they could endure the last grueling stretch.

As they climbed in elevation towards the designated rendezvous coordinates, the wind intensified, bitterly cold drafts swirling down from the icy crags above. The wind lashed Elsa's hair against her goggles and needled through the gaps of her winter gear. She pulled her collar tighter with a shiver while Culper bowed his head low, powering onwards through the building storm.

They curved their way up a narrow ravine, shear rock walls funneling the mounting wind into a tunneling vortex. Elsa could barely catch her breath against the frontal assault of frigid air. Ice crystals pressed against her cheeks at a furious tempo, the cold searing into her bones. She feared her stimulated momentum was the only thing keeping hypothermia's encroaching grasp at bay.

Though Elsa was athletic, the effort of pushing through the snowdrifts was exhausting. Her thighs burned and her shoulders ached from poling.

"Focus on something besides the pain," Culper called over his shoulder, his breath leaving frosty plumes in the frigid air. "It'll take your mind off it."

Elsa concentrated on the hiss of their skis sliding through the powder. All around them, snow-laden pine boughs sparkled brilliantly under the glimpses of the afternoon sunlight. Though the beauty took her breath away, Elsa needed a further distraction from the demanding pace.

"What did you do...before the war?" she panted, her lungs like fire.

"I was a professor of engineering at a state college," Culper replied. "Teaching civil engineering and bridge design."

Elsa raised her eyebrows in surprise and said, "You were an academic?"

She had not pictured the gritty spy as an academic

like herself. She imagined him in a tweed jacket lecturing to students instead of clad in fatigues and commando gear.

"Never expected that, huh?" Culper said, a glint in his eye. "But I enjoyed training the next generation of builders." His expression turned somber. "Though now I mainly teach the fine art of demolition."

Elsa sensed both nostalgia and grim determination in Culper's tone as they trekked onward through the remote snow-enshrouded forest. She realized that like herself, Culper had been plucked from an ordinary life because of talents deemed essential for the war effort.

Elsa and Culper reached the landing site - a long snow-covered meadow nestled between towering ranges. Twilight deepened around them as they hurried to ready the makeshift runway for the gliders. The pair took folding trench shovels from their packs and hacked at the brush and saplings dotting the site.

"We need to properly clear this. No obstacles," Culper declared, digging around frozen roots in the rock-hard soil to fully extract bushes. The grueling labor made Elsa break an icy sweat inside her layers, breath clouding the chilled air as she struggled to remove each root bole surrounded by frozen soil. Her shoulders burned against the resistance while Culper grunted with effort beside her. Culper found a large boulder under the snow. Together, they pried it out of the frozen ground and rolled it out of the runway.

Once finished clearing the meadow, Culper laid out the edges of the runway and handed Elsa a bundle of road flares. She moved to one side of the runway and placed flares opposite Culper's flares. Once the flares were laid out, Culper checked his watch and loaded his flare gun. "They should be here any minute. When I fire my flare gun, you'll ignite your markers and I'll ignite mine."

"Got it," said Elsa.

When aircraft engines echoed between peaks, Culper readied his flare gun and Elsa moved to the first marker on the ground. Just as the two planes and their gliders became visible as they cleared two mountain peaks, a strong gust of wind barreled up through the meadow sending a stinging chill in Culper as he fired his flare gun. The flare wobbled as it headed skyward, then arced as it began its descent. Elsa ignited the first marker and ran to the next.

Without warning, an intense blast of wind shear tore laterally across the valley, slamming into the struggling squadron leader's port flank. The bomber groaned sharply right from the sledgehammer impact, its wing dipping precipitously towards the dark cliffs now scything past.

Behind, the glider rode the violent gust broadside, its lightweight frame whipping violently at the end of the still-taut tow rope. Aerodynamic forces warped the glider's wings to their stress limits as the pilots fought desperately to compensate with overmatched controls. Like a kite torn from a child's helpless grip, the glider fishtailed recklessly behind and above the lead craft's tail assembly. Only rapid adjustments averted wrapping the tow rope disastrously across the bomber's empennage - dooming both entwined vessels instantly.

Despite having narrowly dodged calamity seconds earlier, a hellish gust broadsided the lead bomber once more as it churned blindly through a veil of clouds. Engines howling, the bomber had no chance to maneuver when the craggy gorge cliffs sheered abruptly into lethal view dead ahead.

Pilots Briggs and Petty shouted in vain as the aircraft's crippled wing was brutally embedded into the cliff face at over 280 kilometers per hour. The rending impact detonated fuel stores and munitions in an explosive fireball, vaporizing the cockpit and fuselage instantaneously.

Behind, the towed lead glider smashed horrifically through the spreading debris field of its disintegrated anchor vessel. Buffeted mercilessly, the glider spiraled at terminal velocity completely out of its pilot's control to smash and splinter across the unforgiving mountain slope. Screams echoed amidst the choking black plumes until only silence clung to the frigid Norwegian peaks.

Fiery debris rained down hundreds of feet to the meadow below. Elsa and Culper stared agape in voiceless horror as their eyes misted at the unfolding tragedy.

"My God…" whispered Culper.

In the second aircraft, silence hung bitterly over the static-laden intercom in the cockpit still navigating the deadly Norwegian corridor in the crash's pall.

Croft rubbed reddened eyes hard, emotion solidifying into resignation on his unshaven face.

"Carter, tell the glider pilots we're aborting the landing and heading back to base," he said harshly.

His co-pilot acquiesced quietly, calling the glider on the radio and giving them the news.

Croft searched for clear air to turn both bomber and glider around. The space between the mountains was tight but he was sure he could execute the turn.

As the storm continued pressing in, pilot Croft

banked tightly to reverse their escape course, straining engines and tow rope. Gusting winds sheared treacherously between ridges, lashing the glider violently behind despite its pilots' desperate maneuvers to keep the bucking vessel on an even keel.

Without warning, the over-torqued rope tether snapped with a rifle-like crack, sending the powerless glider plunging with all souls helpless against gravity.

Suddenly unleashed, the bomber pilots struggled to keep their aircraft from smashing into the mountain peaks. There was nothing they could do with the glider released. Croft continued his turn and headed back to Scotland.

On the ground, Culper and Elsa watched as the brave glider pilots angled their aircraft's wings one last time, clearly intending to land his crew and passengers back at the original strip in the meadow with skill and providence.

Nearly reaching safe earth intact, an especially vicious downdraft battered the fragile glider at the final moment. The young aviators inside strove in vain to gain altitude with the jagged pines shearing towards them. The glider slammed into trees below the meadow shredding its wooden wings and fuselage. CRACKING wood echoed across the valley as the glider was torn into dozens of pieces by the forest.

Bolting recklessly toward the crash, Elsa and Culper rushed to the shattered fuselage praying for survivors. Instead finding only broken bodies in the wreckage, they could only bow their heads against the disaster.

"We should bury them," said Elsa.

Culper shook his head. "Ground's too hard and we don't have the time. Snow will cover them for now." said Culper.

"The wolves get them."

"The wolves will get them even if we bury them."

"We can't just leave them."

"Yes, we can. The Germans will be coming soon. They'll be expecting to find bodies. If we dig graves, it may raise suspicions."

Hot tears mingled with the sleeting snow on Elsa's cheeks as she considered the loved ones these men left behind.

"You can be a callous bastard sometimes."

"Yeah. I know. We need to recover as many supplies as possible, especially explosives. We don't have much time."

Culper and Elsa moved through the glider wreckage and mangled bodies of the engineers, recovering supplies. They retrieved explosives, ammunition, and mountaineering gear intact enough to carry onward. Working swiftly as the snowfall thickened, they loaded functional items efficiently into their packs without speaking. The mountain storm pressed heavier around them, driving their efforts more than any need to voice the tragedy before them.

Culper passed Elsa a satchel of timed detonators, mercifully protected inside waterproof pouches that kept snowmelt from penetrating. She saw his jaw clench with anger and frustration as he shifted debris aside, uncovering the shattered transmitter array vital for coordinating their impending strike.

In the distance, Culper heard voices shouting in German above the howling wind. Elsa spotted the beams of the soldiers' flashlights illuminating the cliff where the glider had crashed.

"They're here," said Elsa.

"That was fast," said Culper. "We'd better move."

"We're leaving most of the explosives and gear."

"We can't carry it away. We'll just have to make do with what we have salvaged."

"Maybe we could bury what we can't carry and come back."

"No. Too risky. Let's go."

In addition to the pack already on his back, Culper slung two full packs over his shoulders while Elsa cradled an unwieldy second pack awkwardly across her slender frame. Rising breathless under her double load, Elsa followed Culper's wordless beckon towards the alpine tree line to slip behind sheltering evergreens out of the probing illumination.

As they left the smoldering wreckage behind, Culper and Elsa were careful to cover their tracks. They paused every few meters to brush away their boot prints with pine boughs, erasing any trace of their passage. Where the snow was too deep to effectively sweep, they took turns retracing their steps, one walking backward in the other's footprints to create a confusing and misleading trail. It was a painstaking process, but one they knew was necessary to keep their movements hidden from any prying eyes. With each step, they put more distance between themselves and the crash site. The saboteurs moved as phantom shadows fleeing the harsh roar of a Wehrmacht recovery squad swarming locust-like to pick the corpses already stiffening under blankets of white.

Entering the ridgeline, Culper and Elsa stopped to watch the Germans and make sure they weren't being followed. Satisfied, Culper gave Elsa a nod and they set off again. Icy fingers of sleet needled their cheeks.

Clear of the crash site and climbing past the next ridge, Culper and Elsa came upon the Sheppard's cabin hidden in the trees. Although she said nothing, Culper could see Elsa's eyes begging for respite.

"We should be safe here as long as the storm continues," said Culper.

The single dark room offered relief from the elements. They stacked their packs in the corner. Culper swept snow off a pile of cut timber to start a humble fire within the small stone hearth, while Elsa lit a single thick tallow candle found on the rough-hewn mantel.

Without asking, Elsa searched until she found a kettle. It was empty. She stepped outside, broke off several ice cycles from the roof, and filled the kettle. Closing the door, she moved to the fire and placed the kettle on an iron hook. Moving to her pack, she retrieved a small pouch of coffee grinds.

"You're prepared. I'll give you that," said Culper.

"Damned tooting," said Elsa pouring the grinds into two tin cups.

Five minutes later, the sipping the hot liquid as they watched the fire.

"I'm sorry you had to see that," said Culper.

"Why sorry? It wasn't your doing."

"When it comes to you, it's all my doing."

"You act like I didn't have a say."

"You're right. It was your choice, but still…"

"I still feel I made the right decision in coming here."

"You're making a difference. That's important."

"Are you hungry?"

"Yeah. I've got some dried venison in my pack."

"Oh, you poor man."

Elsa went back to her pack and fished out a bundle. She set it between her and Culper and opened it to reveal aged Gudbrandsdalen cheese wrapped in soft birch bark accompanied with crusty oat bread and pungent cloudberry jam. Culper raised an impressed eyebrow at the spread as she opened a jar of buttery fjord trout in brine.

"Now you're just showing off," said Culper.

They ate like Vikings stuffing their faces. When the last morsels were gone, Elsa once again returned to her pack and drew out small bars wrapped in crinkling silver foil.

"For desert... chocolate," she explained with a sly grin as she broke him off a bittersweet block. "My own concoction - powdered cocoa and roasted almond chunks fused with crystallized pineapple juice, then set firm."

"When did you find time to make this?"

"A little here, a little there."

Culper gamely bit into the exotic confection. Unable to restrain a satisfied groan as the intense flavors jolted his senses awake despite frozen numbness setting into limbs, he had to admit Elsa's creation far outshone his venison jerky.

Stuffed beyond capacity, Culper laid down in front of the fire and belched.

Elsa laughed and said, "Rude, crude, and socially unacceptable."

"That's me," said Culper.

Like an afterthought, Elsa laid down next to him to share their bodies' warmth. Culper offered his arm as a pillow. She laid her head on it. Relaxed her mind wandered, then she said, "Do we have enough explosives to destroy the heavy water plant?"

"No," said Culper. "But we'll do what we can to slow the German's progress."

"It feels like we're falling short."

"We are. That damned fortified mountain plant...the krauts will have repairs underway well before we reach Sweden. But there's not much we can do about it."

Elsa closed her eyes as tears welled up and rolled down the side of her face. Everything they had risked and in the end they had failed.

"I'm sorry, Culper."

"For what? You gave it everything you had. I couldn't ask for more than that."

"It wasn't enough."

"It's not over yet. We have to leave room for miracles."

"You believe in miracles?"

"I believe that anything can happen when you least expect it – good or bad."

"So, what do you do?"

"Adapt to the situation and hope for the best."

"I don't think hoping for the best is going to stop Hitler."

"Like I say... you never know."

"What do you know?"

"We're right and he's wrong."

"I'm sorry. I'm fading. I can't keep my eyes open any longer."

"Then don't," said Culper as he leaned in and kissed her on the forehead.

Elsa looked up and saw a slight smile. She reached up and pulled him closer, kissing him deeply on the lips. He didn't seem to mind.

The next morning, Elsa stirred, blinking slowly as diffused light filtered through grimy cabin windows. She realized Culper no longer lay beside the fading embers in the crude fireplace. Massaging warmth back into her stiff limbs, she hurried to slip on her boots.

Stepping outside, Elsa was relieved to find only gentle snowflakes drifting around the silent peaks. The storms had passed. Scanning for some sign of Culper, she spotted fresh boot prints circling the back of the remote shelter. Following them around the rustic structure, she spied Culper bent intently over a battered wooden sled, twisting torn canvass around a splintered runner.

Hearing Elsa's boots crunch through the crisp outer layer, Culper glanced up. "Shepherd must've abandoned it," he said. "If I can fix it, we won't need to carry the packs."

"You didn't happen to find a team of dogs with it?"

"We're the dogs. But trust me, that'll be a lot better that carrying the packs."

"I'll make us some coffee."

"No. The storm has passed. No fire. The Germans could spot the smoke."

"Right. Then I guess I'll pack everything up."

"Good idea. We should get moving as soon as possible."

Elsa walked back to the cabin. She felt hurt that Culper hadn't mentioned their time together the previous night. But she also understood. Culper was Culper and the mission would always come first.

After lashing the packs securely to the salvaged wooden sled, Culper dusted ice crystals from his gloves. "Right then, up you go," he directed Elsa towards the sled's splintered seat.

"I can help you push the sled," protested Elsa.

"No need. It's downhill most of the way. Gravity will go all the work."

"At least let me help you get it started."

"Fine."

With a resigned sigh, Elsa bent to help shove off, boots digging deep into the powder. The sled scraped forward slowly at first before momentum took over. As their speed built, Culper waved Elsa firmly into the seat. She clambered aboard as icy spray needled her cheeks when the sled lurched over deeper ruts. Teeth gritted against the frigid turbulence, Elsa felt gravity now hurry them onward through the silent alpine sentinels. As the sled gathered momentum, Elsa felt her apprehension give way to awe at their velocity. Culper placed his boots on the back of the runners. Frigid air streamed over her grinning face as Culper deftly banked them along the mountain corridor. She marveled at his skill directing their primitive craft over and around wind-scoured obstacles littering their plunge.

When they hit an icy straightaway, their speed intensified into a thrilling torrent, the sled's rear spraying a comet tail of crystalline flakes. Adrenaline flooding her veins, Elsa shouted exuberantly into the icy bombardment needling her cheeks. For these glorious moments, she transcended her constant anxiety and replaced it with childlike euphoria.

Her spirit soared wildly free of dread and doubt to carve this bright memory under Nature's indifferent gaze. Elsa knew their desperate trial still lay ahead...but for now, she let her hair loose as their wooden vessel raced fluidly along the snowscape - no threats visible across her momentary field of vision save the beckoning valley terminus rushing up fast to meet their skipping craft.

It was in those unburdened moments that scientific formulas flashed before her eyes. Like Culper's missions, it was science that was her first love. As she considered the formulas for heavy water production, she remembered its beginnings at Norsk and her expression turned serious.

Elsa turned to Culper and said, "Culper, I think I know how to destroy the heavy water plant."

"I told you, we don't have enough explosives to complete the mission," said Culper.

"Actually… I think we do."

"What do you mean?"

"Heavy water is not all that is produced at Norsk. Before being transformed into a heavy water production facility, Norsk was used to produce chemicals that required a lot of energy to make. It's primary output was commercial fertilizer using ammonium nitrate."

Culper's attention peaked at hearing the name of the chemical and he said, "Do you think there is any still in storage?"

"Yeah, tons of the stuff. They still make the fertilizer at Norsk using excess power from the hydroelectric plant then transport it to Germany to support their war effort."

Culper's eyes narrowed. "You propose a blast using their own chemicals?"

"Ammonium nitrate oxidizers...combined with diesel fuel scavenged from the railway tankers..." Elsa muttered, visualizing a catalyst cascade. "It yields an order of magnitude of energy more than TNT if properly triggered."

"If we can take out the hydroelectric plant production of heavy water will go dark."

"You're thinking too small, Culper. If we compress the explosion, we can take out the entire production and research facility. It'll take the Germans months or even years to repair it."

"How can we compress it?"

"The armored train coach they use to transport the heavy water from the facility to Lake Tinn, have they replaced it yet?"

"Yes. It's in the rail depot in Telemark. You want to hijack it?"

"If we can… yeah. Is it possible?"

"Yeah, it's possible if we have help."

"The resistance fighters?"

"Exactly."

"How many are there?"

"About forty-five in Telemark."

"What about Oslo?"

"A lot more, but if we start moving rebels around the SS is going to get suspicious. We're better off just using the fighters from Telemark. They should be enough."

"Is this the miracle you were hoping for?"

"It's risky, but maybe… It would be one helluva thing if we pull it off."

"Anything's possible, right?"

"Right."

Ice Wall

As Elsa and Culper topped the ridge, Telemark emerged hazily in the distance below. The town nestled in the far valley like a cluster of toy blocks and dominoes scattered at the feet of an indifferent giant. Even at that distance, Culper could see the SS patrols and checkpoints throughout the small city. On the edge was a concrete barracks squatted defensively next to SS headquarters. "We'll wait until dark before going into town," said Culper.

Night's shadows shielded their approach as Elsa and Culper circumnavigated Telemark's snowy perimeter, avoiding ruthlessly lit main boulevards with their checkpoints and patrols. Hugging shadowed alley walls with their supply sled in tow, Elsa and Culper wound through the silent neighborhoods. Turning a tight corner onto the Ingvaldsen Bakery alley, raucous laughter and boots suddenly echoed from the adjacent crossing street. As SS Squad flashlights strafed storefronts just meters away, Culper yanked the laden sled sideways behind two trash bins, pulling trash and snowy cardboard over the bulging tarp while waving frantically for Elsa to hide herself.

Straining to breathe silently, Elsa listened as echoing boot scrapes halted ominously at the dark alley's mouth. She reeled as torch beams pinned her near the incriminating sled. She backed up knocking over an empty vegetable crate with a loud clatter.

"Who hides there?" came the sharp demand. Elsa froze. Culper unzipped his fatigues, stumbling from behind the bins fastening his pants in an embarrassed rush.

"Apologies, Corporal, just taking a quick leak after one too many beers," Culper stammered as if drunk.

"Watch yourself, sot!" The harsh flashlight beam lingered skeptically on Culper's tousled state before swinging to probe the bins again. Elsa hardly dared move a muscle as beam of light washed inches from her face. After an eternity, the young soldier just scoffed in disgust about drunkards before boots echoed away in the frigid air.

Once clear of the patrol, Elsa and Culper finished their journey, knocking on the bakery's delivery door in the alleyway. Alf answered opening the door.

"You're still alive," said Alf with a grin. "That's good. We were beginning to wonder."

"We need to unload this sled and store the packs someplace safe," said Culper.

"My boys will take care of it. You two get inside. I'll put on a fresh pot of coffee and fetch you some warm pastries from the cooling trays."

"That sounds heavenly," said Elsa pushing past Culper.

"At least you know what you want," said Culper

chiding her.

Culper studied the bakery cellar's rough stone walls in the dim lantern light. Around the table with explosive components spread before them sat Johannes and two other lean members of his underground rebel cell, faces etched with harsh wisdom won raiding Nazi supply lines through Norway's long shadows the past year. Elsa stood by Culper's side.

"I know it's asking a lot and that many of your men could become casualties, but the stakes have never been higher," said Culper. "If we don't destroy the heavy water production plant, the Nazis could very well beat America in the race to develop the atomic bomb. If that happens, there will be no stopping Hitler. Millions could die and fascism will sweep the planet. With that kind of power in his hands, he'll finally have his thousand-year Reich."

"My men are not afraid of dying for the right cause. How sure are you that you can destroy Norsk?" said Johannes.

"I'll be honest… I think the odds are fifty-fifty that we succeed."

"The bomb will work. I'm sure of it," said Elsa.

"Getting it to the heart of the production facility is the problem," said Culper. "There is an entire brigade of SS troops protecting Norsk. We'll be massively outnumbered. If we can get the armored rail car inside the tunnel before the main force counterattacks, I think our odds greatly increase."

"Then let's make damned sure that happens," said Johannes.

"We're gonna need a few of your men to help load the fertilizer once we reach the storage compartment."

"What about the diesel fuel?"

"It will already have been on board at that point."

"Alright."

"How long will it take to gather your men?"

"About four hours. Most are here in town, but a few live in the countryside."

"We need all we can get."

"We'll be ready."

"The longer we wait, the more chance we have of being discovered."

"I agree. We should move quickly."

"Good. Then we attack tomorrow evening."

"Okay. We should solidify your plans."

"Our plans."

"Fine. Our plans."

"What you and your men are doing is incredibly brave," said Elsa.

"It's our country that the Nazis occupy. A patriot has little choice but to fight when the time is right."

"You'll never find a more important cause than this."

"I thought you were a pacifist."

"I am, but when peaceful means and logic fail, even pacifists must make a stand against the development of atomic weapons that could destroy mankind."

"Is there no judgment between good and evil in your philosophy?"

"I didn't used to think so. Now, I'm not so sure. Don't get me wrong. I still believe peace and non-violence are the only ways to save the human race from itself. But we may need to root out the rotten wood before that can happen."

As the rebel fighters gathered Alf started a fire in one

of the old ovens kept in the bakery's basement. Exhausted from her journey, Elsa curled up beside the fire. Culper moved up beside her and said, "Are you okay?"

"Yes, just tired."

"You should get some sleep. Tomorrow will be a long day."

"And what about you?"

"I'm trained to operate without sleep."

"Baloney. You know you'll fight better if you're rested."

Culper sat down beside her. "Maybe you're right."

"You know I'm right."

"Okay. You're right. Happy?"

"Somewhat."

Elsa considered for a moment, then… "So, we're not going to talk about last night?"

"What's to talk about? It happened and it was great. End of story."

"End of story… really?"

"Elsa, in less than twenty-four hours we'll be fighting for our lives. One or both of us will probably be killed. Do you really think this is the best time to discuss our future?"

"Yeah, I mean… I'd like to know what you're feeling before it's too late."

"I don't know what I'm feeling. I'm a bit distracted if you know what I mean."

"That's an excuse… although a good one."

"Okay. If it helps… I feel good about us."

Elsa smiled. "Really?"

"Yeah, really."

"Me too."

"I've got to get back to work. There is a lot that still

needs to be done."

"Do you need my help?"

"Not at the moment, but I'll wake you if I do."

"Okay. Can I at least have a kiss?"

Culper looked around. Everyone seemed busy. He leaned over and kissed her on the top of her head.

"That was a lousy kiss."

"I'm saving up for later."

"I like the sound of that."

"Go to sleep."

Elsa curled up in a ball and closed her eyes as Culper went back to plan the attack with Johannes.

"Any idea where they keep the armored train carriage?" said Culper.

"In a depot just outside of Telemark. It's guarded by twelve to fourteen SS troops to prevent sabotage."

"Good to know. Where can we find a locomotive?"

"There too, along with a diesel fuel storage tank."

"We'll need barrels to store the fuel."

"How many?"

"Forty should do."

"That's a lot of fuel."

"We need a big explosion."

"Okay. There's not much time, but I'll see to it."

"We'll need all your satchel charges to act as a detonator."

"I assumed such. We'll bring them."

"Do you have enough weapons for your men?"

"Yes, but some are obsolete."

"There will be plenty of weapons available from the fallen once the assault starts."

"True. My men understand how to rearm themselves."

"I think our biggest challenge will be securing the

armored coach and the locomotive without alerting the SS. We must capture the depot without firing a shot."

"I agree it will be difficult. But not impossible. My men are guerilla fighters. They know how to keep quiet."

"I hope so. If the SS are alerted and are able to reinforce their defensive positions on the mountain before we arrive, we're gonna have one helluva fight getting into Norsk."

"I suppose some prayers wouldn't be out of the question."

"Bring everything you have to the fight, Johannes. Don't hold back anything in reserve."

"You sound like a man who expects to lose."

"No. I don't believe in suicide missions. We can win this battle, but only if we are fully committed."

"Stop worrying, Culper. We will be."

Culper nodded somberly. "You know I understand your sacrifices."

"We're not doing this for you, Culper. We're doing it for Norway."

"…and the world."

"Yes… and the world."

In the darkened corner of the bakery's storage room, a local printer, Harald hunched intently over a cramped desk wedged near storage shelves and sacks of flour. He adjusted his smudged spectacles beneath the single dangling bulb, scrutinizing the stolen German dispatch record. Meticulously he altered the originator field to "SS-Standartenführer Otto Bauer" using official stamps and Gothic typeset from the false-bottom briefcase at his elbow.

Years setting wedding invitations and society

bulletins attuned an eye now equally useful forging orders sanctioning arms or contraband under the Reich's imposing banners.

As the night stretched on, Harald carefully penned a command for forty empty fuel barrels to be delivered to the train depot by truck - a plausible logistics adjustment from Bauer's staff. When the false inventory order was completed, Harald passed the fabricated document to Johannes's hands for inspection.

"Good work, Harald," said Johannes. "This should do nicely."

As the filtered sun slid behind the great mountains surrounding Telemark, the rebel force gathered in the basement of the bakery. Johannes stood before them with a submachine gun in his hand and said, "For our homes… for our families… for Norway!"

The fighters held their rifles and shouted, "…for Norway!"

Grabbing their backpacks filled with satchel charges, ammunition, and winter mountaineering gear, they filed out of the basement and through the side delivery door. Checking that there were no SS patrols in the area, the fighters traveled in the shadows as they made their way through the side streets of the Telemark.

Under the scarce moonlight, the Reich train depot sprawled before the rebels as a mechanized hive illuminated by towering flood lamps seated atop a guard tower. Squat concrete buildings and giant cylindrical fuel tanks hunkered inside rings of chain link fencing topped with spirals of barbed wire.

Shadowy figures of patrolling guards crisscrossed the open yards between stationary trains, their dogs and cigarette cherries tracing random trajectories between snowbanks. Further out, the greater vacant darkness hinted at maintenance and oil dumping pits tucked discreetly into the pine forest slope.

The rumble of an approaching cargo bed truck startled the watch officer from his thermos. He blinked at the ID papers of the ill-kempt driver whose aged Norwegian face hardly matched Aryan ideals. "What brings you here this late, old timer?"

"Forty fuel barrels, sirs - special depot transfer order. I was told to rush 'em for your tanker loading by a Colonel Bauers." He offered the crumpled dispatch record awaiting clipboard approval.

The officer scanned the unfamiliar form skeptically. "Bauers you say? Standartenführer Bauer handles hydro munitions, not Oberst Bowers..." Still, the stamp and letterhead seemed sufficiently official to avoid his hassle. He continued reading with a dismissive sigh.

"Where is your labor detainee accompaniment to unload the drums?" He peered annoyed behind the second truck. "We've no depot hands at this time of night!"

The driver shrugged innocently. "Had me own lads, sir, but one's caught fever pretty fierce...right contagious still." He extended his rough palms plaintively. "We're due back to Oslo daybreak tomorrow! Maybe your boys could lend some backs to unload my haul?"

Casting an exasperated glance at his teenage corporal drinking surreptitiously by the gatehouse, the lieutenant rolled his eyes waving them inside. "Very well. Franz, grab Metzger. You're conscripted for freight duty!"

The SS soldiers reluctantly stepped onto the trucks' running boards and rode the vehicles into the depot leaving the lieutenant alone to guard the main gate.

The trucks backed up to the loading dock by the diesel storage area. Franz and the corporal hauled themselves wearily from the cab to begin wrestling the unwieldy metal drums placing them on the dock. The drivers of the trucks stood and watched ignoring the protests of the SS soldiers with shrugs of not understanding German.

As the guards rolled the first few containers onto the dock with loud clangs, the old driver wandered between parked wagons, keeping eyes casually diverted. "Hey, where are you going?" said the Corporal jumping down from the dock.

"Just checking the front wheel of my truck. Something felt amiss," said the old driver.

The second driver jumped up on the dock and pulled out a flask from his coat pocket taking a swig then offering it to Metzger. As Metzger took a drink, the driver strategically placed himself between the back of the truck and the SS soldier preventing his view as four rebels soundlessly emerged from empty drums and slipped down off the truck and disappeared deep into the depot without notice.

The four sappers split up – two heading toward the depot's radio tower and two towards the guard tower near the forest's edge.

While one sapper kept watch, the second sapper carefully climbed the ladder to the lookout tower. When he reached the top, he peeked over the side and saw the guard lighting a cigarette with his rifle leaning up against the wooden rail easily within his reach. The sapper waited until the guard turned his back, then silently climbed the ladder's last rungs. With the guard's back still turned the sapper slipped a garrot around the guard's throat as he put his knee in the man's back. As the wire snapped tight, the guard was unable to call for help. He reached for his rifle. The sapper pulled the wire tighter until he heard a CRACK and the guard went limp. He lowered the dead soldier to the floor of the tower, grabbed his helmet and rifle, and took his place as if keeping watch over the depot.

The other two sappers moved silently across the depot to the radio tower and communications bunker. There was one SS guard standing at the entrance to the bunker. One sapper diverted the guard's attention by simply walking toward him out of the darkness, while the other sapper slipped up behind him using his knife to dispatch the guard without any sound beyond a gurgle.

With the guard dead, a sapper moves through the bunker entrance while the other keeps watch outside. The radio operator has his back to the door as he fiddles with the knobs. The sapper uses the butt of his pistol to knock the operator out of his seat, then uses his knife to silence him permanently.

Knowing exactly which were the key components, the sapper removes several hot tubes from the back of the transmitter. For added measure, he takes out his knife and trashes the inside of the transmitter cutting wires and severing connections making the transmitter useless even with replacement tubes.

As he emerges from the bunker, he uses his red lens flashlight to signal the sapper on the watch tower that the radio has been silenced. The sapper on the tower signals Johannes outside the perimeter in return.

With only the lieutenant guarding the main gate, a large and muscular man in civilian clothes appeared out of the darkness and advanced toward the gate. In his hands were a pair of Viking bearded hand axes. Seeing the man and his battle axes, the lieutenant raised his hand and shouted, "Halt!"

The Norwegian hulk kept his pace closing the distance between them as the lieutenant reached for his sidearm.

Without warning the Norwegian raised the two Skeggox and hurled them thirty feet through the night air. Both axe heads landed in the lieutenant with such force he was knocked of his feet and skidded across the ground. With his face filled with shock and unable to catch his breath, he died.

From behind the axe thrower, the remaining rebel force along with Johannes, Culper, and Elsa appeared from the darkness and jogged toward the main gate now opened by the axe thrower. As they entered the depot, they fanned out, each man knowing his assignment and where to go.

Within five minutes, the rest of the guards within the depot including the two by the loading dock were silenced without a shot being fired. Culper's plan was working, but the rebels were not out of the woods yet. The still needed to reach the mountainside facility before the SS discovered their assault.

Culper and Ivar, a rebel train engineer climbed aboard one of the engines in the yard. Ivar gripped the frigid metal controls, flipping switches to build electrical pressure waking the dormant diesel from idle.

The output gauge twitched as current flowed into the enormous engine block. Starter drive engaged, Ivar dialed up the RPMs, fuel injectors pulsing as pistons churned.

At last, he eased the mechanism forward along with its fuel tender car. Connecting rods transferred force down the driveshaft slowly churning immense steel wheels beneath. Generating traction against the icy rails using sand pipes, Ivar rumbled the vessel further through the freight platforms like a stretching feline.

Culper hopped off the locomotive and ran forward to a track switch. He threw the switch allowing the locomotive to switch to another track leading to the carriage storage yard.

Nearing a line of carriages, Culper aligned the coupler and brake lines on the back of the fuel tender car before Ivar reversed the locomotive, locking both buffer frames. The empty passenger wagon settled coupled onto the fuel tender behind the rumbling locomotive. Ivar throttled up again, maneuvering the train to the armored transport carriage beyond which they joined with a secure pneumatic hiss before lurching the now combined train wide along the loading rails towards the main yard.

Ivar slowed the train and stopped next to the loading dock. The rebels loaded the half empty diesel drums into the armored car and closed the steel door. As the rebels piled into the passenger wagon taking up defensive positions at the windows an SS guard thought dead awoke. Seeing the rebels climbing into the passenger car, he aimed his rifle and fired. A rebel was hit in the back and fell off the passenger car into the rough gravel below. The rebels around their wounded comrade fired their weapons killing the

German.

"Shit," said Culper knowing that they would soon be discovered. "Ivar, get this hunk of steel moving!"

Hearing the guns shots coming from the rail depot, the SS commander called the depot communications bunker on the radio. Receiving no response, he ordered a squad to investigate.

Led by their sergeant, the soldiers sprinted from their barracks and jumped into two trucks. At the head of the small convoy was a lieutenant riding in the turret of an eight-wheeled Schwerer Panzerspähwagen armed with an autocannon. The armored car sped towards the train depot's main gate followed by the trucks.

Ivar increased the speed of the slowly moving train as much as he dared. Too much and the engine could stall. Culper hung out the side of the locomotive searching the path in front of them for any signs of Germans. As the train picked up speed and approached the main gate, the armored car and trucks appeared.

"Dammit," said Culper.

Seeing the armored car blocking the tracks, Ivar cut the engine and applied the brakes.

"No," shouted Culper. "Keep going."

Ivar released the brakes and increased the speed of the engine, racing directly toward the armored car.

The lieutenant in the turret swung the autocannon's barrel around and took aim at the locomotive heading straight toward him. Before he could fire his weapon, the engine slammed into the armored car driving the gun barrel into the turret, killing the lieutenant.

The two trucks moved out of the way of the train.

SS troops piled out of the trucks and opened fire on the train.

Inside the passenger train car, the rebels returned fire through the windows. Few on either side were hit as the train passed through the main gate. Instead of heading straight for the mountain fortress, the tracks took the train in the opposite direction. Once clear of the rail switch, Ivar stopped the train while Culper jumped off and switched the track. Ivar put the train in reverse and headed toward the mountain backwards with the armored carriage leading. Culper jumped back on as the train passed.

The SS sergeant radioed the SS commander and reported what had happened. The commander ordered the troops to pursue the train and stop it before it reached Norsk. He barked out additional orders to his staff to send all available units to Norsk. SS soldiers piled out of the barracks and climbed into trucks. Nearly half the brigade raced up the mountain attempting to head off the train.

With the mountain slope steepening, the engine groaned under the strain and the train slowed. The railway turned to switchbacks which decreased the slope but lengthened the journey to Norsk while the troop trucks were able to take a more direct route and gain on the train. Half-tracks, armored cars, and trucks towing artillery followed the troop trucks up the mountain road.

The night sky darkened as thick clouds moved in shrouding the mountain facility. A storm was coming, and the temperature quickly dropped.

Ivar peered ahead through gloom barely pierced by control stand lights, nursing the stolen juggernaut onward into the frigid night.

A pair of Volkswagen Kubelwagens armed with MG-42 machine guns, nicknamed "bone saws," passed the lead troop truck and sped up the mountain. As the train emerged from a switchback and hit a straightaway, the two staff cars pulled alongside on a parallel road and opened fire strafing the train. The rebels ducked down as the passenger car windows were shattered. When the bullets stopped as the Germans reloaded, the repels rose from cover and returned fire. The barrage slammed into the lead Kubelwagen killed the gunner and puncturing the front tire. The flat tire folded under and jammed into the vehicle's wheel well. Unable to control the car, the driver shielded himself as the car swung sideways and toppled over multiple times on the road. The driver in the following car slammed on his brakes, but it was too late. The following car slammed head-on into the lead car in a horrific crash killing everyone and leaving a pile of mangled metal in the middle of the road. The troops trucks were forced to stop when they reached the wreckage. The sergeant yelled for the troops to clear the road. Troops jumped out of the trucks and moved toward the wreckage just as the gas tank in the lead vehicle exploded engulfing both vehicles in an inferno. The troops were driven back. Grabbing shovels from the trucks, they threw snow and frozen soil on the burning vehicles to extinguish the flames. A long line of trucks and vehicles stalled on the road as the train sped ahead up the mountain.

Informed of the impending assault, Colonel Bauer stood next to the rail tracks leading into Norsk. Hundreds of SS troops formed defensive positions around the entry point. To ensure that the rebels failed at entering the facility, Bauer ordered two sections of track to be removed from the railway. It only took the SS troops a few minutes to sabotage their own railway. Once the train had been derailed, the SS troops would be free to slaughter the rebels onboard.

Knudsen, still nursing his wounded shoulder, moved up beside Bauer and said, "Are you sure this will work?"

Bauer, annoyed, replied, "Director, you stick to the research and production. I will handle security."

"That's fine, Colonel. But don't forget the importance of this facility to the war effort. I am sure the führer won't."

"I have always aligned my actions with the führer's interests. It is yours that he will question when all of this done."

"What do you mean, Colonel?"

"Your affair with Dr. Aadland did not escape my purview. Now that she has been exposed as a traitor, I am sure the führer will have questions that you will need to answer."

"That's ridiculous. How could I have known? She fooled you as much as she did me."

"You actually believe that?"

"Of course. You were in charge of security, not I."

"What secrets did you whisper to her while sharing a pillow?"

"Nothing. I shared nothing."

"We will see. The truth always seeps out under the right type of interrogation."

Incensed, Knutsen marched off in a huff leaving Bauer to supervise the defenses.

On the mountain road below, the SS troops finally

cleared the roadway by pushing the wrecked staff cars over the side of the roadway. Climbing back into the trucks, the convoy resumed its pursuit.

As the train entered the last stretch before reaching the Norsk facility, Culper watched out the side of the locomotive and saw the massive blockade created by the SS troops.

"Push the engine to its limit, Ivar. We're only going to get one chance at this," said Culper.

"It's already at full power," said Ivar.

"Then keep your head down. This is gonna be bloody."

Culper took one last look at the tracks ahead before the train came within range and the SS opened fire.

"Oh, shit!" said Culper in a panic as he saw the missing rails. "They've torn up the track!"

Ivar slammed on the brakes. Sparks flew as the steel wheels on the engine locked. It didn't take long for the train to come to a complete stop.

Bauer watched as the train came to a complete stop just out of range. On the road below, he saw the SS troop convoy round a corner and head up the mountain. At their current speed, they would reach the train within a couple of minutes. There was no need to risk the lives of his men. He would protect the facility and let the Telemark SS take the lead in killing the rebels.

Elsa peeked out the side of the locomotive and discovered another set of tracks. She looked at the track behind the train and saw a rail switch. "Culper, look," she yelled pointing at the parallel tracks.

Culper rushed to her side, looked back at the switch,

and said, "Stay low and close to the engine. That's where the steel is thickest."

Elsa nodded. Culper turned to Ivar and said, "Take the train back twenty yards and wait for my signal." Ivar pushed the reverse handle to forward and the locomotive pulled the train back down the mountain as Culper jumped out the engine and ran toward the track switch.

Curious as to what the rebels were planning, Bauer moved to the opposite side of the blockade to get a view of the train's right side. He saw Culper running toward the rail switch and realized what he was doing. He shouted for his men to open fire, then gave orders for the parallel tracks to be pried loose. Grabbing sledgehammers and picks, a team of SS rushed toward the parallel tracks and went to work loosening them.

Reaching the switch under fire, Culper shot off the lock. He waited until Ivar drove the train beyond the rail junction, then swung the lever switching the rails to the parallel tracks. He signaled Ivar to get the train moving backward again. Culper turned to see the SS troops attempting to pry the rails on the parallel track loose. He opened fire with his submachine gun, killing one of the troops and sending the others for cover.

As the train entered the parallel junction, Culper climbed on the engine once more.

The Germans scrambled to pry the tracks loose as the locomotive and cars approached. Bauer ordered his soldiers to block the track with railroad ties. The soldier threw the blocks of oiled woods across the rails to jam the armored carriage's wheels. The soldiers manning the blockade fired at the train as it picked up speed.

With the engines controls pegged to maximum speed, Culper, Elsa, and Ivar hid behind the engine cab's iron sides as bullets ricocheted off the thick panels. Shots smashed the glass on the engine's dials on the control panel. Culper didn't bother returning fire. He knew he would need his ammunition later if they made it to the tunnel.

The soldier prying the rails loose jumped out of the way as the train sped by them. They dove for cover as their own troops fired at the train just missing them.

Smashing through the blockade, the juggernaut continued toward the tunnel. The railroad ties on the rails were easily pushed out of the way by the armored carriage's thick steel panels that shielded its wheels.

The reinforcements from Telemark arrived as the train breached the blockade. The SS troops sprang from the trucks and took up positions joining their comrades firing at the train.

The rebels in the passenger car laid as flat as possible as hundreds of German bullets punched through the car's thin metal panels. Several rebels were wounded and two killed as the train ran the gauntlet of rifle and machine gun fire.

An SS grenadier used a Panzerwurfkorper 42 to launch a HEAT grenade at the armored train car as it passed. The egg-shaped grenade slammed into the armored panels and exploded in huge ball of fire. While it dented the panel it did not penetrate the thick steel plates protecting the diesel drums inside.

Once past the blockade, the parallel tracks converged back into the main track. The locomotive sped toward the tunnel opening, then disappeared inside the abyss with bullets bouncing off the front of the locomotive. The rebels cheered. But the battle was far from over.

Ivar slowed the train allowing the rebels to

disembark taking their wounded with them. Under Johannes's command the rebels took up defensive position inside the tunnel using whatever they could find for cover – anything that could stop a bullet or shrapnel. Once satisfied the rebels were protected as much as possible, Johannes turned off the lights in the tunnel making the rebels poor targets for the German guns.

Deeper in the tunnel, Elsa pointed to a rail junction up head and said pointing, "The fertilizer storage chambers are that way."

Culper jumped out of the engine and pulled a switch allowing Ivar to push the train onto another sidetrack. The locomotive pushed the armored carriage deeper into the side tunnel.

Outside the tunnel entrance, the Germans constructed another blockade, now ten times as many troops, artillery, armored cars, and half-tracks. It was an imposing barricade that the rebels stood little chance of breaking through.

Following Elsa's directions, Ivar pushed the train down an old tunnel spur towards the chemical production area. He braked the engine to a halt by the loading bays as planned.

Culper swiftly forced open doors to long storage rooms packed wall-to-wall with fertilizer bags. He, Elsa, and the rebels hauled bags of ammonium nitrate fertilizer out of the storage vault and into the armored carriage. They sliced bags open and poured crisp orange crystals into the half-empty diesel drums on board, then used rifle stocks to thoroughly mix the ingredients in each improvised explosive container before resealing the volatile slurry within.

Culper opened the pour-spouts on the lids and lowered a detonator into each drum, then connected the detonators' lead wires to a timer.

Once all forty barrels were reconfigured to destructive purpose, Ivar throttled up the engine and drove the train into the maze of decades-old rail lines towards Norsk Hydro's core - the heavy water distillation facility squatting deep alongside thundering hydroelectric turbines.

Elsa directed Ivar to park the armored carriage where the bomb's destruction would be most effective. Culper uncoupled the armored car, then connected the timer to all the drums' lead wires. He kept the timer turned off for the moment.

Climbing back into the engine compartment as the train carefully backed away from the armored carriage, Culper turned to Elsa, "We need to ensure the document archive is destroyed in the blast. But before that we need to retrieve key documents that will help America's efforts to develop an atomic bomb. Only you know which documents are essential. Can I count on you?"

Elsa nodded.

"Good. We'll meet you at the rendezvous point."

As the train slowly headed back toward the tunnel entrance, Elsa carrying a satchel charge stepped off the locomotive and disappeared down a corridor.

A diesel locomotive from Telemark strained up the steep mountain grade, black smoke billowing from its exhausts. The engine hauled five cargo cars loaded with munitions and supplies. The heavy flatbed carriage located behind the tender car bore a secured Tiger I tank, weighing close to fifty-five tons with its weaponry and thick armor plating. Riding on top of the tank, the crew drew their coats closer as the wind and snow picked up. Rattling slowly up the single-lane railway, the train navigated a series of switchbacks and tunnels carved through granite cliffs.

Approaching Norsk Hydro's industrial complex nestled near the top of the rugged valley, the locomotive increased throttle as the rail line straightened. Passing concrete bunkers, the train slowed upon entering the station platform situated just outside the fortified factory grounds. The engine gave short whistle blasts signaling arrival to crews awaiting to unload the vital supplies to be fed into the German military machine waiting outside the tunnel entrance.

The tank crew quickly released the locks and couplings keeping the armored vehicle restrained in transit, allowing the tank to rumble forward off of the rail car under its own weight and power.

The tank pivoted slowly on treads in the direction of the mountain tunnel. Its commander rotated the turret to align the primary 8.8 cm KwK 36 L/56 cannon barrel straight towards the tunnel mouth. The long gun would have clear line of sight down the dark passageways should anything hostile emerge. Behind the idling Tiger, thirty-two SS infantry troops fanned out in standard cover formation, each armed soldier prepared to provide supporting fire if the tank engaged a target. Together, this combined mechanized force stood poised to unleash overwhelming firepower into the tunnel on command.

With the tank and troops in position, Colonel Bauer gave the order for the troops forming the blockade to open fire. It was a broadside like no other – thousands of bullets pierced the darkness inside the tunnel. The troops were not aiming at anything in particular, but the shear volume of lead was bound to have a devasting effect on the tunnel's intruders.

Several rebels were hit, killing some and wounding others. They did what they could to pull the wounded out of harm's way, but the air was thick with lethal projectiles driving them to the little cover they had.

Sensing little residence, Bauer ordered the Tiger to begin its assault. The heavy tank rumbled slowly across the concrete towards the tunnel entrance. Its steel treads ground loudly over debris and ruts in the terrain, propelling the fifty-five-ton vehicle inexorably closer towards the mountain passages within. The tank commander pivoted the turret as he scanned the carved rocky void for emerging threats while his bow gunner peered down iron sights lining up his weapon. Behind the lumbering juggernaut, the platoon of thirty-two infantry troops fanned out in precise phalanx, creeping cautiously in the wake of the armored spear tip trembling the earth beneath its treads.

Inside the tunnel entrance, the sight of the huge beast approaching struck terror in the rebels. The fired their weapons knowing they would do little to stop the tank with its heavy armor plating.

Seeing the muzzle flashes in the tunnel's void, the tank commander ordered the main cannon to fire. The thunderous boom of the cannon shocked the troops around it, many trying to cover their ears after the first shot.

Inside the tunnel, the high explosive shell hit a rock wall shattering stone and sending debris in every direction, pelting the rebels. Johannes ordered the rebels to fall back in a fighting retreat.

As the train approached, Ivar and Culper could see the silhouette of the approaching tank. Both knew the rebels, lacking sufficient weapons to fight armored vehicles, would not last long.

"Ram it," said Culper indifferently.

Ivar smiled at the idea and threw the engine's throttle to full power. Culper grabbed three satchel charges and climbed to the top of the diesel tender. He lit the timing fuse on each charge and set them on the top of the tender.

"Time to go," said Culper as he climbed down the ladder.

"Somebody has to hold the throttle open," said Ivar.

"I'll do it then."

"No. It's not your country, American."

Culper considered for a quick moment, then nodded agreement. He shook Ivar's hand, then leapt from the engine followed by the two rebels that had helped him with the fertilizer bags.

With the train gaining speed by the second, Ivar kept the throttle full forward. Impact was just moments away…

Bauer watched as the Tiger entered the mouth of the tunnel and disappeared into the darkness. There was a loud crash of metal on metal and the tank suddenly reappeared its treads grinding backwards across the concrete, followed by the locomotive pushing the armored vehicle.

His head bleeding from the crash, Ivar grinned in the engine compartment as the locomotive overpowered the Tiger tank. "Go, my sweet, go!" he yelled holding the throttle to its limit.

The SS troops supporting the tank dove out of the

way, trying to get clear of the disaster. Many didn't make it and were crushed by the battle between the two behemoths.

As the railway began its turn across the yard, one of the tank's treads caught on a rail. Carried by the momentum of the 350-ton locomotive, the Tiger flipped on its side, then began to tumble like a child's toy. A moment later, the satchel charges on top of the fuel tender exploded sending a shockwave through the SS blockade, knocking troopers off their feet. The diesel fuel in the breeched fuel tender vaporized creating a secondary explosion many times more powerful than the initial blast. Soldiers recovered from the first explosion were again knocked off their feet. The Germans were in complete disarray.

Inside the tunnel, Culper saw the opportunity and ordered the rebels to withdraw into the tunnel. Pulling back as they had been trained in groups while some covered their retreat, then moved themselves. The wounded were carried by their comrades. The dead were reluctantly left behind to keep the load light. Lead by Culper, the rebels moved quickly through the tunnel. Johannes and a small rear guard protected the tail.

Hearing the explosions toward the tunnel entrance as she opened the metal fire-door to the document archives vault, Elsa knew there wasn't much time. Entering the vault, she placed the satchel charge on a reading table in the middle of the archives where it would be sure to wreak havoc.

Elsa had no intention of following Culper's instructions to collect key documents that could help the Americans develop the atomic bomb before the

Germans. Even after everything that had happened, she was still a pacifist and refused to help either side in the development of a weapon that could destroy mankind. But that didn't mean that all scientific advancement was evil. If handed over to the right gatekeepers, much of the research at Norsk could be used to create nuclear energy that could save and even advance humanity. With unlimited energy, the need to fight over resources would end. World peace could finally be realized.

She knew Culper would be furious. But it was her decision on what to save and what to destroy. She moved through the vault's shelves retrieving the key research documents that could help the Americans develop larger and more efficient nuclear reactors. Decades of heavy water research including her father's. Detailed drawings of newly advanced equipment and piles of data points. It was all so immensely valuable, but she was forced to pick and choose what was most important, what she could carry out on her back.

As she stuffed more and more folders into her pack, she considered what she is doing. She was saving hundreds of thousands of hours of energy research by some of the world's most brilliant minds. But deep down she knew the research was a double-edged sword. She couldn't separate the good from the evil. Science didn't work that way. It had no conscience. How scientific research and data was used was dependent on the ethics of the person using it. She knew that once she turned over the documents she would lose control of how they were used.

It was true, she didn't want the Germans to develop the bomb before the Allies, but she didn't want the Allies to develop the bomb either. Even though she had tried, she could not stop the development of atomic weapons, but she could slow it down. She could give the world leaders time to think through what was happening and the consequences of the scientists' actions.

Moving back to the center of the vault, she reverently set her pack holding the key documents next to the satchel. It broke her heart - nobody would have the research that so many had worked so hard to produce. It all had to be destroyed. It was the only way to ensure that it couldn't be used to develop atomic weapons. Her mind made up with tears welling up in her eyes, she reached for the ring that when pulled would start the timed detonator in the satchel charge. Then, she heard a voice that she recognized behind her…

"What is your real name?" said the voice.

Elsa discreetly pulled the ring on the satchel's timer before turning to face Director Knutsen holding a pistol pointed at her. She needed to buy time to ensure that Knutsen could not remove the satchel charge from the vault.

"Elsa Kristiansen," she said.

"You're Sebastian's daughter?"

"Yes."

"I knew your father. He was a great scientist."

"You stole his journal."

"I admit I did. He was just going to give his research to the Americans. I had to stop him."

"So, you killed him?"

Knutsen thought hard before answering her question. "Yes, and I truly regret it. He was my friend."

"You bastard!"

"Calm down. I can make things right. I want to

switch sides and join the allies. I can be a great help in their development of an atomic bomb. I know everything the Germans have been working on. I will tell the Americans everything."

"Why?"

"After much thought and a change in circumstances, I have become a patriot."

"That's a lie."

"Okay. Let's just say, the Nazis and I have come to a parting of ways."

"My guess is that Colonel Bauer wasn't pleased with your affair with a spy."

"No. He wasn't. The man is a neanderthal."

Knutsen saw the smoke from the satchel rising from behind Elsa. He moved to investigate and saw the satchel charge smoking.

"What have you done?" said Knutsen keeping the pistol pointed at her.

"I'm going to burn it… all of it," said Elsa.

"Fine by me. The less the Americans have of our research documents the more valuable I am. It's all stored in my brain."

"I doubt that."

"It's pointless to argue. I surrender," said Knutsen offering Elsa his pistol.

She took the pistol and said, "How do you know I won't kill you? I should. You killed my father."

"But you won't. Your mother and father were pacifists. I imagine you are too."

Elsa pointed the pistol's barrel at Knutsen's chest.

"There are always exceptions."

Knutsen watched her carefully unsure what she would do.

"We really should leave before that bomb goes off,"

said Knutsen. "If you are going to shoot me, I suppose now would be a good time to do it."

Elsa studied Knutsen like a child studies a wiggling worm. He was no more than that. He was right… without the German's research documents he would be very valuable to the Americans. He would help develop the development of the bomb. She should kill him for that reason alone. His death could save millions.

"Move," she said pointing to the doorway.

"Wise decision," said Knutsen leading the way out of the vault and into the corridor.

She waved him deeper into the facility away from the tunnel entrance.

"But your rebels are that way," said Knutsen pointing toward the entrance.

"Not for long," said Elsa moving past him. "If you want to live follow me."

Knutsen considered for a moment, then followed Elsa down the corridor.

A few moments later, the smoking satchel charge in the document archives detonated. Elsa's pack was shredded as were the documents inside. The explosion tore the fire-proof door off its hinges. A ball of flame ripped through the vault setting the documents ablaze. Smoke poured through the doorway into the corridor.

As the rebels were double-timing it down the tunnel, they heard the explosion. Fearful that it was the beginning of the armored car explosion, many stopped in their tracks. Culper reassured them, "Relax. If it was the main explosion, we'd already be dead."

Following the American once again, the rebels

continued deeper into the facility via the railway tunnel. Culper told Johannes to keep the men moving as he split off from the group and entered the side tunnel entrance to the old chemical facility.

Elsa and Knutsen exited the facility and climbed a stairwell to the top of the hydroelectric plant. Ten giant intake tubes rose hundreds of feet up the mountain to the terminus of Rjukan Falls. The water from the falls fed both the heavy water facility and the hydroelectric plant. The force from the drop created incredible water pressure that drove the turbines deep inside the power plant. It supplied the huge amount of energy needed to operate the facility. The condensation on the outside of the steel tubes was frozen forming a thick ice cocoon.

Knutsen watched with trepidation as Elsa unloaded mountaineering gear from her secondary backpack. "I don't understand," said Knutsen.

"We climb," said Elsa.

"You've got to be kidding."

"Nope. I'm serious as a heartache."

"I'm wounded. I cannot climb. Why go up instead of down? It would be much safer."

"No, it wouldn't. You can stay or go, it's up to you."

Elsa slid crampons onto her boots and secured them with leather straps.

"I have no climbing gear."

Elsa handed him one end of a climbing rope and said, "Tie it tight around your waist... or your neck. I'm okay with either."

Annoyed at her cavalier attitude, Knutsen tied the rope attached to Elsa's leather climbing harness and secured it around his waist.

Using an ice axe Elsa began to climb the ice wall. As she climbed, she used a small hammer to drive iron pitons into ice for Knutsen to step on. Every fifteen feet she drove a piton with a ring into the ice and ran the rope through it as a safety line. Knutsen groaned in pain from his wounded shoulder as he climbed.

Outside the other end of the tunnel, Colonel Bauer rallied his men to form an assault company. An armored car pulled up. Bauer climbed into the cupola and sat in the vehicle commander's seat with his head and shoulders sticking out of the turret. Taking the lead, Bauer ordered the drive to advance into the tunnel entrance. Submachine guns in hand, four hundred SS troops fell behind the armored car and entered the tunnel disappearing into the shadows. It was an overwhelming force that would hunt down the rebels hiding inside.

Culper arrived at the armored rail car and entered. The timer on the fuse was already set but not activated. He considered for a moment, then shortened the time to half - just four minutes. Starting the timer, he jumped out of the carriage, closed the door, and broke off the handle with the butt of his submachine gun. He took off at a dead run back toward the junction into the main tunnel.

As he arrived, he found the German assault force coming down the tunnel. Seeing Culper, Bauer opened fire with the armored car's autocannon. Shell bursts drove Culper back inside the side tunnel. He was trapped with time running out.

Halfway up the ice tubes, Elsa looked down to see

Johannes and the rebels appearing below. They quickly unpacked their gear and started their climb up the frozen pipes.

Hearing the cannon fire coming from the tunnel, Elsa looked down searching for Culper. He was nowhere in sight. Concerned, she drove bad thoughts from her mind and focused on the task at hand. In good shape and weighing far less than a Norwegian man, Elsa climbed quickly. Knutsen was slowing her down. It peeved her that she had to save the life of that piece of garbage. She knew that if she really believed in pacifism, then even Knutsen's life had value and had to be protected. She was obliged to save him no matter what he had done in the past.

Inside the tunnel, Culper abandoned his pack holding his climbing gear and even discarded his submachine gun to make himself as light as possible. With no time to spare, he backed up, then took off running around the corner to enter the main tunnel. Bauer fired the autocannon blowing chunks of stone from the tunnel's wall. Pelted with bits of rock, Culper didn't stop. His legs pumped propelling him down the tunnel, dodging from side to side. A close hit from the cannon blew up next to Culper sending a red-hot piece of shrapnel into his arm. With smoke seeping out of the wound, Culper kept going, ignoring the intense pain until he disappeared into the darkness.

Safe for the moment but running out of time, he pulled out his knife and pried the hot metal from his wound groaning in pain. A small amount of blood flowed as the shrapnel popped from his scorched flesh and fell to the ground. He was lucky. The hot metal had cauterized his wound cutting down on his loss of blood. Without bandaging the wound, Culper continued down the tunnel.

Curious about why the rebel had gone down the side tunnel, Bauer ordered the rest of the assault force to pursue the rebel deeper into the main tunnel, while he took the armored car to explore the side tunnel.

A minute later, he came upon the armored carriage. He climbed from his vehicle and cautiously ventured forward.

Culper sprinted out the tunnel, climbed the stairwell to reach the top of the hydroelectric plant. He saw that Elsa was almost to the top with Knutsen in tow. What the hell was Knutsen doing following Elsa? She must have taken him prisoner or he defected for some reason. Whatever the reason, Culper knew that Knutsen was a prized asset that could help the Americans win the race to develop the bomb. Keeping Knutsen alive until he was turned over to the American military was Culper's new mission.

Johannes and the rebel followed forty feet further up the cliff. With no climbing gear, Culper used the pilons Elsa had driven into the ice to propel himself up the cliff. His wounded shoulder slowed him down. He ignored the pain traveling through his shoulder like lightning.

Seeing the smashed lock on the armored carriage door, Bauer fired his pistol at the mechanism. Emptying the gun's clip, the colonel had broken open the lock. He pulled the door open to reveal the forty diesel drums with wires leading to the central detonator. The timer had twelve seconds left on it. Bauer froze in fear. His mind wanted him to run, but his legs wouldn't move. All he could do was stare at the timer as it clicked down to zero.

The explosion was beyond massive. The carriage's thick armored plates had compounded the blast back on itself increasing its destructive power threefold. Bauer was instantly incinerated as flames burst through the carriage doorway like a blast furnace. The steel plates were sheared from the armored car's chassis and hurled all directions. As the heat created by the explosion instantly expanded the air, the pressure in the tunnel swelled. The cave itself created a compounding affect as the incredible pressure tried to escape. Stone CRACKED. A wall of fire engulfed the SS armored car lifting it up and carrying it down the tunnel end over end until it finally pancaked into a stone wall at the junction. The fire wall split in two heading in both directions in the main tunnel.

All the labs and production facilities within the tunnel were cleansed by fire. The heavy water electrolysis chambers processing heavy water burst as the water boiled from the heat.

The door on the storage vault dislodged as the stone holding the bolts cracked and crumbled. Hundreds of ampules of finished deuterium inside the vault shattered from the intense heat, the precious liquid running onto the floor then evaporating as if it were never there.

The heavy steel doors securing the hydroelectric generator compartment warped and breeched. Fire rolled through the chamber surrounding, then engulfing the huge generators melting their copper cores. The driveshaft driven by kinetic energy from the turbines warped from the heat. It wobbled for a moment, then ripped apart like a headless snake whipping around the cavern and destroying the generators.

The exterior walls and windows of the facility bulged, then burst from the pressure inside. Glass shards and great chunks of masonry wall toppled into the canyon below. Now unsupported, the overhangs and roofs dropped as the buildings collapsed.

The SS assault company was approaching then end of the tunnel when they heard the explosion deep within the facility. Their first thoughts came from ignorance – that the heavy water had somehow ignited and had caused an atomic explosion. It didn't. But it didn't matter. The chemical explosion had created such heat that the tunnel walls were cracking and collapsing. Mercifully, they were not buried alive. Instead, the wall of flame caught up to them for a much quicker death. Screams were snuffed out by the roar of the firestorm rushing through the tunnel. None survived.

Like a gigantic blow torch, the flames shot out of the tunnel on both ends. The SS troops forming the blockade at the mouth of the tunnel ran for their lives. Many were engulfed in the inferno.

On the other side of the facility, the flames burst forth consuming everything in their path. The turbines housed just below the intake tubes were ripped from the mounts as the concrete cracked from the heat. The turbine blades within each machine warped and cracked. The wiring melted. The crankshaft leading to the generators warped and fractured tearing free of its mounts and spinning out of control. The ground ruptured and crumbled from the earthquake cause by the explosion. Slabs of concrete broke free and tumbled into the waterfall's mist below. The intense heat boiled the water inside the enormous intake pipes.

With their faces flushed by the rising heat, the rebels watched in horror as the ice surrounding the pipes fractured from the water boiling inside expanding the metal. Everything was coming apart including the ice wall they were climbing. Two rebels broke free from the wall and fell until their safety ropes caught them. Their comrades moved to help before the pitons gave out.

Culper was shaken by the earthquake and almost lost his grip on the pitons sticking out of the ice. He saw cracks forming in the ice like tree roots. He felt the pitons loosen. He was in trouble.

Knutsen lost his footing as some the pitons broke free. Grasping at the ice for a handhold, he found only broken chunks. He fell backwards. The ringed safety pitons Elsa had driven into the ice and threaded with rope popped out the ice with little effort. With a frightened look on his face, Knutsen accelerated down as gravity took hold.

A moment later, the rope attached to Elsa's harness snapped taught. The leather straps around her waist and chest instantly tightened knocking the wind from her lungs and pulling her from her hold on the ice cliff. Unable to grab the crumbling ice wall, she fell following Knutsen to the abyss below. The rope in the freshly hammered safety ring beside her snapped tight stopping Elsa and Knutsen's descent. As more fire bursts from the tunnel, more ice cracks around the pipes and ice cliff. The safety ring piton broke free and Elsa and Knutsen fell once again. As Elsa fell past Johannes, he reached out and grabbed her harness. He hung on for dear life as the powerful jerk of the full weight of Elsa and Knutsen stretched the tendons and ligaments in his arms. He let out a load groan but didn't let go.

Below, Culper looked over to see Knutsen hanging from the safety rope just a few feet from him.

"Help me," gasped Knutsen struggling to catch his breath.

Culper looked up to see Johannes holding onto Elsa, as nearby rebels tried to reach him before his strength failed. Culper followed the rope attached to Elsa's harness down to Knutsen.

"For God's sake… take my hand," said Knutsen reaching out.

Culper quickly realized that by grabbing Knutsen's hand it would lighten the load on Elsa and Johannes. But knowing that his own hold on the ice cliff was tentative, Culper chose a different route…

Culper pulled out his knife from its sheath and in one swift move slashed the rope above Knutsen's head. The individual strings within the rope unraveled and twisted, then the entire rope snapped. Shocked, Knutsen fell. A few moments later, he disappeared in the dust and watery mist as more concrete, and machinery fell off the cliff. His survival was beyond doubtful.

Culper looked up at Elsa and shrugged as Johannes pulled her to safety. She never loved Culper more as he had chosen her over his mission.

Escape from Norway

The rebels' escape back to Telemark was uneventful. The Germans were in too much disarray to give chase. Safe in the bakery, Culper contacted OSS HQ and informed them of the operation's success - Norsk was badly damaged and heavy water production was shutdown. The rebels losses were extensive, but the German loses were far worse. All the designs and data at Norsk had been destroyed as a result of the sabotage. There would be nothing to further the American's development of the atomic bomb.

Elsa was now the most wanted woman in Norway and the Germans had put a sizable bounty on her capture or death. Culper realized that he needed to get her out of the country before the bounty could be collected. Dying her hair back to its natural color, Elsa returned to being brunette. She changed her clothes from Aadland's glamorous dress, fur coats, and flashy jewelry back to the frumpy sweaters, knit cap, and trousers. On the outside she was Elsa once again, but on the inside something has changed.

Allowing his shoulder time to heal, Culper and Elsa waited until yet another snowstorm hit Telemark before saying their good-byes to Johannes and the rebels. Alf gave them a satchel filled with Norwegian pastries for their journey.

Rebel scouts had confirmed that the Germans had brought in 3,000 extra troops to hunt down Elsa and her American co-conspirator who was still nameless. Escaping through Sweden was risky. Instead, they decided to cross the great mountains to the west and make for the coast where a British submarine would pick them up. With the bottom of their skis waxed, they set out cross country.

Elsa and Culper moved swiftly under moonlight's faint glow trekking through breaks in the towering pines. Fresh snowfall muted their strides across the winding forest carpet, but they knew SS trackers would already be fanning out seeking the saboteurs. Pausing at the burbling ice stream cutting through the valley, Culper met Elsa's eyes with solemn urgency.

"It's going to be a tough haul over the mountains. You need to tell me when you need to rest. Don't try to be a hero. A slip at the wrong moment could cost you your life," said Culper.

"I'll be okay, Culper. I'm stronger now than when I started," said Elsa. "It's your shoulder that worries me."

"It's fine. I heal fast."

"Let me change the bandage."

"We don't have time. We must reach the rendezvous point with the submarine within eight days. Any longer and they'll be forced to leave. U-boats patrol the coast."

"I'm not taking no for an answer. So, you can spend

valuable time arguing with me or we can get on with it."

Culper reluctantly nodded agreement. He knew she was right. If he fell ill because of the wound, Elsa wouldn't survive without him.

Elsa pulled the medical bag from Culper's pack, then helped him unbutton his shirt. Blood had filled the bandage. She gently pulled it off to reveal the swollen flesh around the stitched bullet wound. "That doesn't look good."

"It's okay. It just looks bad."

"And how would you know?"

"It's not the first time I've been shot."

"You sound proud of that accomplishment."

"I'm just saying, I know how I heal. If it was infected, it would smell like rotten cheese. It doesn't. So, I'm okay."

Elsa poured alcohol on the wound more to shut him up than to clean it.

"JESUS!" Culper winced.

"Don't be a baby."

Culper laughed. Elsa joined him as she cleaned up the wound and covered it with a new bandage.

"So, is this what it's like to be a spy?"

"Pretty much. You did real good, Elsa. I'm proud of you."

"Thanks. I'm kinda proud of myself. I guess you really never know what your made of until you're put to the test."

"Well, you passed with flying colors. I'd fight alongside you anytime."

"You're making me blush."

"Have you given any thought what you are going to do once you return to the states?"

"I suppose I'll go back to Chicago and resume my research."

"That's one way to go."

"And the other?"

"Stay in the OSS. We need proven warriors. This war is far from over."

"No. I don't think so. This was a one-off deal for me."

"Alright, but at least give it some thought."

"Okay. I will."

They packed up the medical supplies and set off again toward the looming mountains with their ominous granite teeth clawing one side of the horizon. A harsh gust of wind hit as if challenging their will as they plunged onward into the frigid current, shock biting to the bone. They were traveling where few had gone before. There were no trails to guide them, only waist-deep snow. Their legs burned as they began their ascent up the steep slope.

Elsa focused solely on putting one boot in front of the other as she and Culper traversed the ragged Norwegian mountain passes. The towering pines and snow-laden boulders took on fantastical shapes in the pale dawn filtering through rushing clouds. Numbing exhaustion threatened to overwhelm each step up the endlessly winding slopes.

Culper crushed icy layers underfoot as the cold seeped into his very marrow of his bones. He felt Elsa lagging behind despite her stubbornness to keep up with him. He took her arm gently to support each labored switchback, willing his strength to pass to her worn muscle and sinew. No matter her will, her body could only take some much abuse before it gave out. He made excuses like reading his map or scouting ahead to stop and rest often. He ended the days earlier as their journey progressed. He cut tree branches for a wind shield before starting a fire and setting up their tent. Elsa wanted to do her part and help him, but he insisted on doing it himself. The last of her energy gone, she was too tired to argue. A quick dinner and she was out for the night before the sun even set.

In the morning, Culper would let her sleep in. He knew she would be angry once she awoke, but he didn't care. They were in a fight for their lives, and he needed her strength.

On the eighth grueling day, Culper and Elsa crested the final mountain range on blistered feet and sheer exhaustion. Spreading endless before their ice-crusted vantage stood the slate-gray expanse of the North Sea.

Shading weary eyes against the baleful sunlight punching through racing clouds, Culper spotted a familiar periscope mast scything through white-capped swells. He ignited a rescue flare from his depleted kit to paint a brilliant crimson arc over the unbroken seascape. Elsa murmured silent gratitude when the submarine breached the surface with an answering yellow burst sparked in reply from the bobbing submarine.

Three British seamen boarded an inflatable rubber raft and headed for the coastline as Elsa and Culper made their way down the mountain slope as fast as their legs could carry them. Meeting at the bottom, Elsa and Culper boarded the raft as the three seamen kept watch for the enemy. Moments later, they began the return trip to the submarine battling against the swells and wind.

As the raft closed its distance between it and the

submarine, a German submarine chaser rounded a point and spotted the rescue in progress. With its crew manning its forward deck gun the patrol boat opened fire at the submarine.

Realizing that as the patrol boat sped closer, the submarine captain would have no choice but to submerge without them. Culper joined in the paddling and Elsa quickly followed.

The German gun crew diverted their fire to the raft.

As a nearby shell exploded, frigid water gushed into the air soaking everyone in the raft. The submarine klaxon signaled the crew that it was about to submerge. The captain ordered the ballast tanks flooded and the submarine started to sink rapidly as giant air bubbles surrounded the deck.

"Move it," shouted Culper paddling as hard as his wounded shoulder would allow.

The sea started to swallow the submarine. The rubber raft bashed up against the submarine as a crewman jumped out and secured a line. Culper practically threw Elsa on to the vessel. She scrambled up the conning tower ladder and into the submarine.

Another shell exploded in the water nearby as the patrol boat's gun crew retargeted the submarine trying to damage it sufficiently to prevent it from submerging.

Pulling himself on board the sinking submarine, Culper helped the two crew members in the raft. Waves crashed on top of the deck as the last crewmen was pulled onboard the submarine. They left the raft tied to the submarine's hull as they dashed knee-deep in seawater for the conning tower ladder. Once on top of the tower, they climbed through the tower's hatchway and slid down the ladder without using the rungs. The last crewman lowered the hatch and secured the watertight seal just as water poured over the top of the conning tower. The submarine was below the surface, but not out of danger.

The captain ordered his crew to stop all engines and run silent. He moved to the side of the sonar operator. The patrol boat was right on top of them. They exchanged a worried look as depth charges were launched from the patrol boat. They sank near the submarine and exploded. The crew was rocked. Elsa fell to the deck. Culper joined her as if he could somehow protect her. He couldn't.

The sonar operator motioned to the captain that the patrol boat was moving off. More depth charges exploded in the distance. The boat's crew had lost the scent of the submarine and was randomly firing depth charges into the sea in hopes of getting lucky. The submarine was safe for the moment. The captain waited another fifteen minutes to ensure the patrol was indeed gone. It was. He ordered the engines restarted and set a course for Britain.

Culper turned to Elsa and said, "I think it's okay to get up now."

"Good, cuz that deck is hard on the knees," said Elsa rising to her feet. "So, we're safe?"

"Yeah. The odds of another patrol boat finding us underwater are slim to none."

The captain ordered a crewman to show Elsa and Culper to his quarters where they could rest until they made port.

In the captain's cabin, Culper turned to Elsa and said, "I know there are things we need to discuss —"

"Do we need to do that now?" said Elsa.

"No. It can wait."

"Good, cuz I'd kill for a nap."

Culper laughed, kicked off his boots, and climbed into the captain's bunk with Elsa by his side. Two minutes later, they were both asleep. The mission was over.

Washington D.C., USA

Nestled in the heart of Washington D.C., just steps from the White House, The Willard InterContinental stood as a beacon of luxury and history. With its grand façade and opulent interiors, The Willard had been a cornerstone of American hospitality since the mid-19th century. The hotel's illustrious past was echoed in its corridors, where presidents, dignitaries, and luminaries had roamed.

Elsa woke up to the smell of fresh brewed coffee. Wearing his officer's dress uniform, Culper stepped from the bathroom and said, "I thought the smell of coffee might wake you up."

"You weren't wrong," said Elsa a bit groggy.

"Can I get you a cup?"

"Sure. Unless you have a gallon jug."

"A cup will have to do."

"Cream and a little sugar if they have it."

"It's the Willard. They have it," said Culper moving to pour her coffee.

"It was nice for the White House to spring for such a luxurious hotel. What time's your appointment with the president?"

"Ten AM."

"Are you nervous?"

"I mean… it's the president, so… yeah."

"Do you know what you're going to say?"

"I'm just going to tell him what happened and give a bomb damage assessment, then answer whatever questions he has."

"Are you going to tell about me?"

"No."

"Why not?"

"You'll be safer if nobody knows who you are or what you did. The Nazis have a long reach even in Washington."

"I guess I didn't think about it that way."

"I should be back by noon, and I'll take you to lunch."

"I'm going to need a rain check on that."

"Why?"

"I'm not going to be here. I have a flight back to Chicago."

"When did you book that?"

"Yesterday afternoon."

"Why didn't you tell me?"

"I didn't want to ruin our evening with an argument."

"What does this mean about us?"

"Culper, you know I have strong feelings for you. But I'm not ready for a relationship… or what follows."

"I guess I thought this thing we have was more serious."

"It is serious. It's just that I need some time. These last few months have been like riding a tornado and I don't know which way is up. I know I'm not the same person I was when we started, and I don't want to go back to the old Elsa. But I'm still not sure who the new Elsa is. I don't think it's fair to either of us to jump into something serious before I figure out who I am."

"I suppose I get that. But I don't want to lose you... whoever you are."

"And I don't want to lose you either. I'm just asking for some time, that's all."

"Any idea how long?"

"I wish I knew."

"Well, I'll be waiting."

She pulled him close and kissed him deeply. The phone rang and Culper picked it up. "Yeah. Okay, I'll be right down."

He hung up the phone and said, "I've got to go. It's a bad career move to keep the president waiting."

"True."

"Will you call me when you land?"

"Of course."

"Do you want me to tell the president anything?"

"Yeah. Ask him not to blow up the world."

Culper chuckled, then gave her one last kiss on the forehead, grabbed his hat and left.

Elsa teared up but knew she had made the right decision. She wasn't Aadland, but she wasn't Elsa either. It was time to figure out who she was.

2010 – Stockholm, Sweden

The Karolinska University Hospital ICU was filled with a symphony of sounds, each one a subtle reminder of the drama unfolding within its walls. The steady, rhythmic beeping of the heart monitor was the most prominent, a constant reassurance that Elsa's life still hung in the balance. The soft, whispered conversations of the nurses and doctors as they moved in and out of the room added a layer of urgency to the atmosphere, their voices tinged with concern and determination.

The room itself was awash in the sterile, antiseptic smell that seemed to pervade every corner of the hospital, a scent that was both comforting and unsettling in its familiarity. The walls were a crisp, clinical white, broken only by the occasional colorful painting or photograph, a halfhearted attempt to bring some warmth and humanity to the otherwise cold and impersonal space.

At the center of it all lay Elsa, her still form a stark contrast to the bustling activity around her. Her skin was pale, almost translucent, and her chest rose and fell in time with the steady rhythm of the machines that kept her alive. She looked small and fragile, a far cry from the vibrant, indomitable woman she had once been.

Elsa's eyes fluttered open, the sterile walls of the hospital room slowly coming into focus. As she turned her head, her gaze fell upon a figure sitting beside her bed, a man she hadn't seen in decades, yet whose presence still managed to bring a smile to her face, despite her best efforts to conceal it - Culper.

"'Bought time you woke up," said Culper. "I was being to think you were dead."

"That's all you have to say to me after all these years?" said Elsa weakly.

"Guess I missed a few birthdays."

"A card would have been nice."

"I'm not much of a writer."

"Where in the hell did you go?"

"You said you needed time to think."

"Yeah, a couple of weeks, maybe a month, but six decades?"

"I guess I got a bit sidetracked. You know… the war and everything."

"The war ended."

"And another started."

"You're an idiot. You know that?"

"Yeah. Well, at least I'm a sincere idiot."

"I got tired of waiting. I got married."

"I know."

"You've been keeping tabs on me?"

"Somewhat."

"And yet you couldn't pick up the phone?"

"I thought about visiting, but it just didn't seem right. You'd moved on with your life."

"And you? Did you move on?"

"Married twice, divorced twice."

"Children?"

"A girl. Graduated West Point a few years back."

"Sounds about right. Another warmonger."

"Sometimes people surprise you."

"…and sometimes they don't."

"I'm sorry, if that helps."

"It doesn't hurt."

"I should have contacted you."

"We had been through a lot together. You changed my life."

"In a good way, I hope."

"I was different than before. Maybe a little less naïve."

"War and peace are complicated things."

"We make them complicated. They're really quite simple in concept – just don't pick up the rifle when you argue."

"Bit simplistic, don't you think?"

"Tell me then, what has violence offered mankind?"

"You really want to have this conversation now?"

"If not now, when? I don't know how much time I

have left."

"A lot, I hope," said Ingrid standing in the doorway with two cups of coffee topped with pastries.

"Ingrid, I'd like you to meet Culper," said Elsa. "We've already met, Mom," said Ingrid handing Culper a coffee and sweet roll. "His account of your clandestine activities in World War II were enlightening to say the least."

"You told her?" said Elsa turning to Culper.

"She asked," Culper in between bites of pastry.

"A spy? Really, Mom?"

"It was a different time," said Elsa then turned back to Culper. "You told her everything?"

"I may have left out some of the fun stuff."

"Thank, God."

"What fun stuff?" said Ingrid.

"Never you mind," said Elsa. "I want to keep some things for myself."

"That hardly seems fair," said Ingrid disappointed.

"Welcome to life, darling," said Elsa. "Ingrid, would you mind giving Culper and I a few minutes alone?"

"Sure. I'll go look at the newborns in the maternity ward," said Ingrid leaving.

"So, a Nobel. That's impressive," said Culper.

"Yeah, and a fat check. Speaking of which, I wonder what happened to—"

"Ingrid has it."

"Well, that's not good. She spends money like it's going out of style."

"You can afford it."

"Yeah, I guess I can. What else am I gonna spend it on?"

"You really think this is it, don't you?"

"No, if I was gonna die, I wouldn't have bothered

waking up. But I do get tired of life at times. It's been a tough haul."

"For us all."

"And yet we survived. I guess that says something."

"Like what?"

"We're survivors, I suppose."

"That true... we are."

Elsa studied him for a long moment, then said, "You're a noble man that's lived a noble life, Culper."

"And you're a brave woman. I always wondered how I talked you into going back to Norway."

"I suppose a part of me wanted to go. To do something for my country."

"Well, that you did. That's for sure."

They visited for another thirty minutes before Elsa dozed off and Culper tucked in her sheets. She never woke up and that was just fine with her.

Letter to Reader

Dear Reader:

I hope you enjoyed *A Life Stolen*. I think it's fascinating looking back at World War II and seeing how scientists struggled with ethical decisions about developing an atomic weapon to end the war. I often wonder if they had seen the future and the Cold War if they would have chosen to work on the Manhattan Project.

If you want to learn about what happened to the Norsk Heavy Water Facility and the German's effort to develop an atomic bomb, please sign up for my newsletter and I will send you a free epilogue of A Life Stolen. I'll give you a hint… the Germans rebuilt it.

Here is my newsletter signup link:
https://dl.bookfunnel.com/1vpzij6a8v

Sharing my books with your friends and reviews are always welcome. Thank you for supporting my work.

Regards,

David Lee Corley, Author

Other Novels by David Lee Corley

The Airmen Series - 21 Novels on the Vietnam War

The Nomad Series – An International Thriller Series

Author's Biography

Born in 1958, David grew up on a horse ranch in Northern California, breeding and training appaloosas. He has had all his toes broken at least once and survived numerous falls and kicks from ornery colts and fillies. David started writing professionally as a copywriter in his early 20's. At thirty-two, he packed up his family and moved to Malibu, California, to live his dream of writing and directing motion pictures. He has four motion picture screenwriting credits and two directing credits. His movies have been viewed by over fifty million movie-goers worldwide and won a multitude of awards, including the Malibu, Palm Springs, and San Jose Film Festivals. In addition to his twenty-four screenplays, he has written fourteen novels. He developed his simplistic writing style after rereading his two favorite books, Ernest Hemingway's *The Old Man and the Sea* and Cormac McCarthy's *No Country For Old Men* An avid student of world culture, David lived as an expat in both Thailand and Mexico. At fifty-six, he sold all his possessions and became a nomad for four years. He circumnavigated the globe three times and visited fifty-six countries. Known for his detailed descriptions, his stories often include actual experiences and characters from his journeys.